Also by Frances Collier-Lovell

Bampton Fair and a little bit more: (local history)

King Arthur and the
Dragon of Camelot

Frances Collier-Lovell

Order this book online at **www.trafford.com**
or email orders@trafford.com

Most Trafford titles are also available at major online book retailers.

Printed in the United States of America.

ISBN: 978-1-4269-9783-9 (sc)
ISBN: 978-1-4269-9784-6 (e)

Trafford rev. 11/12/2011

 www.trafford.com

North America & International
toll-free: 1 888 232 4444 (USA & Canada)
phone: 250 383 6864 ♦ fax: 812 355 4082

Contents

For my family, without whom there would be no memories.

Then Sir Bedwere departed and went to the sword and gently took it up, and went to the waterside. And there he tied the girdle about the hilt, and threw the sword as far into the water as he could. And there came an arm and a hand above the water, and took it and caught it and shook it thrice, and brandished it. Then vanished with the sword into the water.

Based on Malory, Works Book XXI

Acknowledgements

To my two brothers who helped with the reading of the text, Collin and Jobey, and my special thanks to Eve Grosse for providing the beautiful frontispiece.

Prologue

One terrifying night in 1942 a German bomber came screaming across the countryside above a West Country town. Hans wrestled with the damaged aircraft as it dropped from the sky. *Too fast*, he thought. *We'll crash.* He could never hope to land it now, and the heavy aircraft would crash into the ground. In front of him the silvered moonlight lit up a small town. *Mein Gott! They will all be killed!* He knew he had to get the aircraft away. Quickly. And jettison the bombs away from the houses.

Throwing his weight to one side Hans jammed the rudder forward, simultaneously yanking on the control column. This would move them off course and the people below would be safe. Nothing happened. The aircraft was still too heavy. He yelled instructions at the bombardier and a few moments later felt the hiss as the bomb doors fell open. Then a moment later felt a great upward lift as the bombs fell away. The aircraft, much lighter now, jerked back under control, Hans completed the turn and they were on their way home.

Beneath them the exploding bombs found a store of ammunition in a long brick building and a red-hot ball of flame shot up into the sky, throwing trees and fields into relief below. But suddenly, all around them, the night sky was rent by high-pitched screeching as if hordes of blood-thirsty demons were unleashed and chased across the countryside in search of quarry. The airmen covered their ears, terrified with fear. Hans tried to see outside the cockpit as the bomb fires burst below. But a ball of searing light burst upon the perspex canopy. He screamed in agony, screwing his eyelids against the pain. The bursting light smashed against the aircraft, which bucked wildly and began to spin as if in a tidal pool of boiling air.

Hans gripped the controls, trying to steady the aircraft once more. He peeped through his fingers, using them to shield his stinging eyes, and saw the strangest sight he had ever seen. In front of him loomed what appeared to be a medieval castle, with decorated white turrets and towers stretching up into the night sky. He rubbed his eyes. He must be dreaming. It was absurd. Nothing like that existed these days. And now the aircraft was heading straight for it. He screamed, throwing his hands in front of his face. They were going to die.

But nothing happened.

Looking again Hans saw the castle had gone, but then gasped as something more terrifying filled his vision. Out of the exploding bombs he saw the image of a dragon, looking larger than a cathedral.

Deep underground an ancient rusting gate with bars as thick as a man's waist loosed its hasp and a frail creature dragged itself around, struggling to repair it. Time was running out for everyone; the medieval beast had been wakened.

Nearby an old woman felt the evil of the beast drawing out her life's breath, and began praying for forgiveness. She caressed a precious blue jewel and waited whilst the cursed prophecy lurched closer.

Chapter 1

The legend in the library

When Maiden and Boy take up the Sword,
Dragon confound and Death to his Horde.

The faded book twitched violently between her fingers as Joan scanned some words and then looked at the cover again. The grim dragon looked back, blood flowing in a crimson arc from its jaws. She jumped, gasped loudly, and the book clattered to the floor.

"Shh!" hissed the librarian behind the counter. "Be careful young lady."

"Sorry," Joan muttered, red faced. Gritting her teeth she snatched the book and ran round the shelves to where her brothers and sister were gathered together, looking for something interesting to read over the Christmas holidays.

"Joan! You're not supposed to run in here!" admonished Timothy, her eldest brother, in a hushed voice just sharp enough for her to hear.

"You must look at this!" she said, her voice trembling, thrusting the book under his face. "This dragon reminds me of one of my dreams!"

He raised an eyebrow snorting with laughter. "Another dream, Joanie? Is it as good as your other one when you told us Father's sheep had escaped?"

Mark, three years older than Joan, fair-haired, blue eyed, and tousled slightly with lack of sleep because he had stayed awake making model aircraft, grinned hugely at the memory. "Do you remember your dream, Joanie? We found our sheep trotting up the lane to Stoodley's farm."

"Of course I do. That was a nice dream. But this other dream about a dragon wasn't," said Joan, stung by Mark's grin which always made her feel foolish and more babyish than her seven years. "You didn't believe me at the time, but it turned out to be true, and this dream is too. You'll see. It's about a sleeping giant, and a dragon. And they both live under a mountain, very close to us. It says so in the book."

Diane, their sister, came squirming around the corner of the tall bookshelves. She was eleven, older than Mark and quite serious. Her cropped dark hair was still damp against her head from their long wintry walk to the library and tiny wisps had stuck up sharply at odd angles as it began drying. "A sleeping giant! Really Joanie! Have you never heard of it before? I've known about it for years. It's Henley Forest."

As usual Diane succeeded in making Joan feel more foolish than ever and she thrust the book into her elder sister's hands. "Look at this. The legend is not just about a giant, there's a dragon too!"

"A Short Book on Local *Legends*," read out Diane loudly, emphasising the word 'legends' with relish and rolling her eyes at Timothy. "Local legends, Joanie The book is about legends. That means it's not true. Not fact, but fiction. In other words it's just a story, like these others on the shelves." She began wriggling between the ends of the bookstand, grumbling, "Oh bother these books! I'm looking for something interesting to read, but I can't see anything here. I'm fed up with the Christmas holidays already." She dropped the book beside Joan. "I do wish we had another adventure planned!" If they didn't think of an adventure within the next few days they would probably end up playing 'Germans and English' or 'Pirates' in the barns, as they usually did. *Bother and double bother!*

Joan reached out to pick up the book, and that's when she felt it. A hundred shooting pains like pins and needles seemed to rip through her veins making her hands tremble.

"Ouch!" she exclaimed dropping the book, and jamming her hands deep into the pockets of her thick coat where they felt safe again. The grim dragon looked coldly from the cover; a twisted smile stretching over huge fangs like a mountain of slime. For one mad moment Joan wanted to run out of the library. 'Don't be silly', she muttered. 'It's only a picture.

It can't do any harm,' and swept the book off the table and onto the floor where she kicked it out of sight.

A woman nearby gave Joan a hard stare before retrieving the dropped book and handing it silently back. *Oh bother*, thought Joan, *I will have to touch the horrible thing again.* She accepted the book, grimacing, and lowered her eyes. "Thank you," she said, feeling the words catch in her throat, and hoping the woman couldn't hear her gritting her teeth.

The woman laughed, noticing Joan's heightened colour. "An interesting choice of book, though you might like to look at the giant on the back cover. It looks far more friendly than the dragon on the front."

"Oh!" Joan flipped the book over and there it was; the giant she had read about a few minutes before, and which she had spoken of to Diane.

A great cheerful splodgy picture of the reddest giant she had ever seen looked up at her. A big red grin split its flat round face, and lovely rosy cheeks beamed like the apples in the orchard, crowned like a halo with lots of fiery red hair. A very red giant, Joan decided grinning back, and stuck her tongue out in a gesture of fun. Perhaps the book wasn't frightening after all. But as she looked at the book again a shadow fell across the face of the giant and suddenly its happy face disappeared, and it began looking sad, then angry and courageous, all at once. At the same time queer sensations began fluttering up and down her arm like a battalion of wild ants. This time she didn't drop the book but sucked her breath in sharply until the sensations stopped and was rewarded by a feeling of sadness. If only she could help the giant be happy again she thought, then mentally shook herself. What a lot of silly notions she seemed to be getting since she had found the book! She was even beginning to feel the book of local legends had a life of its own, which she had awoken as if from a deep sleep. How she wished the book would lead them to a real mystery! Well, she had better not tell any of these thoughts to the others, or they would tease her. She peeped at the giant again, wanting to believe it was only a picture; that there was nothing special about the book, and the giant wasn't trying to tell her anything. But it was already too late for that. With a sickening lurch in her stomach Joan knew life would never be the same again. She also knew she had to take the book home to investigate further. She just had to!

Ten minutes later the children left the library. They didn't notice the unusual cloud following them, nor the rather odd shape at the centre of the cloud, which appeared to be a dragon. However, with the temperature dropping quickly they pulled their coats around them, shivering, then tucked their heads under woollen hats and began talking excitedly as they left the town far behind them. It was over a mile to their home on the West Country farm which ran beside the railway line. If they listened, as they usually did when doing their farm chores, they could hear the shrill blast of the train's whistle as it screeched through the long tunnel nearby, and with this they could gauge the time.

When they passed the last house on the outskirts of Crewkerne Joan fell silent, her mind in turmoil. She knew the book of legends, the giant, and the dragon were mixed up with her dream, and felt something awful was about to happen. If only she could remember her dream! Usually she made notes about her dreams, yet she hesitated to remember this one. *Why?* Why hadn't she wanted to remember it when she awoke that morning a few weeks ago, until it had been jolted back by the sight of the book? Now, with the book tucked in her bag, she would be forced to recall the whole dream. *Well, here goes. I'll try to remember five things about it.* She held up her hand, then counting slowly stuck up a finger. *One, there was a giant. Two.* Up went a second finger and with it came a feeling of being terribly afraid. *Then what? Oh, yes! Three.* As her third finger went up Joan stopped abruptly and nearly doubled over with fear as she felt a big black chasm thumping into her chest. The dream came flooding back in torrents and with it a remembrance of terror so horrid she could scarcely move. There was a vision of the four of them running through dark tunnels desperately trying to escape. "No!" she cried out. It was horrible, and they had all been in grave danger. She tried to blot out the memory, to stop it coming back into her mind. But the fearful images of their terrified faces kept coming back, and with them other horrible, haunting images of strange pictures. Strange people. Faces. Animals. *No*, she corrected, *creatures*, like nothing she had seen before. She suddenly stopped walking as fear gripped her.

Timothy came cannoning into her from behind. "Whoa! Watch out! Your brake lights aren't working!" He teased before noticing the terror on her face. "Are you all right? You look a bit peaky. Is it your dream, Joanie? Have you remembered something else?"

Joan could feel tears welling up in her eyes. *Stop being silly*, she told herself. *Dreams aren't real.* "I, uh, uh, dreamt about various creatures. I know you won't believe me, but I did. They were odd looking things, I don't even know what to call them." She broke off seeing Timothy's face turn from a good humoured grin into a thoughtful gaze and he moved past her without speaking. Both of them realised that her words had broken a powerful spell that had hovered over them since leaving the library. Joan suddenly began running to catch up Diane and Mark who were now some distance ahead. It will be okay if I remember a little, she thought, after all Timothy was there, and he would take care of her. He was her big brother, her fair haired hero. He reminded her of a Greek warrior she had seen fighting in a film on the TV. He would protect them all.

She had no way of realising that her dream would send them on the greatest and most dangerous adventure of their lives.

There was a chance they wouldn't all come back.

But that was later.

Chapter 2

Joanie's dream

"Tell us about your dream," urged Timothy a few moments later, trying to appear interested and wondering why he felt apprehensive of Joan's reply. "Then we can see if it's like the legend in your book."

Joan tucked some wisps of unruly hair behind her ears. "It happened a few weeks ago, after we had walked to Henley Forest looking for holly berries for Mum. Do you remember? It was the day we got caught in all those awful brambles and things. They were thicker than my arm!" And she pushed up her coat sleeve exposing her pale arm, still slightly plump and childish.

Timothy walked closer, feeling very grown up, and wanting to get rid of the prickly feelings he experienced earlier, realising that he had felt as if they were being watched. "Yes, I remember the trip, we called it our 'Adventure for Christmas Food' or something like that. Though we carried off more food from the larder than we brought back!" He laughed, but immediately his smile vanished as he began thinking about what had happened on their last trip to Henley Forest. "We all felt terribly cold, as if we were caught in a winter blizzard. And you two noticed it too, didn't you?" he said turning to Diane and Mark but they were chattering, heads together, and probably scheming. "It felt quite spooky. I was glad to get back!" He stopped short, there was something more menacing about their adventure in the forest, but for the moment it eluded him. He remembered all of them racing through the trees to get away. *Away?* Had something else been out there with them? He shrugged; it might have been other walkers. "I remember it felt unusual. I didn't like it much. Is that what your dream was about, Joanie? Did you have your dream of the dragon that night?"

Her eyes reminded him of dark frightened pools. "Yes . . . no . . . I didn't dream about a dragon. I don't think I did . . . . at least . . . it was a weird dream" She clamped her hand over her mouth to stop herself crying out as a fit of trembling suddenly seized her. She had to stop sounding silly or her big brother would accuse her of being childish, and leave her to walk back on her own. And he would probably never speak to her again about the dream. She had to stop that, because her dream was real. *It was!* And terrifying, and somehow it was all mixed in with the legend she had found.

"We were in the forest, searching for something, I don't know what, when we found some very old buildings behind some brambles. Just like those we saw on our last trip to the forest."

Timothy frowned, feeling impatient. "Is that all you can remember, a bit about brambles? Most of Henley Forest is covered with brambles."

Mark had been listening but now he barged against Timothy, not wanting to be left out of anything interesting, and a bright band of ugly red began spreading quickly across his face. "Old buildings? What were they? Do you think we could find them if we went back?"

Diane could sense the sudden burst of excitement too. "This could be the beginning of a new adventure. You know we've wanted something new to do this Christmas. Perhaps the old legend could become our Christmas adventure. What fun we'll have exploring the forest in our holidays. I'll make some doorstep sandwiches to take with us. And while we're there we can collect pine cones for Mum, and spray them for Christmas decorations! And," with a gleeful look at Joan, "We could look for Joanie's dragon!" And she danced around her younger sister, pulling faces, drooling her tongue and pretending to breathe fire on her. What a notion! To find a dragon living next door.

Timothy's face puckered into a frown, sensing a revolt against his youngest sister. Joan hid behind him for safety; she didn't like her big sister in this mood. Diane and Mark began leaping around Joan like wild natives around a camp fire, making faces and loud hissing noises.

Timothy clapped his hands, taking charge through being the eldest, and wanted his brother and sisters to know it. "Whoa! Slow down everyone. Let's read the whole legend from the book, and afterwards Joanie can tell us everything about her dream." By this time they had reached the school gates at the top of the hill outside the town and Timothy wanted to see if they could create a new adventure from the old local legend before they got back home.

"Let's sit down and have a quick pow-wow about it," he said pointing to the last bench along the pavement. So they all raced the last few yards and somehow everyone managed to squeeze on to it. Joan placed the book on her knees. At once the dragon looked up from the cover, almost smacking its lips with pleasure. Snatching the book she flipped it over so that the friendly giant was looking up. He was grinning again. Once more a silly grin plastered his rosy face and his head looked a mass of curly red hair. Joan's stomach settled and unconsciously she tugged at her little talisman hanging around her neck as she opened the book. Today her talisman was an old shrivelled acorn shell fitted onto a length of string, for after reading stories of Merlin the magician she had endowed her new find of the once perfect acorn with fancies of supernatural powers. She touched it gently, which she usually did when she needed reassurance in times of unease. Though today she realised she also wore her auntie's cross and chain and this too reassured her.

Diane and Mark were leaning across, scanning the book impatiently.

"You can read it to us," said Diane. "Since you found the book."

"Oh, all right," said Joan, feeling her throat shrivel up. She found the beginning of the legend, then cleared her throat and tried to read.

"This legend is based upon a story I heard from my mother, and which she had heard from her mother, and so on. As far as I can tell the story is nearly 800 years old and very few people have ever heard about it. I am concerned that it will be lost, and that is why I have chosen to write it down in a short story book. As with all legends I think there is an element of truth in it, but what it is and who will find it out, I have no idea. However, it is a local legend, and as this book is intended to be about all local legends, this story must go in. Perhaps one day someone can add something more to this short, but interesting tale." Joan rushed through to the end, and upon saying the last word snapped the book shut as if she would stop a bad genii escaping from a jar. The others were looking at her oddly, wondering why she sounded so strange and why she snapped the book shut so forcibly. Did they feel the same peculiar emotion? But before she could ask them a horrid burst of emotion rushed through her so that she realised she was about to start crying. She swallowed rapidly then fishing

in her pocket dragged out a handkerchief and blew loudly into it. She didn't want to read any more.

But Timothy began bouncing impatiently on the bench. "Keep going," he said. "There's more on the next page."

Joan turned the page and read slowly. *"There is a sleeping giant at Crocern who guards a great treasure that once belonged to a Trojan prince and it is said that only a true descendant can keep the treasure. The giant also keeps a watch over the inhabitants of the town, and when any trouble comes it is said that the giant will awaken. Up to now no one has recorded the giant being awoken from his slumbers."*

Joan dropped the book and wondered why she felt drained, as if she had run a thousand miles.

Timothy said slowly, "When trouble comes . . . . the giant will awaken."

"And treasure!" thrust in Diane. "What a terrific adventure this would make! I wonder why the giant hasn't woken before now?"

Mark, who had been sitting quietly, looking very ill, suddenly jumped up, his hands clenched into angry fists at his side. "The town was never under threat before, that's why. Oh!" And immediately a look of horror shot across his face. "Why did I say that?" He slapped his flat hand over his mouth and peeped out above it, his freckled face looking very pink. "Um . . . . mmm! Sorry everyone. Not sure what happened then. Very interesting story though," and he muttered a few more things under his breath before moving off. But as he turned away his eyes were like chips of flint.

Diane grinned. "This is just what we've been looking for! I vote we use it for our Christmas holiday adventure! It's perfect! We can even find the giant's treasure and wrap it up for Christmas gifts." Then, biting her thumb, a faraway expression filling her eyes, added. "I wonder what the treasure is."

Timothy pulled out his pocket diary, eager to take some notes. The thought of finding a giant and the giant's treasure grew more interesting as each moment passed. If they found the treasure they would have solved their Christmas gift problems. "Did your dream tell you where the treasure was hidden? Wow! Just think if we could find it! There might be enough goodies for all of us to have a share! We would have to make it a four-way split of course, so we all got a share." He chuckled. "But being the eldest amongst us I ought to have the lion's share!

Joan clamped her hands over her head, screwed her face up and burst out, "Stop it! It's not a joke!" She wanted to shut out their chatter about searching for treasure and giants. "I didn't see any treasure in my dream, only long dark tunnels, and running, running." The fat tears welled up again and splashed down her face before she could hide them and suddenly the whole awfulness of her dream flooded back as crisp and clear as when she first dreamed it. "All four of us were there. We were trapped in some strange place. It was so frightening!" She ended each sentence with a terrified sob, never wanting to hear of it, or see it, again.

Diane felt sorry for her earlier remarks and passed across a dry handkerchief. "You're not normally so childish, Joanie."

Mark patted her hand gently. "Let's forget it for a while. Perhaps we ought to find something else to do for the holidays." He did his best to look disinterested but a fierce look of excitement had leapt into his eyes at the mention of the tunnels.

Through a series of meaningful looks no one mentioned exploring Henley Forest again as they hurried back to complete their afternoon farm chores. But as each child chased hens, penned up ducks, carried buckets of calf cake, fed cows, and helped their father lug around bales of hay and straw, their minds were taken over by primitive longings of adventure. Primitive longings for challenge, for human courage, and of trials to overcome made their faces glow, and odd chaotic memories tugged at their minds, sometimes remembering how they had found the strange place covered in brambles, and sometimes letting their minds wander on thoughts of treasure, dragons, giants, and adventure. So it was that they gave into their longings for adventure and a pow wow was called for long before their chores were finished and the air around the farm began to throb with the hum of hurried activity.

In the dusk they met at the bottom of the barn beneath the thick oak beams, eager faced, breathing heavily in the cold air, and impatient to begin.

This place, surrounded by large iron grain bins and a cylindrical red diesel tank, was their favourite meeting place when they wanted to plan a new adventure game. It was also the starting point of all their adventures. Timothy stood upright, like a Commander facing his troops before going into battle, whilst Diane, Mark and Joan sat on the top of the bins swinging their legs in some feverish tattoo on the metal sides. The rapid drumming by six legs spoke of their excitement.

Diane thought this adventure promised to be their best one yet, and more exciting than laying disused railway sleepers across the barn floor, between cattle stalls and calf pens, so they could play 'Off ground tig', or 'Pirates'. This adventure seemed to be real; she couldn't wait to begin.

Thrum, thrum, thrum, the six legs drummed on the bins, getting louder and louder.

"Quiet!" Timothy shouted. The drumming stopped and he started to outline his first plan. "Is everyone listening? Right, let's begin. As you know we have just started our Christmas holidays and Joanie has discovered the legend of a sleeping giant who guards a great treasure."

"A *local* legend," put in Joan proudly. "So it might be true."

"We need to decide if we want to find the treasure. Well? Are you interested?" Timothy felt his face flushing as a sense of urgency, mingled with concern, made him step back. He looked at Joan. "Do you still think the legend is part of your dream?"

She tried to say something and for a moment her eyes flickered as though something painful swept across her mind, then she stared out over the barn door to where a few hundred yards away Henley Forest was clothed in winter darkness. She shrugged. "I think I just got frightened when we all began to talk about it in the library. I've got over it now."

"Okay, great. Well, I formally declare this Christmas adventure will be known as 'The Sleeping Giant's Treasure Chest'. And hopefully the treasure chest will be huge, and filled with lots of money and gold. Enough for everyone!" said Timothy, his voice rising in excitement.

"Hooray," shouted the others and kicked the grain bins even louder. "This is going to be fun!" They slapped hands together in a series of secret clasps to seal the pact. Mark spat on his hands and caught Diane scowling at him.

"When we eventually find the giant's castle we must make sure we hide from him, in case he thinks we've climbed up some magic beanstalk!" Timothy hooted loudly at his joke and doubled over, his stomach hurting with the fun of it all. It was such a foolish notion. Mark smirked, and leaping off the bin bowed low to Timothy as if he were a gentleman at court.

"Excuse me kind sir, but I've never met a giant before. Please can you tell me how big you are? Because I can't see your head as it is stuck in the clouds!" The two girls giggled in the background. Mark cavorted around, playing up to his audience, speaking in a ridiculously childish voice, and enjoying the theatrical fun of a new adventure. "I hope you don't like eating children, Sir. You see, we are only small children, and although there are four of us we've not enough meat on us to fill you up. Not even for one meal!" Mark gave a happy yelp and fell on the ground, kicking his legs with exaggerated laughter.

"Okay. That's enough fooling around, Mark. Get back on the bin and listen to what I've decided," Timothy rebuked him, though took the sting from his words by smiling. He put on his severe, no nonsense look. "If this new adventure is to be taken seriously we need to find out several important things. Firstly, who is the giant?"

Diane stopped kicking the bin. "I've already told you."

"Wait!" cut in Timothy. "Tell us everything in a minute. I repeat, who is the giant? Where is he? What is the treasure? And finally, how do we find it? Those are the questions we need to answer. If we manage to discover all of this during the Christmas holidays then I think we will have a fabulous time. We might even get rich!" Timothy took his place on the grain bins beside Mark.

"Okay Diane, your turn now to tell everyone what you know. Stand in the place where I stood and tell us everything you know about the sleeping giant."

Diane slid off the bin, pulling a face. She straightened her coat in imitation of Timothy, cleared her throat, and began. "Here goes. Though I only know a little bit. The sleeping giant is not a normal giant like we read about in storybooks; he's made from the shape of the trees. The trees are those of Henley Forest, and you can see it when you're looking from the railway bridge at the top of the farm."

"Oooh! Let's see." Immediately everyone began sliding off the bins and running to the barn door.

"Wait!" called Diane sharply, bringing them back to the bin. "We can't see the shape of the giant from here; we're too low down in the valley. We need to go to the top of our road. Besides, the giant is partially hidden behind our house and the orchard. There, that's it! That's all I know of the legend of the giant!" She gave a flourish and climbed back on the bin with the others, folding her arms.

Timothy got out his notebook and began scribbling furiously. "Mark, can you add anything to Diane's information?"

"I've only heard the same as Diane . . . ." he began, then stopped abruptly. *It wasn't true.* He had heard something else, and it was there nagging at his memory. Then it hit him. *A giant.* "Actually, I did hear something, a few months ago. It was from the old lady. You know her Timothy, she lives at the bottom of the stone steps between Middle Path and Hermitage Street. Well, she caught me and my friends playing outside her house after school had finished for the day, and blamed us for banging on her door."

"Mum said not to . . ." cut in Joan.

Mark scowled. "It wasn't us who had banged on her door, anyway, it was Steve Dobell, and she said if we didn't stop being a nuisance she would get the old giant to throw us into his dungeon."

Dungeon! Joan put a hand to her head, feeling as if she were suffocating. "Dungeon? His dungeon? Oh, no!" She shook her head furiously as if to blot out Mark's words. "I wish you hadn't told us that. It's linked to another of my dreams! And now you've made me remember! And I'm beginning to remember more and more, and I don't want to!"

"What do you remember?" asked Timothy, his voice tense.

"Oh, don't make me remember any more. Please! It was . . . well, we found a tunnel behind some funny walls, and then there were these pictures, all over the place, and when we looked at them I realised we were being sealed in and we ran and ran and ran." Joan rubbed away the tears that were bubbling up again. Her words didn't make much sense to the others but she didn't care.

Timothy went quiet. He frowned thoughtfully, wondering what had happened to the fun atmosphere of a few moments earlier. Joan's dreams were beginning to scare him with their clarity. "I'll bet we escaped from the tunnels. Right?" He leaped down from the bin and took up his stance again. "All dreams come out good in the end, Joanie. Don't worry. And all of us here will protect you. Even me, aaarrrrghhhh!" and he thumped his chest like Tarzan of the jungle.

Mark grew sharp and defiant. "I'll take my new bow and arrows," he said, thinking of the bow he had made from stripped withy branches and the arrows from hazel wood.

But Timothy cut in, his face pale and set. There seemed to be lots of similarities between Joan's dreams and the legend in the book which he didn't like, and although he knew they couldn't be the same thing, because he was fourteen and boys of his age didn't believe in dreams, nevertheless everything about the legend was intriguing. If it was linked to the forest then he wanted to investigate again, but he didn't want to take the others and expose them to danger. "All of you must stay here, whilst I go back alone."

"No!" protested everyone."

"It's a long way to the forest, and I'll get back much quicker on my own. Besides, the forest is enough to give you the creeps, even on a summer's day! And as I am the oldest I think it would be best for you to stay on the farm, wait for Mum and Dad to get back from market, and wait for my return."

"That's not fair!" shouted Diane.

"We're coming with you!" said Mark. "You might need our help."

"All right. I give in," said Timothy, feeling ridiculously relieved at having company. "We'll go on Saturday, when Mum and Dad are at Taunton Market. But, you must do exactly as I tell you. If not, you'll be sent straight back home."

And so their greatest adventure began.

Chapter 3

The rifle range

Saturday arrived in a flurry of activity and mounting excitement. Diane clattered down the stairs, humming "We're off to see the wizard;" which got everyone in a happy mood and talking about the supernatural and magic, and impatient to begin their big Christmas adventure. First though they had to finish their farm chores after mother and father had gone to market. Diane also wanted to wrap some Christmas gifts she had bought earlier, hoping that their new adventure would fill all of their holidays which meant she would have no time to wrap presents later.

She clattered into the kitchen with lots of little gifts balanced crazily in her hands whilst large shopping bags full of gifts swung from her shoulders. However, what caught the eye were the strange assortment of bandages, plasters and first aid ointments bursting over the tops of her pockets.

She emptied her arms over the table and oohed and aahed helplessly as bottles of bubble bath and boxes of soap, mingled with bandages, plasters, and tubes of ointments, went flying in all directions. She scooped them into a large pile in the middle of the scrubbed pine table and let out a deep sigh. *There, much better.* And she grinned at the pretty pile of tinsel bows as gold jostled merrily next to greens, reds, silver and blues. But then mother's questioning face appeared from the kitchen. "Are you wrapping your presents now?" she asked.

Diane wriggled nervously as flashes of guilt swept through her. "I hope you don't mind. We thought we would stay at home today," she said, wishing she could tell mother their secret plans. But Timothy had sworn them all to secrecy.

Mother nodded whilst tipping boiling water from a kettle into a flask. "I didn't realise I had bought so many gifts already," explained Diane rapidly and more guiltily with each passing moment. "I've got presents for nearly everyone and don't really need to get much more."

"It's a shame you won't be coming, Diane. You'll miss seeing the Christmas lights through Ilminster, and along Taunton High Street," remarked mother. Then seeing the first aid objects began laughing. "I hope you're not planning to give bandages to your friends instead of presents!"

"Oh, no! I'm topping up my first aid box," Diane stammered, checking herself, her eyes large and bright with worry. Had she said too much? Mother knew she only took her first aid box when they were going on adventures. Would she suspect what they planned to do? Diane hated being secretive, and before she realised it blurted out what she should have kept quiet. "When we've finished our chores we plan to go to Henley Forest. We want to find some tre . . . . Ouch!" Diane cried out and fell forwards as something struck the back of her legs.

Mark had come up from behind, heard her, and kicked her knees, then grabbed her cardigan and began pulling her out of the room.

"You clot!" he hissed, when they were out of earshot. "This adventure is supposed to be a secret, and no one is to know we are going to the forest—in case they stop us."

"I heard that," said mother, following them wondering what the upset was. She put down the flask and gave Mark a look. "Your father and I won't stop you going to the forest, but we always tell you not to get up to any mischief, nor run across the open fields, leave gates open, or upset the livestock. And please remember to behave sensibly and carefully at all times." She popped the full flask into her bag. "If you're planning to visit the old rifle range you'll need a warm coat, especially at this time of year. You can shelter against the old buildings if the weather turns wet. Though don't go inside the buildings because the walls won't be safe. And don't climb on anything if it looks dangerous because no one goes there any more and if you fall you may have a long time to wait for help."

Timothy came clumping into the kitchen, peering his head around the door, his Wellington boots thick with mud. "Did you mention the rifle range?"

"Boots off," Mother said automatically. "Yes, if that is where you have planned to go today."

Father had mentioned the rifle range before, usually when telling them real life stories of his first years on the farm, and usually when relaxing after Sunday lunch. He told them army things, about manoeuvrings, target practice and so on, which happened on the farm during the war. But up to now the children thought they had never gone deep enough into the forest to find the rifle range. It always sounded exciting and just the sort of place they wanted for their adventures. But now, suddenly, with mother knowing they planned to go there and giving them various warnings it no longer sounded exciting but rather ominous, and Timothy heard alarm bells ringing. Then instantly it dawned on him that possibly the old walls they discovered on their previous visit might have been part of the wartime rifle range after all. So, they had already found it! Wow! And instantly their planned adventure sounded exciting again because they could investigate the old ruins and look for the giant at the same time!

Timothy looked at mother. "We think we found the rifle range when we went to the forest a while ago. It would be fun if we could find it again, rather than go to Taunton market . . . ." He left the sentence hanging.

Mother smiled. So, her children were up to their old tricks of adventuring, what would they bring back this time? "The rifle range was bombed in the war, and never used again, that's why it will be dangerous to walk into. And I expect it'll be very overgrown with weeds and trees by now."

Timothy jotted a few notes in his notebook. *Rifle range. Bombed.* He raised his head eager for more information. "Have you heard of the sleeping giant?"

"A little."

"Would you tell us? Please?" Sensing a good story he finally kicked off his muddy boots and sidled inside the warm kitchen, his most appealing look plastered on his face. "Joanie found a legend or something about it in the library, the other day, and Diane seems to think it's about the trees in Henley Forest being the shape of a sleeping giant." He pushed his blonde forelock off his face, his blue eyes dancing with fun and all traces of worry pushed firmly at the back of his mind. They were going to have one of their usual adventures today, he decided, and they would probably end up chasing each other around some trees, whooping and yelling like natives, a bird feather stuck in their hair, and playing pranks on one another. "It's the sleeping giant we're hoping to find."

"Goodness me! What a notion!" Mother burst out laughing and the initial fear she had felt when they mentioned the 'giant' disappeared. It was only a childish adventure after all. No need to worry. Most of her children's adventures involved long walks across their neighbouring farmer's fields looking for ancient relics to dig up. Their last adventure found them unearthing spent brass cartridge casings from second world war rifles. And her children were a common sight found waving to the trains as they swept past their farm. This latest adventure would be as innocent as the others she thought. "What does the legend tell you? I'll see if I can add a bit more."

"Oh good!" The four children crowded round.

Timothy began. "The sleeping giant is believed to watch over the inhabitants of Crocern, according to Joanie's legend, which I presume is Crewkerne." He paused, then saw mother nodding. "The giant is said to awaken and help us in times of trouble, and that he watches over a great treasure."

Mother laughed. "I haven't heard that version before. It sounds reassuring to have a giant guarding us; I wonder if we could get his help on the farm sometimes!" She smiled at her joke and continued with her thoughts. "Your legend reminds me of the story of old King Bluebeard, who is believed to be sleeping deep within a mountain. He is surrounded by a host of brave warriors, who live and wait in a large wooden hall, ready to fight when their country is threatened, just like the Saxon chieftains of old, or Odin waiting in Valhalla. Legend tells us King Bluebeard and his men will wake up whenever the country is threatened, and march out to protect it." Mother looked at the eager faces in front of her, liking their interest in stories. "Most legends are made up from bits and pieces of other stories. It's very rare to find a story not based upon another. I expect the legend of your sleeping giant of Henley Forest is a bit like this."

"Is that all, a story based upon another story?" Timothy's face fell. Their delight in finding the rifle range and their new adventure seemed to be fading into a hotch potch of stories that had nothing to do with Henley Forest and Crewkerne.

"Don't despair too quickly!" said mother. "There is often a grain of truth in legends which have become distorted through the centuries. So, for example, your treasure—what do you think it is? A golden necklace?

A rare jewel? Perhaps it is discovering you are a prince or princess of a palace or castle. Or, perhaps your treasure is a store of Roman coins, just waiting to be found."

"Or Cinderella's golden carriage," interrupted Joan with sparkling eyes.

Mother agreed. "Everyone has a different idea of 'treasure'."

Timothy closed his notebook. How would they find the giant's treasure if they didn't know what they were looking for?

But, with their minds focussed on giants and treasure, no one realised mother hadn't really told them about the legend of the sleeping giant and Henley Forest.

Chapter 4

Strange stones

Father's van drove through the gate at the top of the farm track, and the children laughed and dashed into the house to make their final preparations for their visit to the forest. Their parents would be at Taunton market for the whole day and they would be on their own. At last they could start looking for the sleeping giant and his treasure. "Three cheers for the sleeping giant!" they shouted, before giving their secret hand clasps and racing to grab a bite to eat. They would be leaving within thirty minutes. Joan thrust her arms into her thick coat, snatching a scarf against the cold wind, and rushing out tucking a half finished pasty in her pocket. Mark whistled happily whilst munching the last of his pasty as he found out his bow and arrows, and tucked his coat under his arm. Diane and Timothy, being older, were more thoughtful about the items they collected for their adventure. Timothy went to the old engine shed and took one of father's choppers and tucked it inside his overcoat. It would come in useful if he had to cut down the branches and brambles they had seen growing last time. Diane packed her newly replenished first aid kit, as well as a bag of doorstep sandwiches; they were bound to be hungry on their new adventure.

However, before they rushed up to the forest Timothy insisted everyone do their farm chores, so they scooted down to the barns, cleaned out the cow stalls, fed the heifers and took water into the pig sties. Then they had the rest of the day to search for the rifle range, and hopefully find the giant. When they were ready Timothy gave them a nod, locked the door, and set off.

Like a snake they began their trek to the forest, eldest leading, Diane next, Mark in third place and Joan bringing up the rear. There was to be no loud talking, no complaining, and if anyone got sore feet from their Wellington boots Diane would pass them a plaster from her first aid box. They had covered every eventuality.

A heavy drizzle set in as soon as they left the farm and they quickly agreed it was one of the most cold and miserable December days they had had, shrugging their necks as rain water trickled coldly off their hair.

The distance to the forest was about half a mile over broken ground and took them through the apple orchard, a neighbour's sheep field, and then over several wire fences, across a cold stream, and finally amongst the forest trees which were dripping with clusters of hanging ivy and evergreens. They dragged their coat collars together until only their eyes peeped over the tops. It felt really creepy walking under the dense trees and Diane glanced back nervously. Timothy followed her glance and he too began feeling uneasy. Was someone following them? He shook his head wondering, then right up ahead he recognised a tree with a great split through the trunk. They were going the right way after all. But then he recognised nothing else and began feeling sick as they tramped through the dense and dark trees. Had they wandered onto a deer path or fox track?

After twenty minutes he realised they were utterly lost. Diane began making wide sweeping movements with her arms, wanting them to fan out and search for a better path. Timothy glared at her, knowing they were lost; he should have been better prepared and taken compass bearings. He wished he had made some special marks the last time they had come into the forest, like a secret trail. It was too late now. *What a prize idiot I am,* he thought. Mark and Joan stopped chattering noticing the tense atmosphere around them. Timothy raised his hand and everyone trudged to a weary halt, all feeling dispirited and tired. If he told them they were lost Joan would probably start crying, and he knew from years of experience that her crying would upset the others.

Mark swiped his foot at a dried up fir cone. "We've got to keep going. We're nearly there. Come on everyone, follow me." And he rushed ahead, dashing forwards, calling directions over his shoulder and racing into the undergrowth. "Left here! Right here. And then we reach the funny stones."

The children ran after him, wellington boots slap slapping loudly on the forest floor. Mark came to a halt in front of a barrage of ivy. "We're back on the right track now."

"How do you know?" said Timothy. "And what stones are you talking about?".

Mark grinned jubilantly then plunged beneath some heavy gnarled ivy limbs and disappeared. "The stones are here. They're really weird looking."

"Don't touch them," called Timothy. "Remember what Mum said. And we're supposed to keep together."

"Okay. Okay. I'm coming back." A few crashing sounds brought Mark onto the path in front of them again, grinning helplessly and dragging pine needles from his hair. "Wait until you see what I've found!" he laughed, freckles racing across his face.

"Is it the giant's secret world?" piped up Joan excitedly.

"Of course it is," teased Mark. But then he clamped his mouth shut, suddenly feeling uncertain. How did he know about the stones when they couldn't be seen from the path, and why did this dark dense place seem familiar?

Timothy moved in front and began hacking away at the branches to clear a path for the girls. When he reached the stones he hesitated sensing something creepy.

"Perhaps we ought to leave now, and go home."

Diane began to argue, but when she saw the stones behind Timothy her voice dried up in disbelief. Mark's 'weird' stones were huge and stood many hands taller than Joan. They were ragged around the edges and looked like a giant's hand had ripped them from a gigantic quarry in some mad satanic frenzy, before heaping them in a crazy profusion of lines, one on top the other. These ghastly stones formed a vast wall that seemed to push its way into the forest before disappearing beneath a dense wall of giant vegetation. Many of them were thick black in colour Joan noticed, and they gave off a feeling of evil

"What is this place?" she whispered.

Mark pressed closer to the strange wall, noticing a faint mixture of lines and odd markings gouged into the surface of each black stone. The nearer he got to the wall the stranger he felt.

"Be careful," said Timothy, closely following his younger brother.

The girls tucked in behind the boys, once more in single file, and once more with Timothy taking the lead as they found themselves on a thin path running alongside the wall. Sometimes Timothy missed his footing and all the while a growing sense of fear swelled through him. How he wished he hadn't brought the others; Joan was far too young to cope. Soon she would grumble she felt cold, and he would get the blame. He shook away his doubts and hoped they would soon find the rifle range. He remembered how the temperature had dropped on their earlier visit to the forest, and how it felt as if they were entering a world of winter. It was dropping now. Plummeting faster than a broken icicle. Every now and then his hand touched a stone through the mounds of ivy that had grown up around it, and as it did a tremor rushed through him.

He could feel the stones changing shape beneath his fingers as he moved along the black wall, becoming newer, modern, and identical in size. Rapidly he started hacking at the ivy anxious to discover what was underneath. Now he realised the stones were different, red, oblong. Then he burst out laughing, the horrid weird stones were gone and in their place were normal, red house bricks. What a relief!

However, Mark was disturbed. He halted so quickly Diane nearly cannoned into him whilst Joan collided into them both.

"Ouch, mind where you're—going!" Mark snapped, struggling to control a sudden breathlessness.

"Shh!" said Timothy. "I think we've found the rifle range."

"I know. That's why I brought you here," Mark spat crossly.

Timothy stared at his brother's bad temper. "This must be all that survived after the bombing in the war. I wonder if we can get inside." He noticed how his voice seemed to echo with a haunting quality as if being sucked into nothingness by the wetness of the forest. Then suddenly his fear returned and it was more frightening than before because he felt someone else beside them. He whirled around, eyes peering into the darkness. Mark, Diane and Joan were looking at him strangely. *Don't be silly,* he thought, forcing himself to breathe deeply. *There's no one else here.* "Is this the same place we found on our last visit?" he asked. No one replied. The odd sensation passed and Diane had taken the opportunity to put her pack on the ground, massaging her aching shoulders.

Joan dumped her duffel bag beside Diane's and yanked off a Wellington boot, complaining about blisters on her heel. Diane silently passed her a plaster, but she was looking at Mark who had gone white around the eyes. Her younger brother looked as if he were listening for something, then flung up his hands and leaned forwards like a startled rabbit bolting to its hole.

"Mark! What is it?" she hissed, keeping her voice quiet and wondering why she did so. His eyes flickered in his white face; they seemed to be pleading for help. Then the moment passed and Mark relaxed. Somewhere a blackbird shrieked in alarm and once again the sharp sound broke the unnatural frozen quality of the forest.

Timothy shook himself, wondering if he had imagined the strange sensations, then began hacking at the ivy again. Mark bustled around clearing twigs and rotting leaves from beneath their feet. Diane grabbed Joan's arm and together they began tramping down the dead vegetation to make a suitable place for them to sit on and eat their lunch. Joan reached to touch her acorn talisman beneath her coat then realised she was still wearing her pretty gold cross, and without realising the enormity of what she did clenched her fingers around the tiny piece of gold, and it made her instantly feel better.

Timothy had chopped down a pile of ivy and thrown it behind him. "Diane, stack these branches to one side so we can clear a passage to the stone wall. If we're lucky we might see a door or something leading us into the rifle range. Mark, you can help Diane, and Joanie can look after the food. We'll be stopping for lunch soon. Mum thought we could sit just inside if the weather grew worse. Though no climbing." He broke off, shivering violently. Diane and Mark dragged their coats tighter, pulling the collars up around their ears and tucked their scarves under their chins.

Beside them Mark did a very peculiar thing, he picked up his bow, notched a tiny arrow into the string, and fired, aiming directly at the brick walls.

Timothy called out. "Mark! No! What are . . . ?" But his cry was too late. A faint thud followed the soft twang of the string as the fragile arrow broke itself against the dense ivy and fell to the ground.

"What did you do that for?" asked Timothy, looking bewilderedly at the broken arrow. He thought how the fragility of the arrow had been abused by its impact of the ivy, and how the ugliness of Mark's weird stones stood in sharp contrast to the simple beauty of his hand-made arrow. For a moment Timothy felt horrified at the destruction of the arrow, remembering the care Mark had spent in making it, and finally admitted to himself there were many horrific things in the world, of which he as yet knew nothing. And quite suddenly he knew that in these last minutes his youthful innocence had been lost forever, and lay in pieces with the arrow.

The two girls were looking with wide eyes at Mark. *What had he aimed at?*

Then, "Shh!" Joan whispered sharply, feeling her stomach doing somersaults. "Something's groaning behind the walls."

"Don't talk nonsense," grumbled Diane. "You're only trying to frighten us! And it's not very funny. We know there's no one here because Mum told us no one goes to the rifle range any more."

"There is, Diane. I heard something. I know I did!" said Joan, starting to stamp her foot but remembering in time that young girls didn't so such things.

Mark brushed past and collected the broken arrow before tucking it into his bag. He appeared to be inspecting the brick walls for damage. But how could a home-made toy do any damage? He gave a shuddering sigh and his shoulders sagged with disappointment, but then quite suddenly he grabbed one of the thick ivy vines and tugged, really hard, until a piece broke off.

"Get back, Mark!" barked Timothy roughly, who by now really wanted to go home and get everyone to safety. "You'll end up pulling the whole wall down!"

Mark hesitated for a moment, his eyes wild, and then he yanked again with a vicious twist of his lips. This time he wedged his foot at the base of the ivy for leverage and with much groaning the vine broke.

"Good!" Mark's face beamed. Immediately a thin rumble was heard deep inside the ivy. Then a small section of the rifle range wall came bursting at his feet. He laughed and tugged again, completely ignoring Timothy and his sisters who were wondering what had gotten into him. Now he grabbed a thicker piece of vine and as he yanked it towards him a great length of wall buckled and began toppling downwards. It was falling directly on top of the children.

"Move!" Timothy bellowed, catching at Joan' arm. His nails bit into her sleeve and he dragged at her as if he were wrenching off a branch. She came jerking her off her feet towards him, shocked into immobility but suddenly finding herself being propelled sideways. Timothy used this momentum to help him with his next movements for as the two of them went crashing to the ground he forced their combined body weight to one side, juggling with the need to go crashing towards Mark and the thought that he would land very badly and could end up hurting himself.

He couldn't worry about that now. He had a fraction of a second to put his next idea into action and get Diane out of the way also. The wall buckled alarmingly above them and on either end of the twisting brickwork loose red bricks were beginning to fall. Soon the whole thing would go.

Timothy raised his free arm, awkwardly twisting it and punching Mark in the shoulder, whilst simultaneously kicking Diane to send her flailing into the mound of leafy branches she had collected earlier. He braced himself for a bad landing and moments later a sharp stabbing pain exploded through his left hip causing him to cough and gasp. Before he could yelp with pain however Joan came crashing on top of him, her sleeve still caught in his hand, and all the breath in his lungs shot out of him as he was sandwiched between his sister's weight and the hard ground. With an agonising thump the four children hit the ground in a mess of tangled limbs and branches, well clear of the bricks.

For a split second there was silence before Joan let out a shrill howl of indignation, wriggled from Timothy's grasp and stood up like a fiery imp, eyes popping crossly to protest loudly. Diane slithered away, her face thunderous, and hit out at her brother's hand as he offered to help. Then she hurried over to Mark who was on his knees a short distance away and seemed to be in pain. He got to his feet, rubbing a sore shoulder, and planning a return attack. But their grumbles were cut short as a thick sliding sound like oozing mud roared in their ears and drowned everything out. The rest of the rifle range walls were moving.

"The whole thing's falling down!" bellowed Timothy. "Don't move! Stay where you are."

They didn't need a second bidding, they were frozen to the spot and staring helplessly at the red wall collapsing in front of them. Timothy gauged the destruction of the walls and shoved them further away. "That's better! Wow! That was close."

"Mum warned us about messing around!" snapped Diane, glaring at Mark and simultaneously brushing dirt and leaves off her coat. "She said the place had been bombed, and now we've finished it off. We should have left it alone; we could have been hurt." She ended her little speech in the grown-up voice she had begun to adopt when trying to impress upon the others that she was in charge, especially of their health, as

Mum's eldest daughter, and therefore knew best. After all, she reasoned, she was the one with the first aid kit. But Timothy noticed her white face and felt sorry for her. She had been scared as hell too.

"We nearly got hurt, Tim, and you hurt my arm," wailed Joan, near to tears.

Timothy gave her arm a distracted pat; wondering if he looked as sick as he felt. "Good shooting Mark!" he said, adopting a false light quality. "You looked like William Tell shooting the apple with his bow and arrow. Well done."

Mark stuttered, blushing horribly, "I'm sorry." Then his voice went thin. "What's this behind . . . . ? Another wall, and those stones . . . ." He broke off sharply, his voice now rapid and changing to furious excitement. "Come here! Quickly. Look at this!"

"Whoa! Wait!" exclaimed Timothy. "Wait for me." Then his voice changed too. "What *are* those? Mark! No! Don't touch anything," But Mark had jumped over the pile of red rubble and was looking at a large patch of jet black stones. He began rubbing his fingernails over the black surface of each one, a thoughtful expression on his face. "These stones are like the ones we found earlier." And then he added something that sent shivers up and down everyone's back. "These stones have been carved. Many years ago. I wonder why. And what does it mean?"

"I can't see any carvings," said Timothy leaning closer.

Mark ignored him and began pushing along the length of newly uncovered wall. There appeared to be no end to it. As fast as he pushed along its length a barrage of ivy and ancient trees stood in his way, almost as if they were shielding the wall from prying eyes, like a secret wall.

"These stones are monstrous!" said Timothy. "This wall is much too big to investigate now. Perhaps we ought to go home before we get lost."

Mark had a rapt expression on his face. "I wonder who carved them," he said. "They're very old. I think it would be a good idea if I made drawings of them."

"What for?" Timothy frowned.

"Because I think I've seen these carvings before."

"I can't see any lines, well, nothing much."

"We may as well have our lunch here," said Diane, spreading a blanket over the soft pieces of ivy they had cut earlier.

"Okay," said Timothy, coming back and munching on a pasty whilst he looked thoughtfully at the strange stones in front of them. "I suppose the rifle range was built against that black wall for strength," he muttered between mouthfuls. "Though I can't see the lines you mentioned Mark. Perhaps you're imagining them."

"I'm not!" Mark snapped, snatching out his notebook and sketching furiously. "There! Surely you can see this line," he said pointing. "And this, and this."

Timothy shook his head. A moment later he gasped, stumbling back, his head craned upwards. "Cripes! Look at that! Up there! I've never seen a wall so big." The black wall, since that is what it was, went up as far as Timothy could see. In fact it went so high it disappeared into the huge canopy of trees growing overhead. "It's not just a wall, it must be something else," he said.

The girls followed his pointing finger. "Oooh!" And they too craned their heads, trying to see the top of the strange black wall.

Moving as one the children inched away, their faces working under a barrage of emotions, flickering from surprise to shock, from awesome wonder to excitement as they realised they were beneath an ancient castle wall, from a forgotten civilization.

"Oh, my goodness," gasped Joan. "It looks like . . ." and stopped, feeling shocked.

"It can't be," said practical Diane.

"But what is a castle doing here?" said Timothy voicing their thoughts.

So it was they gaped at a castle wall and everyone forgot the groan Joan heard moments earlier.

Mark became more convinced that he had seen the peculiar lines on the stones before, and sketched furiously, wondering if he would remember where, and perhaps find out more about the castle walls. Timothy experienced a queasy feeling; knowing they ought to have gone home earlier, and feeling their Christmas adventure was getting out of hand. "From now on we are to be more careful. And as Diane rightly said, Mum did warn us," he said with emphasis. Then, realising how cold he felt he made a quick decision. "I think we have done enough for today. We have found the rifle range and the brambles Joanie mentioned as part of her dreams, and we have found a mystery wall. Let's all go home now and we can have a pow-wow in the orchard."

An immediate protest began, though it was half hearted as Diane and Mark huddled, cold and miserable into their coats. Diane didn't want them to get indigestion from moving too fast after eating, and Mark wanted to complete his drawings, but Timothy remained adamant. "There's something unpleasant going on here, and I don't like it. Until we've sorted out a proper plan of action we're going back home, in one piece, just like I promised Mum."

After a hasty tidy up the tired little group of brothers and sisters left Henley Forest far behind, trailing their way back to the farm. They decided to finish their lunch at the pow wow, in the wooden stable that stood on the hill in their apple orchard. The stable, originally built as protection for the farm's beef cattle, was made of four sides of rough wooden planks nailed together. It had a small window along the front and a sloping roof covered with black felt. The inside always smelt of hay and dried earth. Today it was cold but dry and they quickly made themselves comfortable as they spread out the blanket which Timothy shook out. Diane slipped her haversack onto the floor in front of them and everyone contemplated sinking their teeth into the last of the sandwiches, and the jam tarts, and then going over the first part of their Christmas adventure. Though their faces glowed with excitement no one could utter a word. It was as if something had come back from the forest with them and frightened them into silence. Mark sat on the blanket, his eyes black and gaunt, fidgeting with his broken arrow, curling his arms around his knees protectively, and looking secretive. Joan felt for her tiny cross at the base of her throat and quickly hid the book of local legends inside her coat pocket, as if she thought looking at the gruesome dragon on the cover was enough to conjure it.

Timothy looked grim, and paced the inside of the shelter like a caged animal. Diane packed away the lunch bags, then sat back looking confused. She could feel the tense atmosphere, but didn't know what had created it. Mark hunched his shoulders and turned away from the others to hide his drawings as though he didn't want anyone to see them. The others watched silently, feeling dismayed, since it made them feel as if they had returned empty handed from their new Christmas adventure.

Then slowly Timothy opened his hand.

Nestled in his palm lay a dark, metal object. Later he would discover it was an ancient weapon, used during the battles between King Arthur and his enemies.

"I found this. It must have fallen out when the brick wall crashed down."

Mark sucked in his breath, looking at what appeared to be the metal tip from one of his arrows. But the object in Timothy's hand was much larger, heavier, and hammered into shape, and obviously made of iron. "Can I touch it?"

"No!" the word exploded from Timothy's lips and he snapped his fingers over the object. Immediately he felt a strange sensation, and thought it was an electric current, pulsating through his palm. He jumped, nearly dropping the arrowhead in the process. *What was that feeling?* There weren't any cables or batteries attached to the object, so why did he think of electricity? Anyway, the object reminded him of a relic from some long gone age, and more fitted for a museum. Perhaps it was a piece of some asteroid which had dropped from outer space, like a UFO. Or, could it be something worse? He tried to look as though everything was all right. He didn't know what the object was, he only knew it was important and might be linked to Mark's drawings, and Joan's legend. He plopped the arrowhead, since that was what he thought it was, back inside his pocket, and the burning sensations disappeared until all that was left was a little tingling running up his arm, reminding him of tiny spiders dashing away when their nest had been disturbed. He nearly laughed out loud in relief.

Then the air hushed, and it seemed to the children as if a gentle sigh escaped from Henley Forest as if someone felt happy, and it wafted softly to the children in the cattle shed. "Ohh!" Mark said, lifting his head with a radiant smile on his face.

And suddenly the tingling sensation along Timothy's arm exploded again. "Aah!" he shouted in surprise, then leapt up darting quick backward glances over his shoulder as if looking for someone following him.

"There's no one there," Mark said, his voice sounding like an echo in the cattle shed.

Diane screwed the empty paper sandwich bags into a ball. She had noticed nothing unusual, but the rustling of the paper sounded harsh and brittle. "Make sure you wash your hands before you eat one of my special tarts; especially after touching that thing," she said prosaically. The boys laughed and the tension around them rushed out with a whoosh. It was getting late, but no one had noticed. Mark relaxed his shoulders, Joan yawned and stretched her arms above her head. "I felt a lot of sadness about the place," she said, thinking of the black wall. Then she snuggled down on an edge of the blanket, longing to fall asleep.

"I think we need to investigate the old rifle range further," Timothy said.

"Are you sure you want to?" Mark would be very happy if they never went back to the forest.

Diane took a big bite from a piece of fruit cake, nodding her head enthusiastically. "I thoroughly enjoyed our walk up to the forest, even if I did get worn out carrying everyone's lunch." She looked at the others, not noticing their white strained faces. "I wondered if it would be helpful if we could find the author of the book? Perhaps we could ask them some questions about the legend; find out more about the sleeping giant of Henley Forest."

Timothy could have kicked himself. "Why didn't I think of that myself? Good idea, Diane. Perhaps we'll discover there's more to the legend than we know already." *It might also explain the weird feelings he had been having,* he thought. He couldn't wait to begin.

Chapter 5

Can we find the author?

Tracking down the author proved impossible. The library assistant appeared too busy on the Monday morning to help four children wanting to speak to an author of a book written over 75 years ago. Didn't they think the author might have died by now, she suggested? Timothy thought he had been rather silly missing the obvious clue of the publication date inside the front cover, and to make matters worse, it seemed as though the librarian tried to snatch the book out of Joan's hand. "I'll have the book back," she said, giving them all a glare. "You shouldn't have taken it out; it shouldn't have been on display. I remember getting rid of it ages ago. I don't know how it got back on the shelf stacks."

Her eyes suddenly started snapping frostily at the children and her fingers were wrapping themselves around the book. Joan knew she had to cling on to the book and responded by digging her nails into the book cover. They needed the book for their Christmas adventure and she wasn't going to give it up so easily.

"I'm not returning the book, Miss," blurted Joan, shaking her head at the librarian until her fair curls danced furiously. "I've got two weeks left on the ticket and I'm still reading it." She tugged it again and the book came away in her hands, and Joan raced outside, clutching her prize.

"Well!" exploded the librarian, spluttering crossly at Diane who was standing in front of her. "I suppose your sister can keep it another week; I know you children have walked a long way into town. But that book oughtn't to be out at all. It's out of date and out of print. Make sure you don't keep it too long." Flickering emotions chased themselves across her face as she began wondering why she suddenly felt so upset. It didn't make sense. She had felt really happy coming to work in the library today, having had a pleasant weekend preparing her Christmas cake and planning a party, but as soon as she saw the old book about local legends she had come over bad tempered and didn't want the children to have it. She tried to explain herself to Diane. "Don't take too much notice of the stories in there; most of them are rubbish and the product of a fevered imagination."

Outside again Diane shooed Joan down the street. "I don't think she like us! Let's run."

"She didn't want us to have the book," said Joan. "I wonder why not?" And the little group broke into a gentle trot down the hill and along Market Street.

Timothy felt puzzled as well. "Let me have the book, Joanie. I'll have a quick glance through it as we walk home," and he slowed their pace until they were walking briskly. Soon they would begin the long hill up Hermitage Street and they would need all their breath to keep up a good pace. But as Joan handed him the book another odd feeling rushed up his arm, making him nearly drop it. "Ouch. What was that?" he yelped. The book had grown so utterly cold. *As cold as a tomb*, thought Timothy. He could see the ugly green dragon glaring at him, evil and threatening, and quickly he tipped the book over. The red faced giant looked back, rosy, very red, and very happy. Gradually the book began to get warm and Timothy could feel his face stretching into one great big grin as wide as the grin on the giant's face. *Very peculiar* he thought, turning the book again. And then again. And every time he turned it over he felt icy, or warm, according to which creature was looking up at him. Dragon. Giant. Dragon. Giant. Cold. Hot. Cold. Hot. He felt the book was giving him a sinister warning, but it seemed rather foolish to feel alarmed at a book, so he ignored it.

"'*Local Legends*'," he said aloud. Legends weren't supposed to be true although mother suggested they might be based on fact. But this legend couldn't; no one believed in dragons and giants these days. He noticed there were ten legends in all, usually containing mythical beasts, ghostly apparitions of people in silver, or telling of disappearances of children in previous centuries. *All very silly*, Timothy decided, and retuned the book to Joan without saying anything about the icy feeling he had experienced earlier.

Diane complained, feeling miserable and downhearted. "I don't know why you bothered to bring the book, Joan; the librarian said it was printed a long time ago, so the author has probably died! And if we can't speak to the author, or find out anything more about the Sleeping Giant, we won't need it and we won't have much of an adventure."

Later, their mother handed them the telephone directory. "If the author's family still live nearby you might find them listed here."

"Why didn't I think of that?" Timothy exclaimed rushing upstairs with the thick book, and the others dashing up after him. "Thanks Mum."

"It'll be near the end," Diane added helpfully. "Under V. We're looking for Vanstone. Elizabeth Vanstone."

Timothy flipped the directory open, muttering loudly. "'Vann', 'Vanovitch', 'Vanrymen', 'Van-Stein', '*Vanstone!*'" Then he waved the book at them, nodding eagerly. "Here it is, Vanstone." Then his voice fell. "Uh oh! There are five of them."

"Try telephoning them all," called mother. "Ask politely if they know of Elizabeth Vanstone. If they say 'yes', ask them if they are related to her. If they're unsure about speaking to a group of youngsters over the telephone, tell them they can speak to me instead. I'll be happy to vouch for you." And she moved away laughing.

A few calls and a few minutes later and they narrowed the search to one remaining person. This time they were lucky; Betty Vanstone, of Hill Farm Cottage, Misterton, turned out to be the daughter of the author. But when their mother spoke to the lady over the telephone and explained her children were interested in knowing more about the Sleeping Giant, Betty grew worried. She said 'yes', she did know more, though wouldn't tell them over the telephone, instead she would call round later and speak to them with mother present. The children felt they were getting somewhere at last.

"Hooray!" Timothy scribbled out a few questions for Betty Vanstone, such as: How old was the legend? Did it have anything to do with the trees at Henley Forest? Did the picture of the dragon have anything to do with it? Had Betty ever touched the book herself? But as he wrote the last question he paused, remembering the strangeness he had felt earlier.

Diane busied herself making fairy cakes for their visitor, whilst Joan hugged the book as if she had a secret, it's eerie chilliness forgotten.

Mark had his own questions for Betty Vanstone and looked at the ancient arrowhead that Timothy had brought back from Henley Forest. It intrigued him because it reminded him of the weird stones they had seen near the rifle range. Perhaps they had come from another world. The arrowhead and the stones were connected in some way and he determined to find out how. And he wanted to know who had carved the lines on the rocks, and which he had copied. *Or,* he sucked in his breath, if not a *who,* then w*hat* had made them? Mark needed some answers and dashed upstairs, but as he reached his bedroom he suddenly became alarmed at all the unusual happenings, and dived beneath the bedclothes until their visitor arrived.

Betty Vanstone arrived mid afternoon. She caused a bit of a stir in the farmhouse as she arrived in a lovely red car covered in unusual stickers of stars, crescent moons, and magical signs, reminding Joan of the type of clothes Merlin the magician might have worn.

Her car looked like a red cube, which intrigued the children until they noticed Betty had difficulty walking, and her compact little car had been adapted to take a wheelchair. Betty got out slowly, using two strong walking sticks, and when outside she unclipped an electric wheelchair from the back of the car, fixed it firmly on the ground, and settled herself into it so it looked as if she were in an armchair. Then she drove it inside the large farmhouse kitchen, which was large enough for her to manoeuvre around. Mother helped her get near the table and everyone gathered round, chattering and excited.

Betty had a lovely beaming smile which she bestowed on them all and made the children love her at once. Diane grinned back, mighty pleased she had made the cakes and within moments the children began firing their questions.

Mother clapped her hands sharply. "Hold on, all of you," she cried, dismayed at the torrent of noises headed towards their visitor. "Let Betty have a drink and something to eat before you badger her for answers."

"Okay."

"Sorry, Mum."

The children slumped, fidgeted, smothered sighs, and watched Betty concentrating on her cup of tea. She looked calm, yet beneath her lowered lids closely studied the children. Though they didn't realise it Betty's hopes had been raised by their telephone call to her earlier, and now she was looking for a special child, one she had sought for many centuries, the child who had been named 'The Chosen One'. If she could find this child then perhaps the evil prophecy might be laid to rest forever. But, whatever she found or hoped for, here in this warm farmhouse kitchen on this December afternoon, she knew that life would never be the same for these children again. *Unless* . . . . Her thoughts stopped. Making up her mind she gave a faint nod, at last she realised there might be a way in which she could help. Timothy saw the nod and jumped up, "Can I ask some questions now?" He stepped up to Betty's chair. "First we would like you to tell us everything you know about the legend of the sleeping giant," he said.

And carefully Betty began to speak. And so it was the children first heard the real untold story of King Arthur and his knights, and how they came to be at Crewkerne many centuries ago, and how it all happened near their home, and how the sleeping giant legend grew.

Chapter 6

The legend of Crocern

"Did King Arthur really come to Crewkerne?" Joan demanded to know, her mouth opening and closing in amazement, not sure whether to 'ooh' or 'wow' every time Betty told them a little more. "I always believed King Arthur died at Glastonbury."

"According to some legends he is buried there, yes. But, is anyone really sure? Hundreds of years ago a priest found some bones and buried them in the old Glastonbury Abbey, but can we believe their claims? Are they really King Arthur's bones? Who can say? What if King Arthur was too badly injured to make it back to Glastonbury? What if he died somewhere else?"

The children were shocked. Joan could feel her eyes nearly popping out of her head. They had never expected their Christmas adventure to be this exciting!

"Try to imagine King Arthur, badly wounded, floating away on a boat, never managing to reach Glastonbury. Try to imagine the impossible; that the lake was in a different place." Betty entranced them with wonderful visions of new possibilities. "What might have happened to him if he died before completing the boat journey? Remember, he had just had a furious battle with his son Mordred and most of his heroic knights were dead or badly wounded. Later, knowing he was about to die, King Arthur asked his faithful knight Sir Bedivere, to throw his sword Excalibur into the lake. Then he said his farewells. Who knew what happened to their king when the boat went out of sight?" Betty's eyes glittered at her audience.

Then she sprung her real secret on them, and it changed their world forever. "Hundreds of years ago a large lake existed nearby." Pause. On the south west of Crewkerne?"

Stunned silence greeted her words before Timothy looked up sharply. "A lake? Near Crewkerne?" Then he remembered his orienteering exercises with the scouts. "But our farm is on the south west . . . . We live there . . . . I don't know of any lake . . ."

"Are you certain?" asked Betty levelly.

Timothy gave a shout and thumped his head with the palm of his hand as he recollected something else. "Yes! There is! Or was. Though now we call it a pond! When father bought the farm a huge pond stretched from the house to the barns, and all the way to the clay pits." The younger children remembered they had heard the story too. "Father had it filled in and grassed over for feeding the cows." His eyes flashed excitedly. "Do you really think it was King Arthur's lake? And how do you know?"

"I have proof," said their visitor, flourishing a battered map from her bag in front of them. "When I realised who contacted me earlier today, and where you lived, I thought you might like to see this. It shows the site of your farm. This is a seventeenth century tithe map I found several years ago, and look here, where I'm pointing my finger." She brushed her finger over the faded ink. "These wavy marks indicate areas of bog or marsh. See how big the area is! I think the marshlands are about a mile wide by about three miles long which proves that at least four hundred years ago a vast marshy area existed on the south west of Crewkerne. Since then it has been drained by intensive farming, to leave the little we have today. Your pond! If a huge lake existed here it might have been the Lake of Camelot! Nothing else like it existed in this area, except at Glastonbury where it flooded the levels across to Bridgwater." She paused. "Perhaps King Arthur's sword was thrown into the lake somewhere near here."

There. She had done that which she intended and which she knew had to be done, namely planting the seed in the children's minds, which would lead to the prophecy. It was up to them to take it further.

Timothy raced out of the kitchen and up to his bedroom, anxious to prove Betty's theories. He didn't realise he would add another piece to the puzzle for Betty, and they would step closer to the prophecy and the point of no return.

He came back brandishing his arrowhead. "What do you think of that?" He thrust it towards Betty.

"Where did you find that?" Her voice dropped like a bell of doom.

"At the rifle range," muttered Timothy, reddening. "What's wrong with it? A wall collapsed and this must have fell out. I found it on the ground."

Betty reached out, desperate to touch the object, but finally letting her hand fall limply into her lap. "So, it has finally begun, as I predicted when you telephoned earlier. Well, we shall just have to do the best we can."

"What do you mean?" asked Diane.

Betty's eyes grew dark and fresh worry lines etched across her face as she looked at the faces of the children, reading their confusion. She had wished for this day, yet dreaded it. "I'll start at the beginning. The object Timothy has found is an early medieval spearhead. Quite worn, through age, but definitely a medieval spearhead and finding it here may prove my theory of King Arthur and the whereabouts of Camelot."

Mark was scowling; as usual his elder brother had managed to find something special. "This spearhead is not old enough for King Arthur!" He complained, then stopped, and clamped a hand over his mouth. "I'm sorry. I didn't mean . . . . what I meant was . . . . didn't Arthur live much earlier?"

"When we talk of King Arthur we're talking of the very early medieval period rather than the later period, towards the end of the fourteenth century, and yet, some historians are not sure if Arthur existed at all."

"Of course he did!" Joan offered.

"Some say if Arthur lived at all it was around the seventh century, which was probably the same period as this spearhead. Remember, this spearhead would have looked similar had it been made one or two hundred years earlier, so we can't date it exactly without taking it to a special laboratory." Timothy tucked his arrowhead into his pocket and felt the air grow cold. Betty was watching them all very carefully. She was looking for a sign, but when she saw nothing she continued as though nothing had happened. "The legend you found in the book is a small part of a larger tale, sometimes known as a prophecy, which begun during the time of King Arthur. The prophecy talks about what may occur in the future, and tells how the Sleeping Giant of Camelot will awaken on Christmas Day. If the giant awakens then the world is doomed."

"Doomed?" Joan gulped.

"It's nearly Christmas now," said Diane.

"Yes. And from what you've told me if the walls are being revealed then the prophecy will come to pass, the giant will awaken and the world will end. Unless someone can stop it."

"Can anyone stop it?" asked Timothy.

"Yes. Someone special, someone known through the ages as the 'Chosen One'." Betty looked at the eager faces in front of her. Joan, she thought, looked scarcely seven, and the others were hardly old enough to be facing the challenges that she believed were waiting for them. Surely they weren't the chosen ones! They were much too young to overcome the horrific things which were still in the forest, lying in wait for the final Christmas. She wanted to stop them. "You must not to go to the forest again, it's no longer safe. Perhaps it never will be again." And saying that she hurried out, just pausing briefly to have a word with mother.

Left alone the children began blaming themselves for Betty's warning.

"If only I didn't shoot the arrow," groaned Mark.

"If only I hadn't found the book of legends," whispered Joan.

"If only I didn't like adventures," bemoaned Diane, following everyone into Timothy's room and biting her nails, which she always did when she was worried.

Timothy cut in. "If only, if only . . . . but think! She said it's too late *now* because things have already begun happening. But, what if we all try to stop the prophecy?"

"How?" asked Diane.

"By going to the rifle range again."

"No! We mustn't," gasped Mark, going white in the face.

"Betty told us not to," Joan said. "And I don't like the forest; it's creepy."

"Then don't come with us," Timothy snapped. He felt unusually impatient with his younger sister, as if he was being controlled by a mind stronger than his own. "You're too young anyway. It's a shame, because you will miss out on our Christmas adventure, which is getting more intriguing by the minute!" Now his eyes were sparkling as he banged about his room, snatched up his note pad, and banged downstairs. The odd sensations of earlier completely forgotten. "Follow me, well, anyone who's not afraid of the creepy forest!" He was being horrid, and he knew it, but he couldn't stop himself. He also knew he ought to listen to Betty's warning, but he was caught up with the excitement of the unknown and powerless to stop it. "Let's go outside to decide the next part of our adventure."

The children snatched a torch from the annexe locker and hurried to the stable in the orchard for another pow wow.

"I'm definitely going back to the rifle range," said Timothy. "Even if it's on my own. Whether Betty likes it or not."

"But Tim, there is something dreadful in the forest," said Diane. "I can feel it. That's why Betty told us not to go there again."

"Well, I think Timothy is being brave," said Mark, feeling a new respect for his elder brother.

"I don't feel brave," he replied, noticing flutterings in his stomach and just beginning to understand a little of what dangers surrounded the prophecy. "I think Betty was trying not to alarm us by not telling us too much. But there is more, I'm sure of it and I think it's tied up with my spearhead. It frightened her and stopped her telling us another bit about the prophecy. She wants to keep us safe, but on the other hand she knows something must be done if we are to prevent the world from ending. We must speak to her again. Perhaps we'll end up saving the world!"

They all laughed, delighted as only children can be.

"Yes, lets." Diane shrugged into her coat; the stable had grown cold and the pow wow ended.

Mother looked worried when she heard their plans. "When Betty left she wanted me to tell you to make your decision carefully."

"We have," said Timothy grandly. "We're off to Betty's place. See you later, Mum. And he raced out, the other children following, grabbing their bicycles from the engine shed and within moments they were on their way, coats billowing against the cold wind, and pedalling furiously.

Chapter 7

Betty's secret

Betty Vanstone's cherry pink cottage stood in a walled garden full of trees shrouded against the cold winter frosts. Tiny mullioned windows peeped beneath creeping vines of rose and jasmine. During summertime a mass of pink rambling roses covered the front making the cottage resemble an old chocolate box top. The children propped their bikes against the back wall and were soon chattering excitedly on the scrubbed pine stools in Betty's kitchen, between slurps of hot chocolate. Betty took a stool between them and began to tell them some of the secret things she knew.

"First I must tell you a little about myself and the history of Crewkerne, since it's important you understand as much as possible about what is happening. I have known about the prophecy of the Sleeping Giant from childhood, but a few years ago I discovered a bit more." She took a deep breath and continued. "I taught history at the Ilminster Girl's Grammar School, and my special interest is the medieval period. For reasons I won't bother you with I have a passion for uncovering secrets and long forgotten legends; a trait I inherited from my mother. Then, a few years ago I discovered a piece of Latin writing in the school's attic and realised it referred to an old prophecy, mentioning Cruaern."

"Cruaern? Isn't that name similar to the one we found in the legend book? Crocern? Or Crewkerne?" broke in Timothy.

"Yes. Crewkerne. The Latin text referred to this town. I translated it as best as I could and couldn't believe my luck when I recognised the legend my mother had told me of. It referred to an evil battle which had been fought near Cruaern hundreds of years ago, and it said that the evil had never left, but when certain events happened it would return. It didn't describe how or what the evil would be, only that it could destroy our world."

"Do you think it is happening now?" Diane looked pale. Mark clenched his stomach, feeling sick.

"We want to know everything," burst out Timothy. "It's our new game; we want to find the sleeping giant for our Christmas adventure."

"Game? Adventure?" exploded Betty. "Believe me, you'll find this game is more than you bargained for!"

"Sorry," said Timothy quietly, ashamed of his outburst. Why had he said something so foolish when he already felt they were heading into danger?

The children waited as Betty began telling them of long ago events and how legends grew up around the warrior king, Arthur.

"The prophecy of Crewkerne's giant is linked to a medieval curse. They say because Arthur was murdered by his own stepson, and killed by his beloved sword, that the land around cried out in pity, and feeding upon the evil deed became evil itself. It was prophesied that in time the evil within the land would spring to life and destroy the whole world. Some people believed that the evil would awaken during Christmas festivities, when all the magic of the old world comes to life, when days are dark, and nights are long and cold. People here today sometimes imagine they are being taken over by strange sensations." Timothy's eyes swung round to face Betty. Did she know about the strange feelings he had felt?

"It's a horrid prophecy," complained Joan. "Christmas is a time of fun and laughter."

"As it was in the medieval period," agreed Betty. "It was a time for people to celebrate their hopes that spring would return. But, it was a time of dark superstition, of horror and death, with evil beings stalking the land."

"People don't believe in that nowadays," said Diane in a brittle voice.

Betty changed her voice and carefully spread her tithe map on the table in front of them, and a few crystal objects were placed around the edges to flatten it. "Do you see the large areas of marshland around Henley Forest, as well as the lake?"

The children nodded.

"Can you see Henley Forest on the top of a hill? Hundreds of years ago, before the Romans came to our country, the people built their forts on high ground so they could see their enemies attacking them. Later, the Normans built their castles on high ground for the same reasons. Where the ground was marshy, especially in the south west around Bridgwater and Glastonbury, the high ground and hills would appear like islands in a large lake especially after long months of rainfall. If you look at the trees of Henley Forest today they are much higher than the surrounding fields, and would have appeared as an island."

"An island! That's why you think the Isle of Avalon might be here!" gasped Joan.

"Of course it's not! Avalon is at Glastonbury," said Timothy.

"What do you think?" asked Betty, her eyes piercing into Mark's.

He twisted uncomfortably. "I don't know much about islands and King Arthur. I like engineering."

Betty clapped her hands, angry at his reply. "Has anyone heard of Sir Gawain and the Green Knight?"

Joan nodded.

"Then you'll remember how a large green knight appears at Arthur's court during the Christmas festivities and sets in motion a series of magical events. The green knight is a bringer of magic, and possibly a prophet of death. It is he, and not the knights of the Round Table who reminds them of the knightly code of truth, honour and chivalry." Then Betty gave her chilling warning. "Beware; Christmas is nearly here. Perhaps a stranger will come bringing magic and unnatural events. If that happens they can only be stopped with magic or courage."

Silence greeted her words that had sounded like a death bell tolling. Somewhere a clock ticked noisily, and Mark swiped nervously at a dribble of sweat coursing down the side of his face. Betty's mug clattered noisily, upsetting the eerie quiet which had crept into her kitchen, and the moment passed.

"There was a scrawled note on one corner of the parchment, hastily added at a later date, as if someone else had discovered more about the legend and wanted to help future generations. It said that the prophecy could only come to pass once in every hundred years, and at Christmas time, and it described how a 'chosen one' might have a chance of stopping the evil by solving a riddle. As the centuries passed people began to believe nothing would ever take place, and the prophecy passed into legend."

"Could the evil thing happen this year?" asked Timothy.

"I think the evil *is* happening," emphasised Betty. "But our problem is that we don't know what it is, or how it can be stopped. And we don't know the identity of the 'chosen one'."

"It's only what you've found in an old torn manuscript," scoffed Mark rudely. "Who believes that stuff these days!"

Betty ignored him and delivered her final bombshell. "The legend declares the chosen one to be a child."

Crikes! A child? Joan nearly fell off her stool, her heart pounding. Who was it? Was it one of them? Was it one of their friends?

"Christmas is less than three weeks away," gasped Diane, wondering what other mysteries and horrors their Christmas adventure would reveal.

"When Timothy found the medieval spearhead it confirmed the Arthurian connection with Crewkerne, and we know that Crewkerne, or Cruaern has been at the heart of the prophecy. If the prophecy is medieval, and refers to Henley Forest, as I suspect it does, then there was someone or something in the medieval period, and on that spot, which caused it. Perhaps we can discover more about it from reading the Arthurian legends, and then perhaps we can discover how to stop the destruction before it occurs. I tried myself, many years ago after my mother died, much as you are hoping to do now."

"What happened?" asked Joan.

Betty tapped her wheelchair. "I got this for my pains. I was standing beneath a big oak tree near the rifle range when a branch crashed down on top of me. It broke my back. She smiled weakly. "I survived, in a fashion, albeit I can hardly walk and have to use a wheelchair everyday of my life. I never returned to the rifle range. The forest didn't want me prying. I decided to keep to teaching history, rather than solving it." She brightened suddenly, hopefully. "Now you're all here and already you have a medieval spearhead, perhaps you can solve the prophecy, even if danger threatens. Can you do that?"

"Of course we can," said Timothy without thinking.

"I can't wait," said Diane, forgetting Betty's warnings.

Mark kicked her sharply, hissing in her ear. "Don't be a fool, Sis. Didn't you hear it could be dangerous?"

Diane gave him a murderous glare. Who was he to tell her what to do? Then she deliberately smiled sweetly at Betty. "This is going to be a really exciting adventure. I'm looking forward to it."

Betty touched Diane's arm, her fingers burning hot. "This may be an adventure for the moment, but it may prove more dangerous than you realise. You ought to listen to your brother. However, promise me one thing; you must be careful and don't take any risks. Keep together at all times; a family unit is the strongest possible defence to evil. Will you promise?" Her eyes were piercing as she looked at Timothy.

He felt a wave of fear washing over him and swallowed hard. "Is it that bad?"

"I can't say, but you could find you are dealing with a medieval world where everything around you is strange and dangerous. You should prepare yourselves as much as possible. Go to the library and read as many Arthurian legends as you can. Look for references about magic, prophecies, and objects of good and evil. Perhaps being children you will notice something I missed. Then come back to me here and I will guide you if I can." Betty closed her eyes, grey with exhaustion, and added so softly they wondered if they heard anything at all. "One of you must finish it on your own." Her head fell into her arms and within moments she looked asleep. The children left hurriedly, speeding away on their bikes. But as soon as the door closed Betty got up. Suddenly her face had changed beyond all recognition; the cheerful bloom on a pink smiling countenance had been replaced with gouging deep lines spreading from her mouth, over her cheeks and around her eyes. The once soft mousy hair was turning into matted locks dragging messily about her face, and had the children returned they would have thought another person sat in Betty's place.

A dirty ragged old lady pulled herself heavily to her feet, then dragged the thick curtains over the windows, blotting out the pale December light and turning the kitchen into a shadowy mysterious world, until it resembled a hermit's hovel. But this was no hovel; this was a cavern, sculpted into a holy site many centuries ago; a place where holy men and women spoke to the spirits of the forest.

Gradually the air calmed to a place of reverence, and incense tingled in the motes of dust that floated around the woman's head. She moved to an old cabinet that stood hidden behind the stairs and her hands began shaking as she rested them on the wooden lid; it had been a long time since she had held the object that lay inside. The sides of the cabinet were adorned by astrological markings, and she noticed how the heavy top and the roughly hewn sides were cracked, with large gaping holes appearing in many places, as if the object inside had tried breaking out. The wood had become darkened with age and centuries of polish, and as the old lady lifted the lid she felt the roundness of the edges, grown smooth with use. She was eager now, reaching deep into the dark, until her hands cradled a much smaller casket, snuggled softly by a shroud of decaying leather. She was nearly there! Inside this ancient casket was what she sought. She lifted the lid and suddenly as she grasped the object her body went rigid and her mind exploded with images of the past. She threw back her head and laughed letting the wonders of the past roll over her, wash through her mind, suffusing her whole body until she remembered just how it had been. How she had felt when she had been in love. *Oh, let the ancient power do its work!* This was what she had longed for, had waited for, since she first fell in love with him. She let her memories flood back.

A few moments more and another transformation took place; her face began to glow, her body straightened until she looked completely transfigured, graceful and beautiful. *Please let the prophecy work this time!*

"Come my love," she breathed, rolling the strange blue object over and over in her hands. This was the secret of the casket. And wiping the beautiful gem until it began to glow she placed it gently in the centre of the table. Almost instantly sharp blue beams exploded in all directions, bursting like thin rays of turquoise sunshine, bouncing off the walls and rebounding like a miasma of colour until the whole room was drenched in blue. Moments later the kitchen begun dissolving, swirling round in blasts of ethereal mists until all that remained was the sense of another world; an ancient world, where the sound of soft rain trickled through a great canopy of gnarled trees, and the urgent tramping of many horses could be heard, pounding the carpeting of fir cones and rotting leaves beneath their hooves. Occasionally the clink of horseshoes could be heard striking against loose stones, or the laboured breathing of winded horses barging through the undergrowth; they were the sounds of a large army on the move, galloping ever nearer. Startled birds shrieked, taking flight and wild animals shot into holes or hid themselves amongst the forest trees. The woman crooned, gliding her hands gently over the object, nodding her head back and forth, back and forth, back and forth, rocking her whole body in some mystical ritual.

"Uahm. Uahm. Uahm. I am here. I am here, beloved," she sighed softly, scarcely breaking the unnatural atmosphere around her, until her words flowed like honey with promise to a lost love.

She stopped. It was time to speak with the ancients.

Chapter 8

The sword

"Did Betty really say Camelot might have existed near our farm?" cried mother alarmed, when the children congregated once more around the large table and told her about the strange meeting and the links with Arthur and the lake.

Mother had been pounding a fistful of dough, though now she stopped, lines furrowing her forehead. "I'm sure you ought to leave well alone, rather than investigating these old stories and legend. You don't want to embroil yourselves in anything sinister."

It was just what Timothy had been thinking, and he found himself trying to keep a straight face rather than look alarmed as mother began voicing his own fears. He felt a torrent of words bubbling up, threatening to tell everyone their Christmas adventure was cancelled because he thought it was too dangerous, but as fast as he wanted to blurt the words a tight band of pain gripped his head telling him something different. This tight band seemed to be urging him to investigate further, to explore the secrets of the past and heal the ancient prophecy.

"Sinister things don't happen these days, Mum," he managed finally, draping his arms around the back of a chair and managing to look casual. Mother responded with a solemn look, noting his white face, but saying nothing, and the moment passed.

Taking Betty's advice, the children returned to the library the following day, eagerly collecting every Arthurian story they could find. There were copies of Morte Arthur, written in the lovely poetic style that told of Arthur's triumphant battle over the Roman Emperor Lucius, and ending with his death at the hands of his stepson Mordred. There was the evenly versed stanzaic Le Morte D'Arthur which told of Lancelot's love for Guinevere and the destruction of the Round Table, and they also discovered a book of Arthurian romances, written by someone called Malory. This last was thick and heavy, and they drew lots as to which of them would carry it home. The librarian, feeling more relaxed today, laughed at their intense faces. "You've got a good holiday's read there." Timothy bit his lip, feeling the enormity of their task as he opened one book and then another, to be met with some unusual version of the English language he couldn't make head nor tail of.

Racing back home they each chose a book and began reading it and making notes of what was inside. Mark chose one of the Morte Arthur books and quickly slipped off to read, but he found he couldn't settle down. Instead he kept pacing around his bedroom looking at his drawings of the weird stones in the forest, before tossing them back on the bed. He tweaked and twisted them, looked at them one way up and then another, before giving a 'Humph' of disgust and tucking them out of sight. Where had he seen these particular lines before? A deep frown scarred his forehead, it was no use; he couldn't remember. The lines were symmetrical, forming triangles or rectangles, and yet in between were combinations of long strokes, short stabbing strokes, and several softer flowing strokes, as if carved with great care. Thirty minutes later he dashed whooping onto the landing. "Success! I've solved it! I'm a genius! I know where I've seen these lines before!"

Timothy, Diane and Joan emerged from behind their doors, one after the other like popping peas, just in time to see Mark bolting back into his bedroom. He began what appeared to be a bizarre ritual, throwing himself on the floor and wriggling under his bed, with his legs floundering behind him. A few grunts of effort later and one after another shoes boxes and battered old storage boxes came tumbling out as he dragged out everything he could reach: toys, books, comics, and even the odd lost sock which he ruthlessly pulled out and dumped behind, until his bedroom floor resembled a rubbish tip.

"Have you discovered the answer to the legend?" Diane asked, wondering who would be clearing up the mess he had created.

"I've found something much better; the answer to the unusual markings on the rocks!" Mark began inching backwards like a raggedy worm until he appeared again, hair tousled and his arms full of secret cardboard boxes filled with favourite, but often broken, toys and souvenirs. These he threw onto the bed before disappearing one last time to reappear a few moments later dragging a battered square metal tin. This tin was dark red, dented badly, and scratched in many places, and the lid didn't quite shut properly, but each side bore proudly the word "*OXO*". Underneath this Mark had written in white gloss paint "*TREASURES*". His eyes were glowing with success. "I'm looking for the piece of thick metal that I got from the fair, which had unusual markings on. I recognised them from my drawings."

Timothy stepped into the littered room. "Whoa. Slow down, Mark. What piece of metal? What drawings?"

Mark could hardly contain his excitement. "The drawings I made of the funny marks on the rocks at the rifle range! They're exactly like those on the strange piece of brass I got from an old lady at the October fair, two years ago. Don't you remember? I went to her stall, saw it, told her I liked it, and she just handed it over. I mean it was really funny. I didn't even have to pay for it! She said the brass had been in her family for hundreds of years, but they'd never got rid of it because they said one day someone would need it. Since I asked her for it she thought I was the one who had need of it. Wasn't that strange?" Mark was laughing now, feeling everyone's eyes on him and loving it. "Why would I need a piece of brass? I didn't even know what it was. But look!" He rummaged in his 'Treasures' box amongst pebbles and tiny metal tin cars, and even a few ancient coins he had dug up, until he found what he was looking for. Then he held it up, his face glowing. In his hand was a thick piece of brass that had been worked into a soft oblong shape and scored many times. Mark leapt up and thrust his pencilled drawings beside the brass for the others to see. "They match exactly."

Timothy looked impressed. "You're right. The markings are the same." Well done, Mark!"

Mark's eyes suddenly drew together until they resembled two suspicious slits, and with a quick movement he gathered up the brass, and the drawings, and slid them under his pillow. "I'll take the metal thing when we return to the rifle range. I know we just have to go back; and soon."

Timothy began breathing deeply, realising another piece of some dramatic jigsaw puzzle had slotted into place. Firstly he had found his arrowhead and now Mark had this strange piece of brass. What next?

"Okay everyone, back to reading; we need to make some sense of these Arthurian stories before tomorrow. There are lots of stories to read before then."

Diane wrinkled her nose at Timothy's retreating back. "My eyes are tired."

"Mine are, too," added Joan, rubbing them tiredly. "There are almost no pictures to look at in these books, and I wish we hadn't promised to read *everything* on Arthurian legends!"

Mark banged his door shut when everyone had left. He flopped onto his bed and wondered how much he could remember about the old lady at the local fair who had given him the brass. She hadn't been there last year he recalled, because he had looked for her to say Thank you. What had been more confusing he remembered, was asking the other stallholders about her, and them telling him they couldn't remember seeing her at all. Perhaps Mark had been mistaken, they suggested. Mark scowled; his memories were beginning to feel thin and unreal, and after a while he wondered if he had imagined the old lady after all.

But *someone* had given him the brass, and if not the old lady, then who?

Timothy could be heard striding around his bedroom making preparations for their adventure. Every now and then he tacked up a large piece of white paper on the walls and covered it in chunky writing or rough sketches of his notes from the last few days. One sheet contained a rough drawing of their farm with a red cross to the north which marked the site of 'Henley Forest'. Beside this he stuck a bright red pin and wrote 'rifle range'. On another sheet he listed the information Betty Vanstone had given them, whilst a third sheet was devoted to their unusual discoveries. "Mark's large piece of brass" headed this section, and beside it "(Strange markings on the stone wall)". Below that, in thick red ink and underlined, he wrote "Spearhead". Finally, to make their new adventure official, he created a cardboard banner from a flattened cereal box that he suspended above his window. It gave a new title to their plans; "Christmas Adventure: The Sleeping Giant of Henley Forest". Entering a few minutes later the three younger children nudged themselves and grinned.

Timothy had turned his room into a command centre, similar to those they saw on television crime dramas, and by reading the large sheets of paper they immediately saw the areas that were most important to explore further, such as Mark's large piece of brass.

Timothy held up a fresh sheet of paper. "This is for making notes about the things we've discovered from reading the Arthurian legends. Diane? Do you want to go first, and write up what you have found out?"

"Me?" She shook her head, feeling miserable and useless. "I found the texts difficult . . . . It was hard to understand . . . . some of the words were gobbledy gook! I just wrote down a few names, places and that sort of thing. I've got a small list . . . ." she faltered.

"Well, let's put up a few things to start with," cajoled Timothy.

"I've found the names of the 'good' knights. Gareth, Gawain, and Agravain," said Diane. "I've called these 'good' because they were faithful supporters of Arthur."

Timothy wrote their names on the paper. Green ink for good; black ink for bad.

"There were also treacherous knights," continued Diane. "Lancelot . . ."

"No! Not Lancelot," cut in Joan. "Lancelot was a good knight, and a brave one."

"He fell in love with Queen Guinevere," snapped Diane, angry at having her ideas doubted by her younger sister. "He was the cause of the quarrel that eventually destroyed Arthur and his knights."

"Don't argue, you two, I'll simply write 'Lancelot' on both lists, 'good' and 'bad'. In green and black ink," said Timothy. "Anything else? Joanie?"

Joan had spent hours struggling with the battles between the Arthurian knights and the Emperor Lucius. Was there a clue to be found in the battle, he wondered? Had his own spearhead been used in that last battle?

"There was a lady called Fortune. She was a prophetess of doom," Joan said, making her voice low and gloomy like a death knell, and making the others laugh.

"Why was she a prophetess of doom?" asked Timothy.

"She decided when King Arthur would win his battles or be defeated," Joan replied, having already guessed what Timothy would ask. "There's also Mordred. He's the bad guy." Timothy's pen squeaked again and 'Mordred' was quickly added to the list, this time in black ink.

"What about objects?" queried Timothy, "Betty asked us to think about those too."

"Excalibur," cut in Diane.

"Good. What else?"

"A cross," said Joan, touching her own cross at her neck. "Arthur was a Christian king."

Timothy's head shot up, the hairs on his neck bristling. "What did you say? Arthur was a Christian? Are you sure?"

Joan nodded.

"That might explain something that's been puzzling me since our last trip to the forest. Joanie, tell me, do you always wear your tiny crucifix?"

"Usually, though not if I think I might lose it," she replied somewhat unhelpfully.

"What has that to do with King Arthur?" Diane and Mark wanted to know.

Timothy scribbled 'Christian' and 'Christianity' on the large sheet of paper and his hands were shaking. "I'm not sure, but it might explain why we felt cold at the rifle range. Diane, you did, didn't you? And you Mark?"

They nodded.

"But you didn't complain of the cold, did you Joanie? Which is odd, since you always like to be wrapped up with hats and scarves and things." Timothy's eyes glittered like black diamonds.

"I might have felt cold; I can't remember," said Joan, lowering her face to escape her big brother's piercing look.

"Try to remember. It's important! It might give us our first clue to what is behind that black wall of stone."

"Okay, I don't think I did feel cold," she muttered finally.

"Hooray!" whooped Timothy. "Don't you see what this means? I felt cold, just like Diane and Mark. And none of us wore a cross. If King Arthur was a Christian king he would be protected by his faith. When Joanie wore the cross she didn't get cold like the rest of us because she was protected by her faith, just like King Arthur. In fact, to be on the safe side, I think we should all wear a cross when we go to Henley Forest next time."

"Like a talisman, you mean? Well, if it keeps me warm I'm all for it," laughed Diane, taking it as a huge joke and enjoying how everyone was getting into the spirit of their latest game.

"And a talisman will protect us against evil," agreed Timothy.

"Evil? Ugh!" Diane pulled a face.

"I could make some wooden crosses for us to carry," said Mark. "I can also join two metal strips together to form a cross."

Diane suddenly looked up. "Can I add another word to your lists, Timothy? It's from the Arthurian books, and it's *giant*," she said, stretching her mouth to emphasise it.

"A giant!"

"Oh, of course there had to be a giant because there's one in my book of legends," said Joan.

Then something happened which nobody noticed much at the time, yet which caught Mark unawares and left him feeling as if he had been punched in the stomach. "UhFF!" he grunted.

Timothy continued. "I wonder if your Arthurian giant is the same one that's written about in Joan's book on legends?" he said to Diane. "If it is, perhaps we'll find a giant in the rifle range when we go back!"

Diane bit down on her lip, her face full of confusion. "I hope we don't find it. The Arthurian giant is not a nice one. In fact it's an evil giant and is known as the Giant of Mont St Michel."

"That's French for St Michael's Mount," clarified Timothy, writing the words quickly on a sheet of paper; in black ink.

"There's a St Michael's Mount near Montacute," put in Joan. "We went there with Mum and Dad last summer."

"There's also a St Michael's Mount in Cornwall," added Mark.

"Three Mounts, and all named St Michael's Mount," pondered Timothy. "One in France; one in Montacute, and one in Cornwall. I wonder if there are any more, and I wonder if each Mount has a giant? Do you know, Diane?"

She shook her head.

"This might be another important clue for our adventure," said Timothy, growing excited. "The word 'Mont' is French for mountain, or hill, so we know the giant is always linked to a hill." Then a thought hit him and his voice rose as his thoughts came tumbling out. "Henley Forest is on a hill, Betty told us! I wonder if Henley Forest is another St Michael's Mount? If so, it would link the forest to a giant, and explain why people talk about the Sleeping Giant of Henley Forest." Timothy spun around, eyes blazing. "Joan! Read your book on legends again! Find out any reference about St Michael's Mount."

Joan rushed off, heart pounding. But events were moving quicker than they realised, for the giant had already begun to awaken.

Chapter 9

Strange adventures in Henley Forest

Thinking of a giant living nearby made the children so excited they lost all sense of danger, and forgot Betty's warnings to leave well alone. Realising there were just over two weeks left before Christmas the thrill of such an adventure made them careless of danger.

"Diane, what else did you discover?" asked Timothy.

"The giant had to be killed by Arthur before the knights could travel past and fight the Emperor."

"So, the giant was killed by Arthur. That could be relevant. Did the prophecy come about because Arthur killed the giant? No, that can't be right; the giant was killed in France. So, why would it affect us here? At Crewkerne?" Timothy stopped, realising how futile their efforts were and how they seemed to be getting embroiled in something menacing. *If only Betty could help us.*

"How can Arthur kill the giant and yet one still exist today? If we believe that the giant is the one in Joanie's legend," declared Diane.

"Perhaps there's a whole army of giants!" said Mark, voicing everyone's fears. "One for each Mount! Maybe Arthur killed one giant and let the others escape."

Timothy's pen squeaked again. *'Giant: evil: killed by Arthur. Possibly another giant, which survived'.*

"Let's think about the 'sleeping giant' of the forest for a few moments. If we say that the giant is the trees that form the forest; then it means the giant *is* the forest. The forest and the giant are one and the same thing.

Therefore if the giant is evil then the forest is evil," declared Timothy, trying to understand the relevance of what he was saying. "Perhaps we have to destroy the forest."

"Don't be silly," snapped Mark, for once countermanding his elder brother. "How can we destroy the forest? Or the giant for that matter? We're not King Arthur with his sword Excalibur! We're only children."

"I think it's a friendly forest," cut in Joan, and she glared at the boys and stamped her foot on the bedroom floor.

"It's a shame to think the Giant is evil; it looks so lovely on the hillside, lying on its side, almost as if it is asleep," said Diane reluctantly.

"It is asleep!" defended Joan.

"We must go there again," said Mark. "I want to take my piece of brass with the markings on it," and his eyes glittered dangerously.

"We'll go after lunch. Quickly everyone, get your chores done and meet in our orchard pow-wow site," said Timothy, and they scattered in different directions to feed the farm animals, but before they left Timothy had something he needed to do. He took the medieval spearhead and strapped it onto a stout piece of willow. *It looks just like a medieval jousting lance,* he thought, feeling pleased with his work, and realised he felt strangely complete. Whole. As if before he had been missing something. Which was a foolish feeling. *Wasn't it?*

By early afternoon they had reached Henley Forest again. All carried crosses either wooden or metal. Mother had found a cross on a chain for Diane to wear and Mark had been as good as his word and bound metal strips together so they carried at least two crosses each. As they entered the forest no one felt cold; the temperature remained the same.

"I can't hear any birds singing," whispered Diane, looking over her shoulder.

Mark was walking slower than normal; his piece of brass seeming to weigh him down; but he felt very important. He had taken the lead and seemed to know exactly how to find the rifle range. As they arrived at the site everything looked forgotten and desolate, and they noticed how the bricks were beginning to crumble amongst the forest vegetation, as if they had been lying there many years instead of a few days. Tilting back his head Mark saw the wall of black stones looming high above them.

He pulled the brass from his rucksack. "Let's see if it matches the markings on the rocks." He wiped his forehead, feeling strangely exhausted, and his fingers left a dirty trail across his face. Walking to the rocks he slid the brass piece over the surface as if he had done it hundreds of times before.

"Do you know what you're doing?" asked Timothy.

"Not really; I just have a peculiar feeling that this is what I'm supposed to do," said Mark, pushing the brass higher. "I hope something happens soon, my arm's beginning to ache."

"I'm about to burst open with nerves," said Diane wringing her hands.

Just as she spoke Mark located some marks on his piece of brass with identical marks gouged into the rock surface and a deep rumbling noise echoed around them. It grew louder and louder until eventually the ground began to shake beneath their feet as if an earthquake was about to start. As the children stared, frozen to the spot, the black rock face broke apart revealing two black wooden gates behind. Each gate was the size of a house, and now they stood open, inviting and welcome.

Joan cried out in awe and horror. "It's the inside of a castle!"

Chapter 10

A lost world

There was such an overpowering amount of black all around they thought for a moment they were standing at the entrance to the underworld. In front stood a towering castle different from anything they had seen before. Black topless walls and huge black gates filled their vision until the blackness seemed to leech into their very souls. Timothy felt his knees trembling; what terrifying place was this? He knew he should move, should grab the others and run away, but every muscle felt like jelly and he could only stare, wondering what would happen next.

Then the black rock rumbled to a halt, a great mass of rock standing on either side of the group of children, menacing and evil, and forming a secret entrance into Joan's 'castle'. He galvanised himself into action, snatching his arms around the younger children. "Get out!" he yelled, trying to move them back.

But Diane didn't want to be moved. The blackness made her hesitate but after the initial fear passed she felt intrigued. Peeping past Timothy's shoulder she gasped with wonder. "Ooh! It's like a cathedral!"

Mark hunched his shoulders, his eyes large in his white face.

Joan slipped her hand into Diane's. "I don't like it, Sis; it's so big. Something horrible might be hiding in there."

But Diane wanted to explore further. "Come on, let's go inside," and began creeping forward slowly, moving past the heavy black gates and entering the castle depths.

On every side were high walls of honey coloured granite making the inside of the castle turn golden after the blackness behind them. She gazed up, speechless, staring at the walls which were covered in monstrous paintings of Arthurian battles.

"These pictures are just like the ones I've seen in the books we were reading," said Joan, inching forward with her sister and clutching Diane's hand tightly, yet desperately longing to touch the knights in armour or the galloping horses. In some paintings men were grappling in hand to hand combat whilst others stabbed, lunged and killed one another in a gory display of war. It was a terrifying sight.

Their eyes grew like saucers as they moved between long lines of rough wooden tables and benches. They were set with bronze and wooden platters as if a huge banquet had been suddenly interrupted.

"Be careful, Diane," said Timothy, following behind and wondering why his sisters always wanted to investigate things.

But as he and Mark moved through the gates the black rock walls suddenly started shutting, as if an unseen hand was pushing them together. They begun to move slowly at first, and then with increasing speed seemed to rush together with a bang.

Diane was the first to react and began screaming. Timothy appeared to be frozen in shock then he raced back and snatched at the black rock with his bare hands. Quickly he began ordering and controlling everyone as he usually did when things became difficult or dangerous on the farm. "When I count to three all PUSH. Two. Three!" Timothy rammed his shoulder against the rock edge and the girls slammed themselves beside him also. They pushed and pushed but it was useless. Timothy turned to Joan and gave her a hard shove, trying to propel her through the last tiny gap. "Get out! Run!" But it was too late. The gap locked shut and he yanked his hand away before it could get caught.

Mark's voice broke across their screams as he sauntered over to them. "Why are you screaming? I've got the key, remember?" And he waved the heavy brass object with the unusual markings in front of their faces. "This is what made the rock walls open, and how we got in, so it must be a key. Or, rather, *the* key." And he gave a chilling laugh as if to say, I'm in charge now. The others fell silent.

"You had better be right," muttered Timothy when he could catch his breath, and wondering what was happening to his little brother. Before he could speak however a faint light started to glow around them, getting stronger and stronger until it felt as if they were once again bathed in daylight. But that was odd, because there appeared to be no windows. The evil of the place seemed to roll away so that within moments it appeared to the children as if they were standing in a grand medieval hall with nothing more sinister than a flight of wide stone steps in the far distance. As the light grew stronger they saw again the huge paintings along the walls and counted more than twenty scenes from Arthurian legends, all gorgeously depicted in bright colours of red, blue and gold. But they were not all of battle. Some paintings were of Arthur's court, some of love, and others telling the story of Arthur's life. At odd intervals a snow white pennant appeared to flutter over the honey stone, as if caught in a breeze, and leading the knights into battle.

"It's beautiful," breathed Diane walking through the cathedral-like cavern.

Joan bit back the last of her frightened sobs and followed. "I can see pictures of King Arthur. And look! Over there! It's King Arthur with Queen Guinevere, and they're both wearing a crown." Moving slowly into the medieval hall, for that was what it was, she pointed to a golden haired knight with a very intricate suit of silver armour on. "I think this is Lancelot. See how he is gazing up at Guinevere; you can almost see little stars shining from his eyes towards her. Oh, it is so beautiful!"

"Trust you to be romantic," teased Timothy lightly, though in truth he wished they were outside again.

"She's not Guinevere," corrected Diane. "In my book she was called Gaynor. Though she is beautiful. See, she is raising her arm towards Lancelot as he looks at her, and longing to touch him." Diane sounded wistful and reaching up involuntarily laid her fingers on the feet of the golden haired knight.

"Don't touch it, Diane. We don't know anything about this place yet. There might be more hidden catches and hidden caves here which will swallow us up forever."

"Now who's being romantic," teased Diane.

"If we disturb something the giant of Henley Forest might come to life," said Joan going pale. "Mum wouldn't be happy if she knew we were in here."

"I agree, Joan. However, now we're here I suppose we could investigate a little," said Timothy. "But, remember what Betty said, and keep together. And, if we concentrate on thinking about good things then our good thoughts will combat any evil here."

"I can't feel any evil in here," said Diane.

"Not in here, no," said Mark.

"What do you mean by that?" Timothy snapped.

Mark shook himself, feeling as if he had been sleep walking for a few moments. "I don't know. Sorry. Just forget it." He moved away from the others, aware his strange behaviour and comments were making everyone uneasy. He forced himself to focus on the huge paintings. He recognised Gawain and his brothers, all looking alike as peas in the pod, then he noticed a knight, half on his knees, struggling to protect himself, armoured in beaten gold and wearing a small crown, which had to be the emperor Lucius, fighting for his life, before being defeated by Arthur.

As the children moved further into the chamber they saw a black knight, half hidden by a gloomy corner. The style of this painting was quite different from the other bright, vivid paintings because the knight did not wear armour of gold or silver with red, gold or blue insignia on his shield, but was painted in black. Everything about the painting was black; helmet, armour, lance, shield, gauntlets and boots. Even his eyes glittered blackly behind a black helmet and his black arm was raised in anger and hatred. "Mordred," whispered Mark. "Look how large he has been painted in comparison with the others."

"And he's evil," declared Diane.

They decided to keep their voices hushed as they walked across the large chamber until they came to a knight throwing his sword into a lake. "Sir Bedivere," said Joan.

Mark moved to the middle of the chamber, turned to look at the others, then looked up and shouted. "Hey, everyone, look on the wall behind you."

It was the most magnificent painting, and the largest, they had ever seen. Painted in the softest gold with silver filigree and glittering with many coloured jewels, was a sword. There were engravings of fabulous creatures filling the length of the shaft, and a glow, like a golden halo which made it look like a fiery talisman. But the most amazing thing they noticed was that the sword seemed to be suspended above them.

"Excalibur!" Mark sighed. "This must be one of the magical signs we were told to look for."

"An omen of good," Timothy said.

"An omen of God," amended Mark, because the upright sword appeared like a fiery cross of the crucifixion.

After a few moments they moved further along the walls. Diane pointed out the final display which was a scene of Arthur, in a flat bottomed boat, swooning, but obviously making his way to Avalon. "Here he is, on his final journey," said Diane. "How sad. And there's . . . oh, he's not going to Glastonbury. I can't see the Tor. It's a castle, and how strange, he's moving away from it. I wonder where the castle was?"

"It's here of course," put in Mark quietly. "We are in King Arthur's castle. At least we are in one of his castles. Perhaps the treasure we are looking for is Arthur's sword."

"But the sword was thrown into the lake nearly fourteen hundred years ago, and the lake has been lost," said Diane matter of factly.

"Except for the last bit of the lake," said Timothy. He paused, waiting for their attention, since what he would say next would make their adventure the most thrilling yet. "If the treasure we are looking for is Arthur's sword it might still be lost in the lake. And the last bit of the lake, according to Betty, is, (pause) our pond."

Chapter 11

The Guardian's Chamber

The younger children sucked in their breaths and gave a great silent Wow! Could they really believe their pond was King Arthur's lake? Then another thought followed, where was the Isle of Avalon? Could that be near their home also?

The pond on the children's farm measured about twenty metres across by thirty metres long, and in lake terms was relatively small, yet it appeared large and forbidding in the winter when melting snows and heavy rainstorms flooded the banks. That's when the resident moorhens built their nests high above the waterline in the centre of the pond, and as the nests grew taller mother would tell them how the moorhens knew how high the water level would be throughout the coming year, and would build their nests high enough to stay dry and safe. But the pond could be walked around quite easily; so if anything had been thrown in it would be easy to find. However, the lake Betty had showed them on the tithe map seemed to be several miles in length. If Arthur's sword lay at the bottom of such a lake, thought Timothy, *how can we find it?*

"This place is beginning to feel scary," said Joan, pulling her coat around her shoulders. "The air's got colder."

"Who's worried about being cold?" scoffed Diane. "All this mystery is making a terrific adventure for us."

Mark gave a slight cough. "I think we're being watched," he said.

Timothy could see nothing. "There's no one here. This place hasn't been lived in for hundreds of years."

Mark moved abruptly to get out, and as he did so a sharp shock raced up Timothy's arm. "Ouch!" he yelped. "Who did that?" He spun round crossly. "Mark, did you do that?"

"Do what?"

"What did you see?" asked Diane, an anxious look on her face.

"Oh, nothing. No one," said Timothy forcing a peculiar laugh. "Silly me. I got an electric shock from the wooden handle on my lance and thought someone was behind me. Where shall we explore now?"

A shock from a wooden handle? Mark stood as if turned to stone, and his face was deathly white. "We must go, before something awful happens."

"What?" asked Timothy.

Mark didn't reply. Timothy stared around nervously, unsure of what to do. He knew he wanted to leave this strange medieval hall yet for all that he sensed something in the chamber with them, something wanting them to stay.

"Let's have a final look around, Mark. After all, if you have the key we can open the entrance and go home any time we choose, but for the moment please stay a while longer. I think that electric shock was telling me to stay."

"Humph!" Mark grunted ill-naturedly. "More like warning us to get out."

"If we want to solve the prophecy before Christmas we'll have to hurry," said Diane. "Because it's only thirteen days away." The realisation that this might be more than a jolly adventure, and might in fact be dangerous, and be limited in time, served to dampen everyone's spirits until Mark's attention was caught by a painting of a silver knight. It was smaller than the others. Soft, beautiful and childlike and the young fair-haired knight had a golden glow around its head as if it were an angel. He didn't wear heavy gauntlets like the others but raised his hands in supplication, his fingers splayed across the wall, delicate and rosy tipped, facing outwards to touch hands with the onlooker.

Mark stretched a hand upwards placing it lightly upon the hand of the painted knight. His hand fitted perfectly, almost as if it and the painting were the same hand. "Aahh!" a shuddering sigh escaped his lips as if he had come home after a long voyage.

A moment later the stone wall grated loudly and swung back revealing a hidden passage. Inside was a short narrow tunnel with a rounded roof, smelling of moss, and very dark. Through the far end of the tunnel the children could see an ancient portcullis gate with iron bars as thick as a man's waist, rusted with age and buckled as if by a huge explosion.

Joan gasped, "It's like an Aladdin's Cave! I wonder where this will take us." She surged into the tunnel. "It might be full of treasure! Can we go inside, Timothy?"

"No!" he snatched her coat. "What have we found now?"

Mark clutched his stomach, doubling over. "I'm going to be sick."

"Oh Mark, not here!" said Diane pulling him away from the tunnel. "Take a deep breath and count to five, then put your head between your knees for a few minutes. I'll get out Mum's smelling salts."

"Thanks," muttered Mark, quickly following it up with a snort of disgust, "Ughhh!" And he screwed up his face as Diane swayed the pungent salts beneath his nose. As he jerked upright he gave a gasp at something through the portcullis in the distance. "What's that?"

Everyone turned and stared. Through the portcullis they could see what appeared to be another chamber, and it was glowing with a pea green light such as they used for Hallowe'en. Then with a tap-tap-tapping like rapid hoof beats the sound of scurrying footsteps came rushing through the tunnel.

"Whoa! What's that? Quick everyone, get back!" Timothy shoved everyone behind him, eager to protect them, but by the time he turned back a tiny faun-like figure had appeared, bobbing its head up and down, and looking half like a man and half like a goat. This funny creature was dressed in a short bright harlequin waistcoat like a jester in a circus whilst covering its goatlike legs were knee length brown leather hose.

"A faun!" Diane gasped, as behind her Joan giggled nervously.

"Don't be silly," scoffed Timothy. "Fauns don't exist."

"This one does," Joan said, feeling brave, and popping out from behind her sister clapped her hands gleefully. "He's like a little jack-in-the-box. Up and down he dances. Up and down." And in fact the faun did look a little like a comical figure, bouncing up and down on its feet, and every now and then giving a sharp joyous shaking of its head. Then, much to their surprise it spoke!

"A good day to you all. In fact it's a terrific day for everyone!"

The strange little creature rocked from side to side, nodding continually, before making up its mind and made several bobs and bows towards the children. All its movements were done in such a quick manner that an odd red cap, perched upon its head, with two long ears poking through, bounced up and down in an agitated manner, threatening to fall off. In fact, after the initial surprise the faun looked such a comical and friendly animal with its smiles of welcome and agitated movements that all the children began to relax. His eyebrows were so thick they joined across his forehead and hung in tendrils on either side of his narrow face, ending in a mass of confusion amongst his beard that hung like a mat to his waist. He was the strangest and merriest creature the children had ever seen. Mark gasped, his face deathly pale. "Never mind fainting young man; we need to sort out what's happening due to your arrival." The faun put his hand under Mark's elbow and led him through the open doorway beneath the silver knight.

They were going through the tunnel into a whole new world beyond. With hearts popping nervously the others followed as docile as sheep, their eyes large and alarmed as they dipped their heads beneath the jagged prongs of the portcullis.

Once inside the new chamber the faun appeared happier as if he had overcome a difficult task. Timothy knew that there was something going on which he didn't know about and he didn't like it one bit. He glared crossly at the faun even though that little creature was now skipping around excitedly and settling a fur covering across Mark's shivering shoulders. "Thank goodness you children are here! I had almost given up hope of seeing you."

"You expected us?" Diane squeaked. "But how could you know we were going to be here? We didn't know ourselves. We came here by accident. Anyway, who are you?"

"What a lot of questions!" scolded the faun good naturedly. "I'll answer them all in good time, young miss. First, let me introduce myself. I am Eorldormann, Acting Lieutenant to the Master." He bowed and swept off his ridiculous hat in one small movement.

"The 'master'," repeated Diane. "Who's your master?"

"Are you really a faun?" interrupted Joan, bouncing excitedly from one foot to the other. "My sister thinks you are."

"Shh!" Timothy dragged her back behind him where he felt she would be safer. "Who's your master?"

"I'll explain later; no time now. Don't worry though; I'm a friendly faun. I'm delighted to see you; you're my first visitors in over 500 years. Welcome to my home." He bowed with one swift movement and clapped his hands delightedly before twirling the long fronds of his moustache.

His genuine enthusiasm at seeing the children helped to make them feel at ease with him and Diane and Joan were especially enchanted with him as he reminded them of an enthusiastic puppy.

"If you really are a friendly faun then tell us where we are," said Timothy irritably, not at all appeased by the declaration of friendship. "Then explain how we get out of this castle or whatever it is."

"You are now in the Guardian's Chamber, young man. Before that you were in the Outer Chamber. I am the guardian, and this is my chamber. In fact I am the only one left." The faun looked sad suddenly but forced himself to brighten. "Well, are you all here? Let's see." Eorldormann bounced around clapping his hands again (which seemed to be a habit of his when very excited), and began counting the children as they lined up. He bobbed up and down so quickly his hat threatened to fall off. "Good. Good. I was expecting four of you, though my memory is not as good as it used to be. I have been expecting you for hundreds of years, but never mind that now. We have lots of work to do."

"Work!" echoed Timothy feeling dismayed, thinking he already spent many hours working on the farm each day.

"There is a great deal to do. First we must find the sword."

"Sword?" Timothy glanced at the faun and wished someone would pinch him. "Did you really say 'sword'?"

Diane broke in. "We were told it was at the bottom of our pond, whoops, lake. Anyway, our pond has been filled in, except for a little bit, which is on our farm. And so we don't know how to find it."

"Whoa, slow down, young lady," said Eorldormann laughing. "Maybe I ought to explain things. It is true that many centuries ago your pond was a lake. It was Arthur's lake, as you all realise by now, and this whole land belonged to Arthur of the Britons. The paintings you saw in the outer chamber are of Arthur's world; they must have given you a clue. Especially as you enjoy reading about King Arthur." The faun broke off, fixing a hard gaze on Joan who reddened with embarrassment.

"How did you know?" she stammered.

"I know everything," Eorldormann replied mysteriously, "because I am a being from a magical world." He peered darkly at her beneath his thick bushy eyebrows and Joan found herself catching her breath in fear and amazement. *The faun must have read her mind!* It was frightening, yet the faun also reminded her of one of her favourite schoolteachers; it had a trace of something in its voice as if it were a great dollop of kindness, and she realised she wasn't afraid of the faun at all.

"Can you tell me who painted the pictures in the Outer Chamber?"

"I did; nothing else to do for hundreds of years. I've had no one to speak to and nothing to do, except guard the you-know-what for fourteen centuries. And as you can see, I'm getting old. It's about time the old prophecy came to pass. I feel so tired at the moment I don't think I could have lasted another hundred years."

This was all a bit too much for Timothy who realised with ill humour he would have to reprimand his sisters for speaking to the faun as if they were long time friends.

"Hundred years? What prophecy? I don't understand."

"Of course you don't understand; you're the eldest one here, apart from me, and just when you think you're starting to get too old for all your childish games, hey ho, it's too late. You've grown up, and you never believe in magic and things like me, again. It's such a great shame, but all children grow out of believing."

"I won't," Diane cut in bravely. "I'm nearly as old as Timothy, and I still believe in magic."

The faun paused and its smile softened. "Enjoy your dreams while they last. One day children simply grow up and pooff! They turn into adults." When he stopped his face looked like a sad deflated balloon. "The world will never be a happy place until people keep believing in magic, and creatures like me. I never stop believing in children, and it is only their dreams which make me real. But sadly I am the last of my kind." His voice grew soft and he wrenched his hat from his head, screwed it tightly in his hands and wiped his eyes. It came away moist with tears. Joan would have run to him but Timothy glared at her. *We don't know if this faun is friendly yet,* he seemed to say.

Eorldormann pretended not to notice, though Joan's gesture gave him a warm feeling around his heart. "Let me explain why and how I came to be here."

He waved them all to sit on the heavy couches nearby, then taking up a position in front of them he gave a tiny cough and began to speak. With his thin reedy voice he conjured up images of a time when scribes wrote on parchment, when man shared his world with colourful and exotic creatures, and when knights fought in ancient battles swearing loyalty and honour.

"I am Eorldormann, chosen to be a king's guardian. I was just one of many such eorldormen. Our duties were to control, and imprison if we could, the evil dragons that lived upon the earth and roamed the countryside, killing and maiming everything they came across. Many centuries ago, before Arthur ruled Britain, there were three dragons. They were the biggest, most wicked creatures that ever stalked the earth. No one could get near them, and they created havoc. Then one day a brave young Christian knight called Sir George, you call him 'St George', came to our land, and managed to kill one of the evil dragons. But still there were two more stalking the countryside, killing the people and slaying their cows and sheep for food. The land looked for another champion to rid the world of the dragons, before the people starved. At that time there lived a strong youth in a country village who left home to find his fortune. On his way he saw a sword rising from a huge lake, which he grasped and took for his own. Now this sword was a very special sword and belonged to the enchanted ladies of the lake. They were very jealous of anyone who touched the sword, but when the young man took hold of it they gave him the right to keep it for his whole life, as long as he returned it to them on the day he died."

"King Arthur," whispered Joan, feeling the hairs on the back of her neck bristling like pine needles.

"King Arthur," agreed the faun. "With his enchanted sword he sought out and slew the second dragon. In later years it became known as the Giant of Mont St Michel."

"Oh, my goodness!" Diane bounced up from the couch, eyes flashing. "I've read about the Giant of Mont-St Michel! It's . . . . it's. . . . ."

"Shh!" Eorldormann's voice crackled sharply and he wagged his head to be quiet. "I never talk of *those* beasts, not in here," and he twisted head to look behind them.

"What happened to the last dra. . . . beast?" asked Timothy, holding his breath and realising he dreaded the answer.

Eorldormann paused before replying as if he was weighing up something of importance. "There was one left; only one in the whole world, and it lived in Camelot. It was completely alone, without family or friends of its own kind. I know . . ." He broke off. "I know how it feels to be lonely," and a tear splashed down his face. Diane passed him a clean handkerchief which he used to dab his eyes before continuing. "The beast, realising it was on its own, and being continually hunted by knights and fortune hunters, longed to revenge itself, and plotted to destroy the world."

"Oh, that's sad, and awful, all at the same time! Couldn't King Arthur kill this horrid beast too?" asked Joan.

"Arthur was old by this time, and the land needed another great champion; one who was strong enough to defeat it. But the only knight heroic enough had been banished from Camelot because of his love for the queen."

"Lancelot," shouted Diane jumping up and thinking of the beautiful knight she had seen as they first entered the castle.

"Yes, Lancelot! He seemed invincible. But, his love for Queen Guinevere amounted to treason against the king, punishable by death, and the most unforgivable of all knightly sins. If caught he would forfeit his life. However, rather than take his life the gods took his great strength and he became as weak as a baby." The faun's head drooped lower and lower as he told his story, until his large eyes swam with tears, and taking out a handkerchief blew his nose loud and long. "Lancelot had to leave Camelot and the king, swearing to forego his love for Guinevere if only the gods would return his strength so that he might fight the last *dragon*," and Eorldormann breathed the last word as if he had mentioned something terribly evil in a sacred place.

"Did the gods give him his strength back?" Joan asked, crossing her fingers in front of her face.

Eorldormann wagged his head in such a sad manner that his red hat lay like a flat pancake around his ears. "He regained some of his strength for a short time, and straight away he rushed off to fight the beast in a dark hollow, where a great river crashed down over a bed of rocks. It was there the beast made his home. For three days and nights the air echoed with their screams, neither one showing mercy. Lancelot wielded his lance, by now coated with gore, continually thrusting it into the creature's belly, but it was so powerful it only became incensed, he swished his tail into Lancelot's face, wounding him gravely. Finally Lancelot began losing ground, weakened by loss of blood and tiredness."

"Poor Lancelot!" said Diane, looking green.

"Lancelot made a final rally, calling on the gods to help him one last time, and for one final moment his great strength was restored. Lancelot thrust his lance into the side of the beast, and as it was withdrawn thick black blood flowed after it. When the battle was done the dreadful creature crawled deep inside the earth to lick its wounds."

"What happened then?" whispered Timothy.

"King Arthur ordered the best builders in the land to build great chambers around the dragon, thus imprisoning it forever within its cave. Then I, with the rest of my kind, took it upon ourselves to guard the beast forever. Now I am alone, and no longer strong enough to keep the beast imprisoned. Soon it will break free, and the castle walls will crumble. It must be stopped."

Dumbfounded Joan thought of the Book of Local Legends which she had found in the library, and remembered that it had a picture of a dragon on the front cover and a picture of a giant on the back. She tried to shout a warning to Timothy, but no words came. At that moment she realised Henley Forest was home to both the giant and the dragon of her book.

Well, they knew the giant was the shape of the trees of the Forest, but what about the dragon, this horrid beast that Eorldormann was so nervous of? When would they find that?

Chapter 12

The circle of magical thread

"Tell us how the beast can be stopped," said Timothy, not believing for a moment in such things, and finding himself wishing he could bite his tongue rather than ask any more questions. Everything the faun said seemed to bewitch the children into the greatest most terrifying adventure imaginable. Equally Timothy thought a trap was being woven and he, Diane, Mark and Joan were the prey caught in the middle.

"Someone must bind it with the magic thread," said the faun quietly.

"Magic thread? What are you talking about?" demanded Timothy, feeling a strange sensation engulfing him and threatening to sweep away him, Mark and his sisters.

"Did I forget to tell you about the magic thread?" said Eorldormann with wide innocent eyes.

"No," snapped Timothy, frightened and out of his depth. "You purposely did not mention the 'magic thread'. If there is such a thing. Well, you've had your fun, little faun. Now I'm going to have mine. I'm going to get you out of my imagination and never think of you again. We are all going back home, and we will never come back!" He snatched Joan's hand and began to march off; it was about time he got everyone out of this weird place and home safe and sound. But as he moved to go Eorldormann looked at him carefully, for a long moment, his expression full of helplessness as fat, shining tears splashed from his eyes and fell like raindrops to the floor.

"I'm sorry. Please forgive me," the faun sniffed and gurgled. "I would like to send you all home, with my blessing, to where it is safe. But I can't."

Realising this was not what she wanted to hear Joan yanked herself out of Timothy's grip and her young voice suddenly filled the chamber with a simple plea. "I want to see my Mum."

Eorldormann looked pityingly at her. "And so you shall, but not for a little while, little one. Please, be patient. I'm sorry if I frighten you; it's a frightening situation, and I'm not used to dealing with children." He wiped away the last of the tears which still clung to his long nose and sniffed one last final sniff.

"We're not used to dealing with fauns," said Timothy feeling flustered, and realising he needed to make friends with the strange creature again, but not really understanding why. "And it's not as if we're afraid . . ." He stopped. Was he lying? No, it felt true. His fears of a few moments ago had completely gone. Whatever tension or feeling had been in the air was no longer there. Eorldormann felt it too. He began to sound brighter and happier, becoming the light footed skipping little creature they had met a few minutes ago, and to prove it his little red cap began bouncing up and down again, quite merrily, as if freed from something. "Oh, I see I shall have to explain everything. That's all there is to it. We have so much to do, and so little time, but, it can be done!" He ended confidently, then quickly his mood changed and his voice ended on an irritated note. "Do you see that?" He indicated a green pile of something behind him. "That's the magic circle of thread; it's what you'll need for binding the beast."

"What!" The children gave a collective sound of horror. Somewhere in the chamber behind the faun they could see a huge luminous green bundle rather like a giant untidy ball of thread on the chamber floor.

"Wow!" Mark pushed past and went straight to the thread. Letting it slip through his fingers he decided, "It's nothing special. It looks like cotton." However, when he touched it again his voice changed, it became cautious, worried. "Ohh! It's getting warm, like it's got electric current running through it."

Eorldormann rushed across. "Careful, young man, we don't want to awaken its magical powers yet."

"Crikes!" Mark yelped, and flicked the thread from his fingers.

"This is a unique and magical thread," the faun said. "It's the only thread that can keep the beast imprisoned. If it is allowed to break free of its prison then the Giant of the forest will awaken, and finally the prophecy will come to pass when the two beasts of legend will fight at the end of the world, unless the *dragon* can be bound for all time." Eorldormann waved a threatening finger. "Be warned, children, because whatever, or whoever gets bound up by the thread, will never break free."

"Get back everyone! Don't anyone touch it!" yelled Timothy, bursting into action and pushing Mark away from the green fibrous mound.

Eorldormann smiled. "It is best to keep clear. However, the thread is safe at the moment. It has no ends with which to tie it together, and therefore it has to be cut before it can be used."

"You mean, that pile of thread is all one piece?" exclaimed Mark. "Just one great big circle, that is all twisted round and round together! And no one can use it?"

"That's right. I've been spinning it for centuries. It's magic thread, and has to be spun in one big loop or else it will not be magic. When the you-know-what became my prisoner I knew that if ever it broke free I would have to stop it from destroying the world. So I tried to think of something which could bind it forever. That's when I remembered the magical thread which we the fauns invented, and which made us famous all over the world. Nothing will ever break it once it has been used, and that can only happen when it has been cut. Up to now I have never needed to cut it, but that will happen soon."

"When?" Mark wanted to know.

"You ask too many questions, young man." Eorldormann glared and stamped a foot. It was clear the faun could be happy, irritated, worried or friendly at a moment's notice, swinging from one mood to another without warning. "Let's pray we never find out! The beast can destroy a town before breakfast, and everyone in it. My thread, once cut, is the only means of stopping it."

"Miss Vanstone never told us about that!" exclaimed Diane.

"Why don't you just cut the thread and bind him yourself?" asked Timothy who felt it was the most obvious thing to do.

Eorldormann lowered his voice, and looking over his shoulders deliberately moved the group back towards the narrow tunnel where he felt he was able to mention the dreaded *dragon* word again. "It's not as simple as that. Remember, the thread is magic, and therefore nothing on earth can cut it. I think it has to be a magical object from the lost lands of Camelot. That is why you are here, to find the enchanted sword of legend. Excalibur." The word whispered and echoed around the chamber seeming to bounce off the walls and come back at them from all sides.

Timothy pounced, feeling cross and foolish. "*Think*! You *think* the sword will cut the thread! Don't you know?"

"How can I, until it has been tried?" Eorldormann shook his head. "I hope my belief is the right one. If it's not, then what can we do? How will the dragon be stopped from destroying the world? Already it is stronger and rocks are falling from the chamber."

"The rifle range."

"Yes. The rifle range was the beginning. Many more stones have fallen in recent days. I fear the castle is beginning to collapse. We must bind the dragon as soon as possible. The thread must be cut. Also," Eorldormann paused, quite out of breath after talking so much for the first time in hundreds of years. His eyes searched the young faces in front of him and at the back of his eyes was an expression of sorrow and pity, and when he spoke next the children understood why. "The prophecy states that only a child will be able to find the sword, and when it is found it will cut the magical thread."

"That's why you can't cut the thread," said Joan, though no one heard her.

Mark looked quite green as if he was going to be sick. "Betty Vanstone said something about a child." Turning to Timothy he said, "What must we do?"

But Timothy swung away from Mark's bleak look feeling angry and unhappy; they were demanding answers he couldn't give. "Why must I always make the decisions?" he said, realising he had no alternative since they were relying on him. What could he say to them? Any decision he made could endanger all their lives. *Would our parents give their approval to help the faun? If I don't help the faun the world will be destroyed.* Did anyone ever have such a difficult decision to make, he wondered? He looked around at the strange surroundings, a large chamber that looked much like a medieval hall, but filled with an ethereal glow from the green magical thread, and he was not really sure how or why they came to be in such an odd and dangerous place. Yet somehow it had become familiar in the short time they had been there, as if he had been there before. His brow furrowed as he contemplated the luminous green thread. Was it magical? Would it bind the dragon? Was there really a dragon? He was almost an adult now, why did he think he could believe the word of a faun? Surely all his friends at school would laugh if he told them a faun had told him to look for King Arthur's sword; the whole thing was ridiculous. He would tell the faun 'No' they couldn't help him, and run from this cavern as fast as they could. But just when Timothy was about to speak Eorldormann stumbled, his legs buckling beneath him. He looked frail and ancient, his little red cap looked faded and lifeless, and his jacket ragged and worn. Suddenly Timothy understood something he should have noticed before; the faun was dying. The sense of urgency, the changes of mood, the merry eyes and lively actions, were an extravagant show put on by the faun so as not to alarm the children to the seriousness of the situation. Timothy's earlier words died in his throat. If they ran away now the faun would die and the dragon would escape and destroy the world. It was as simple as that. They had to help Eorldormann.

Taking a deep breath Timothy tried to analyse the situation and what could be done. He began by picturing all those diagrams and questions on the large pieces of paper in his bedroom. If only he could think the problem through logically he knew they would have a chance of success. Item one; the faun said they needed a child. Well, there were four of them, so there were plenty of children! But, item two, which one was it? Could he assume it was one of them? Mark had proved his involvement in the quest by ownership of the strange brass key that let them into the castle chamber. Timothy himself felt his involvement because he had found the medieval spearhead from a real Arthurian lance. He let his hand slip to the cold metal, delighting in the feel of the ancient weapon, and wondering if perhaps Arthur himself had used it. Item three; Mark's hand had fitted the hand of the boy knight exactly, and led to another chamber. Item four, and here Timothy paused as an icy shiver of fear raced through his stomach, Eorldormann had been expecting them. Surely none of this could have been coincidence? With dread certainty Timothy accepted that they were the ones chosen to find the sword.

He braced his shoulders and looked Eorldormann in the eye. "We'll do it! We will find Excalibur."

Chapter 13

The painted dragon

"Hurrah!" Eorldormann began dancing around so jubilantly, and cavorting so furiously, that his tiny red hat threatened to topple off. "Hurrah for the children!" Joan dashed over and caught the toppling hat just as Eorldormann began pounding Timothy on the back, his pleasure giving way to an outburst of speech which grew faster and faster with each word. "Well done my boy. Well done indeed! I'm so happy! I knew you would help. I said so all along. I wish my dear Mrs Eorldormann could be here to see it. Bless her soul. She didn't think you would help you know. She believed human children were only interested in themselves and not interested in helping us down here. But I told her she would be proved wrong one day, that we all need to help each other if we're to survive, those from your world and those from mine, and that no two children were alike. I said there were good children and bad ones." A faint frown clouded his features and he paused thoughtfully, looking at the tiny group of children who stood all in a row in front of him. "You're not like the others at all."

"What others?" cut in Joan, giving Eorldormann a startled look as he nodded his thanks to her, grabbed his hat and placed it back in its precarious position on his head.

"Shh! Not so loud; you must only speak in whispers when you're in this chamber." Eorldormann raised his rather thin long faun's arm to his lips, shook his head at her and turned to stare hard at the far end of the cavern. They all followed his gaze, expecting to see some children. But they saw no one. Diane wrapped her arms around herself as a premonition gripped her. Was there something dreadful lurking there?

She whispered to Eorldormann, "I can't see any children. Did you see somebody else? Were they here? What happened to them?"

"They came to a bad end. Oops! Sorry, I ought not to have told you that." Eorldormann clamped his arms over his face and peeped through his fingers, looking like a startled rabbit, and Timothy thought how his eyes seemed to be boring into the deep gloom behind them. "You must forget what I said. It's vital we don't say anything about the *others*," and his voice dropped to a rasping whisper before becoming brisk once more, as if he had made up his mind. "You'll be all right. You all look much braver. You're good and kind, nothing selfish about you at all. Yes, everything will be fine, I'm sure." Eorldormann couldn't look them in the face. A long pause followed. "There are . . . . difficulties. There always are . . . . I don't know what they will be, I only know I should warn you that you will all be facing great danger." His cheerful smile disappeared in an instant and he looked like a drooping flower.

Timothy spun on his heel. "I don't like this one bit. I'm not even sure what we are supposed to do," and he started pacing the floor in the sharp, irritated manner that the younger children recognised as meaning 'trouble' with a Capital T. Two scowl marks appeared on his forehead. "It seems to me the answer to the problem of cutting the magical thread is Arthur's sword. Therefore we must find the sword, before thinking of anything else. And if we find it, will it cut the thread?" He planted his feet squarely in front of Eorldormann, glaring hard. "Will your special thread bind the dragon?"

But Eorldormann hadn't heard Timothy; he was concentrating hard on something behind them.

"Can you help us find it?" asked Timothy, wanting to shake the faun with worry and hating the way his voice rose higher like a frightened child's. "Do you know where the sword is? If you do, you must tell us." He could feel hysteria rising up in him as he tried to grapple with the insurmountable problems of being in a magical world where creatures talked, knights appeared on walls, and giants and dragons walked the earth.

"Shhh!" Eorldormann started flapping his hands like an agitated hen. "Hush, I tell you! Not in here. Not in front of the you-know-what." He darted another look behind him. This time when the children followed his gaze to the back of the chamber they saw in the darkness a huge shape towering upon the walls, rippling over monstrous stones until it seemed as if it were gyrating in a grotesque ballet in the shadows. Joan screamed. She was certain she was looking at another painting but it looked like a monster, and a very large one.

"The dragon," she shrieked, taking cover behind Timothy, and pointing directly at the menacing beast.

For a moment time itself stood still as if petrified by the waves of fear which engulfed the children. They could only look at the hideous painting on the back chamber wall in horror. Billowing flames of molten lava seemed to hurtle from the creature's jaws, cascading in slathering streams to the rocks at its feet. But more horrors awaited them for swarming beneath the dragon's trunk-sized legs were twelve black ugly creatures the size of buffalo. Their leathery skins were black as jet and covered in rows of razor edged scales which bristled and writhed like undulating serpents. They had snake-like heads which lunged towards the children as if ready to tear them into morsels for dinner. But, however horrifying these creatures were, the size of the monstrous dragon made these strange black creatures look like puppies.

"I've never seen anything so big! It must be the size of King Kong," breathed Timothy, backing towards the tunnel.

"It's the size of a castle," gasped Mark, turning a peculiar puce colour as if he were going to faint again.

"Did you paint it, Eorldormann? The same as you painted the knights?" Diane asked, her eyes popping. "I have never seen anything so ugly. No wonder it's the creature of myth and legend." She broke off and turned to ask Eorldormann more questions, but he was gazing intently at the dragon.

Joan was gasping, her mouth working furiously. "A painting? Are you sure, Diane? But it looks . . . ."

Eorldormann glared at her, twisted his fingers around a piece of her coat and thrust her tightly behind Timothy, his voice low and furious. "No more talking! Now, quickly, get out of this place. Run! Into the tunnel!"

They didn't need a second bidding; Eorldormann caught hold of the girl's hands and they raced under the rusting portcullis and out through the tunnel.

Once back in the Outer Chamber Timothy, Diane and Joan collapsed in a small circle, panting and wide eyed.

"Fancy us being scared of a painting!"

"It was big!"

"I never saw it when we went in!"

"I hated those horrid black creatures around its legs . . ."

"I thought it looked very real; I can see why Lancelot couldn't kill it."

Diane suddenly screamed, "Where's Mark?"

Chapter 14

Mark acts strangely

Mark never reached the tunnel. He started following the others but found his coat being held by something invisible. "Hey, let go!"

Though no one answered him he felt he wasn't alone. A second later he found himself being catapulted through the portcullis where he sprawled on the tunnel floor.

"Hey!" he shouted. "Help! I can't move."

"Mark? Where are you?" called Diane.

"In here. I fell."

Timothy dashed back into the tunnel. "I'm coming."

"What happened?" he asked when he reached Mark, slipping an arm under Mark's arm and helping him back to the others.

"I don't know. The key seemed to be holding me back. And I thought something was tugging my coat."

Eorldormann began looking alarmed. He trotted over to the boys, his head nodding furiously and his hat toppling dangerously. "I shouldn't have let you inside the Guardian's Chamber. I'm sorry, but I had no choice!"

"What do you mean?" Timothy's voice turned cold.

Eorldormann stuck his head in the air and began reciting something he had learned hundreds of years previously. "All who seek to rid the world of the dragon must enter its chamber," he chanted. "Now you see why I had to get you in there; you had to see it."

"See it?" ground Timothy, glaring at the faun, whilst goose bumps rushed like a rash over his back. "What did we have to see?"

"The painting. The dragon . . ." Eorldormann gulped so violently his tiny red hat fell off.

Joan scooped it up, passed it back, and asked, "The painting. that one through there?" Her little fingers were shaking as she pointed to the deep shadow beyond the tunnel where they had been standing moments before.

Eorldormann didn't have chance to reply as Diane chose that moment to touch Mark's bag with the key in it. Mark pulled the bag away angrily. "Leave it Diane. It's mine, and I'm the one who must carry it!"

Diane stopped at the harshness of Mark's voice. "I was only trying to help. Why is everyone so grumpy today?"

"Sorry," muttered Mark, feeling normal again. "I don't know why I yelled at you. It's just that I feel no one else is allowed to touch the key."

"He's right," said Eorldormann, beginning to puff up and down the chamber like a runaway train, his hairy legs thump thumping the floor, as he explained how the key worked. "The key belongs to him since it was passed over by the last 'Keeper'. It's the key to the castle, as Mark discovered. In ancient times the holder of the key was known as 'The Gatekeeper', and no one else must hold it, or use it, or it loses its powers."

Timothy looked thunderous. "That's all very well for you to tell us now, but why did Mark say it felt heavy?" and he glared at Eorldormann simultaneously surprising himself by sounding like their father.

The faun laughed lightly and his voice tinkled like tiny bells. "Oh, that's simple. It's magic. Merlin created it to respond to one keeper; Arthur. Since Arthur's death it has passed through generations of successive keepers right up to your brother, Mark."

The other children looked bemused, not sure whether to feel outraged because the key didn't belong to them, or pleased they had something between them which was once King Arthur's. Joan moved closer to the others for reassurance, deciding never to go back into the chamber with the *you-know-what*. She shivered recalling that she thought the painting was alive. Which of course it wasn't. She was foolish to even have thought it. Wasn't she?

Mark snatched the key close and his eyes glittered at Diane. Timothy began feeling uneasy, what precisely were they getting into?

Eorldormann trotted away, looking helpful and guilty in equal measure. "Just now you asked if I could help you find the sword. My advice is to look at the paintings in here."

"Do you call that being helpful?" snapped Timothy.

"Trust me! Please."

"Why should we?" growled Timothy.

"I think he would help us if he could," said Diane.

Then Timothy remembered his scout camps and felt in his pockets for a small round object. Yes, it was there. "My compass!" He popped it into the palm of his hand and stared disbelieving as the needle began revolving. "Wow! I can get a reading in here! North, South, East, . . . everything. It might help," he said, and quickly began jotting down a variety of co-ordinates and linking them to the paintings.

Joan realised she wouldn't be needed for a while and allowed her emotions to draw her towards the tunnel and the green mound of magical thread. Although she seemed to be in a trance her mind was racing with thoughts, wondering if she could solve the mystery of how to cut it. *Was there another way?*

Eorldormann chattered around the four children, sometimes fussing, and always sounding cheerful and full of importance, but on one thing he was adamant, no one was allowed near the painting of the dragon in the Guardian's Chamber, nor to walk into any of the dark tunnels, without him. To do so might awaken the sleeping giant. At this the children stopped aghast. *The Giant!*

Struggling with their concerns about the dragon they had quite forgotten the giant. Timothy clapped his hands sharply; they had to have an emergency pow-wow.

"If the giant *is* the forest and the castle is in the forest."

". . . . then we're walking *inside* the giant," finished Diane.

"Everyone be very careful!" cautioned Timothy.

All chatter ceased as they moved like nervous shadows around the outer chamber, stepping lightly in case they woke the sleeping giant, wondering if they would find any clues to help them in their quest, and staring at the magnificent paintings but not knowing what they were hoping to see.

Timothy called them together after another half an hour had passed. "This is hopeless. We can't do any more here. We'd better walk home before Mum and Dad return from the market."

No one argued. It had been a long day and they were feeling tired and disappointed. They agreed the paintings were pretty, magnificent in fact, but nothing gave a clue as to how they might find Arthur's sword. Mark hid a sly smile and popped his notebook inside his coat pocket, as if hiding a secret. Whatever he was hiding, thought Timothy grimly, he didn't want anyone to look at it. Within moments they said their goodbyes to Eorldormann and filed out through the black rock, which Mark opened using his magic key. The castle wall banged noisily behind them and once again they were looking at an ivy covered mountain, with a thick canopy of trees above. King Arthur's castle had disappeared. Their adventure had failed. It might have been a dream.

Mark kept flexing his aching shoulders as they walked and occasionally hummed off-key, thinking of his simple drawings; especially the one of a large knight throwing the sword into the lake which intrigued him most of all. Ten minutes later they were back, running, careering, and laughing with relief through the apple orchard.

"Home again," Diane shouted jubilantly, giving the garden gate a welcoming thump. But as she did so the winter sun dipped beneath the tree line and the countryside was plunged into darkness. The children discovered they were left standing in a pool of mist that filled their orchard with a sinister glow.

"The air has grown cold again," said Mark.

"Yes, the temperature has plummeted just as it did when we were in the forest," agreed Timothy. He looked around with a lump of fear stuffing his throat so he could hardly breathe; *surely something had followed them home.*

"Look!" called Joan. "The rays of the sun are lighting up the surface of our pond. I've never seen it like that before."

"Neither have I," said Timothy. "Wait! It gives me an idea. Now I know how we can find the sword!" and forgetting the presence of *something* he raced through the back annexe and up the stairs, leaping three at a time. The others followed after, gasping, laughing and running to catch up.

"It's the sunlight. In the paintings."

What could he mean? Timothy quickly spread his rough map of the farm upon the bed. "It has something to do with the direction of the sun's rays. Did any of you notice the sunshine in the wall paintings?"

Mark collapsed onto a chair, nodding and breathless. "I did see yellow lines that looked like sun rays, glittering and bright. I've sketched it in very poorly; I didn't think it would be helpful."

"Anything could help at the moment. Let's see your drawings."

Mark passed them over and Timothy flattened them out. He turned them about, twisting this way and that, and then began adding directional arrows on his large pieces of paper.

"The height and position of the sunlight in the paintings will tell us the time it was thrown into the lake. We'll be able to see the position of the sword in relation to the lake and what's around it. For instance, we can locate the sword by looking at objects in the background of the same painting, such as the hills, the chapel on the site of Glastonbury Tor, and anything else we noticed. I'll do some compass co-ordinates and hey presto! We find the sword." Timothy finished with a triumphant flourish and ran out of the bedroom. "Come on everyone! Follow me, and leave your notes here!"

Diane snatched up a coat just in time to see him disappearing out the back kitchen.

"We need to get our chores done," Timothy said, stamping his feet into his Wellington boots. "Then we'll meet again to make more plans. Diane, organise some food for us. Mark, don't bother putting your boots on, grab your trainers and then telephone Betty Vanstone and tell her what we've seen today; Mum might let you cycle to Misterton again. I'll do your farm chores so you can leave immediately. It's vital you ask Betty for her help; we can't do this alone." Timothy paused briefly. "When I've finished my chores I'll set to work on the compass headings from your drawings, Mark."

Much later, after feeding calves, watering pigs, cleaning out cows, and bringing a fresh jug of milk in for their mother, they all reassembled in Timothy's room. Mark had returned from his cycle ride to Betty's, armed with more large sketches, and now they were sitting on Timothy's bed munching cakes and 'doorstep' sandwiches.

Timothy sellotaped all his large drawings underneath the window and alongside these placed a rough map of their farm and the forest. Finally he tasked everyone to write up the things they had learned from reading the Arthurian library books.

Diane wrote up: *Camelot; lots of knights; banquets; Christmas; chivalry; battles, pretty dresses, castles, lakes,* and *lots more stuff.*

Mark sketched in the ancient lake of Crocern according to Betty's tithe map, and with a red ink marked in their pond. It looked so tiny beside the ancient lake, how could it be part of the Lake of Avalon?

Joan wriggled tiredly. Her notes were just single words, but she also had lots of stuff from the Encyclopaedia Britannica about Mont St Michel and St Michael's Mount. But she found nothing in the encyclopaedia about the giant of Henley Forest. So she sucked in her bottom lip and eventually wrote: *Winter; Sarum; Last Battle; Chapel; Excalibur; dragon; giant.* "How can we hope to find anything?" she said with a loud yawn. "The books never mention Crocern, Crewkerne, or anything like it, only forests, hills, battles, and things. And I'm tired." It was all too much for her, being just seven and three quarters, and she leaned back into the pillows and went to sleep.

Timothy took his map and Mark's copy of the tithe map; if he was going to pinpoint where the sword had been thrown then he would have to do his next markings very accurately. First off he added the directions North, South, East and West before taking father's Ordnance Survey map of Somerset and pinpointing Glastonbury. Beside this he added a thick black dot for the Tor.

Next he took a protractor, popped it over the centre of the medieval lake, and very carefully he drew four lines, using his compass readings. Finally he removed the protractor and continued all the lines backwards until they all crossed at the middle of the lake. At this point he drew a little sword.

"I think the sword is right here!" And as he grinned at them all it struck them that their adventure was coming true.

"The sword really is on our farm!" exclaimed Diane, waking Joan with her loud shriek.

"It's in our pond," said Timothy complacently. "Just like I said." And after that everything changed.

"How can we get it out?" asked Joan, stifling a last yawn. "We mustn't disturb the moorhen's nest."

"The sword is not on our farm," grumbled Mark. "We're much too far away from Glastonbury and the Isle of Avalon." But no one took any notice.

Timothy pored over the maps again, checking and rechecking his readings. He needed to be as accurate as possible if they were going to do what he was about to propose. "We're talking about something that might have happened nearly 1400 years ago, and might or might not have happened in the lake, or in our pond," he groaned. "There are so many 'mights and 'ifs'. What if we're wrong? What if there were more lakes, or if we're in the wrong place? Though, looking at my drawings of the compass co-ordinates, and comparing the pictures in the castle chambers with the location of our farm, we're almost on top of the sword! Oh, I wish I knew what to do!" He threw down his pencil, crossed his arms over his stomach and blurted out his proposal. "Let's at least try to look in our pond for the sword. If we don't find anything then Mark might be right, perhaps our farm is too far from Avalon." He rolled up the large sheets of notes. "I'm going to put them in my wardrobe for safekeeping." *And so Mum doesn't see them and start worrying.* "Let's focus on what we have discovered so far."

"Arthur's castle," broke in Diane.

"A prophecy," said Joan.

"An ancient creature; a faun, Eorldormann, who has declared our castle is one of King Arthur's secret castles, and told us more about the prophecy," added Timothy. "Also, we need to find Arthur's sword to cut the magic thread."

"So we can bind the dragon," said Diane feeling nervous.

"Lastly, the clue to finding the sword is in Eorldormann's paintings," finished Timothy. He thumped his head and laughed, realising what he had just said. "If the sword is in the paintings then Eorldormann must have seen it, since he painted it." He stopped short, understanding the full significance of his words. "If Eorldormann painted it, then we *are* looking in the right location." He glanced at Mark and bit his lip sharply. "If we don't find the sword what will happen? How can we stop the dragon escaping? We must find the sword before Christmas."

There were fifteen days left. Then what? Nobody wanted to ask the question.

Timothy took charge. "Bring all your spades to the pond at first light tomorrow. We're digging for Arthur's sword."

Chapter 15

Taking up the challenge

The following morning the farm was a frozen wasteland, and icicles like crystal talons hung heavily from the corrugated roof on the red brick barn. Rolling like a misty blanket the morning light inched into the valley and the children trudged out to the pond, swathed in a colourful collection of coats, hats and scarves. They laughed, jumped and crunched their way through every frozen puddle along the farm tracks, enjoying the noise of the ice crackling around their Wellington boots. On the way they collected the heavy spades from the woodshed and dragged them to the side of the pond, all ready to begin digging, only to discover that digging up the pond was going to be more difficult than they had imagined.

To one side of the pond stood a large willow tree, almost at the centre of Timothy's coordinates. They wouldn't be able to dig the tree up. Its branches were huge and thick and covered a large area of ground right up to the wall of the pig pens. Then another problem occurred to the children because the pig pens were covered in a flat base of concrete! They couldn't dig anything, and they wouldn't find the sword.

"This is hopeless!" groaned Diane, flinging her spade to the frozen ground then watching whilst it bounced and slid along the path.

"I agree," said Mark, tossing his spade crossly after his sister's. "What now?" He blew hard upon his mittened hands to keep them warm. "I'm going indoors to get a hot drink."

Timothy glanced across, feeling utterly miserable, but saying nothing. He finally understood the impossibility of their task. Snatching his drawings and maps together he screwed them into a tight ball and rammed them deep into his coat pocket. *What now indeed?*

Then he remembered the dark tunnels leading from the chamber beneath Henley Castle. Where did they go? The faun had told them to keep out of the tunnels. Why? Was the answer to the prophecy in those tunnels? If it was then he had to get inside them and find out if he were right. Slowly a crazy thought began to grow inside his head, and like a ripple on a pond one thing led to another, and another, until a whole flood of ideas and questions bubbled on the tip of his tongue. Did the tunnels run from the castle? Beneath the fields? To their farm? If they did, could they walk *from* the castle to their pond by using the tunnels? It wasn't a far-fetched idea; the farm and their pond were rather close to the castle. Timothy looked up at the others, who by now were kicking at frozen tufts of dirt, his excitement mounting.

"Everyone, follow me. Take the spades back; we're going to the castle again." His mood was infectious.

With coats flying they threw their digging tools back in the shed and raced back in the house, hurrying after Timothy who began giving orders. "Diane: pasties, hunks of cake, biscuits and apples. Joan: four bottles of lemonade. Be ready in ten minutes."

He snatched up his lance, compass and notebook, Mark grabbed his brass key, and they were ready in eight.

"Okay. Let's go!" Timothy was anxious to be moving, and desperately hoping he was making the right decision. But when he weighed up all that had happened to them over the past few days realised that the legend of the sleeping giant was no longer a myth, but grounded in truth. And as this dawned on him he wondered if the tale of binding the dragon with the magical thread might also be true. It was too terrifying to think of now, so he pushed it to one side.

As they got closer to Henley Forest Timothy caught Mark looking at him with a strange look on his face. Did he guess how scared he felt? He realised that being the eldest meant the success of their venture would depend upon him. A chilling thought shot through his mind; what would happen if they failed? They might all be killed, and it would be his fault.

Other frightening thoughts crowded into his head. Dashing off like that he wished he had told mother and father where they were going. What would happen if they didn't come back? What had been happening in the castle? Eorldormann had been scared of something in the chamber. What was it? Timothy chewed his lip in an agony of indecision. If they didn't try to stop the prophecy who else would? It had to be a child Eorldormann had said, and it had to be now, because the key to the castle had been found. So, if it wasn't them, then who? There was no one, other than themselves, and they were running out of time. Normally Timothy, Diane, Mark and Joan eagerly looked forward to Christmas, sewing decorations, stringing paper chains across the sitting room, but this year their thoughts were being taken up by the strange goings on at Henley Forest and Christmas didn't feel like a time of play at all. Timothy ground his teeth, worried about the outcome, yet knowing he would protect everyone as best he could, and when he turned to face the others his lips were white with suppressed emotion.

"We are looking for two things: the sword; and someone to find it." He took deep gulps of icy air. The others were all puffing after their run up the hill, their faces damp. "The prophecy mentions a child (*gasp*) who is supposed to stop evil coming into the world. (*gasp*) Mark has the brass key to the castle (*gasp*) and I found the medieval spearhead from Arthur's last battle. All of which means we must be special. Betty talked about a special child; Mark and I are both children! Also, Mark's hand fitted the painted hand giving us access to the Guardian's Chamber."

"And to Eorldormann," grinned Joan.

"Yes. And Eorldormann recognised *us* as being his only hope. *Us!*" Timothy emphasised noting how they were beginning to look as if they were knights on an Arthurian quest.

"This is fun," laughed Joan.

Timothy snorted, his reply scathing. "This adventure is not 'fun'; we are in earnest." He snatched at Joan's hand and gripped it tightly. "This is not an adventure any longer, Joanie. You must understand that." He shook his head as if to ward off a bad feeling. "Oh, why did I let you come? You're so young. You can go back if you want to."

She snatched her hand back, her eyes sparkling angrily. "I don't want to go back! I want to go with you. I don't want to be left behind. You always say I'm too small to join in your adventures, but I'm seven now. And that's quite big really." She bit hard on her lip and moved closer to Diane. Timothy suddenly burst out laughing; they were only children after all Why had he become so serious? He pushed the last of his bad feelings aside, ready to indulge in the fantasy of their 'adventure' once again.

"Okay. You win. You can go with us." Then he began to outline his plans. "We have no choice but to accept the challenge! But we need to be very careful. I suggest we return to the chamber within the castle then perhaps we can find a tunnel to take us under our pond. If we do we might find the sword. I also think, well, *hope*, the sword is hidden at the spot I worked out the co-ordinates for. It must be in the tunnels. We must find a way underneath the castle." Timothy stumbled with the last words, feeling himself slipping back into the feelings of fear and chaos. He shook his head, convinced he was only exhausted from their dash up the hill. But Diane's reaction hammered home the reality of the danger facing them.

Her head shot up. "No! We can't go into the tunnels! I don't like the dark. Besides, Eorldormann warned us about them. We shouldn't plan to do something he warned us against." She stopped suddenly, threw her bag to the ground and fixed Timothy with a hard stare.

Joan stumbled into Diane's back, her face puckering up and frightened. "Tim, you're going in the tunnels? Oh no! Diane's right! We can't do that! Eorldormann told us not to. And don't you remember? I had an awful dream about tunnels, and running away, and screaming and things. You know I did!" she gave a violent shudder. She hated it when their games got out of hand, and remembered when she had played on the roundabout in the town play park and the boys had pushed it faster and faster until she screamed to be let off. It felt like that now. This game didn't seem funny any longer.

"We were told not to go into any tunnels," said Mark, and his voice had an ugly edge to it. For several days he had suffered strange sensations, alternating between elation and impatience at the new adventure, and feeling moody and cross with everyone. He dreaded going back to the castle, and he felt resentful about having to use his new brass key. Well, he wouldn't! And he didn't want to go back!

Timothy shrugged his shoulders at the stormy expression on Mark's face. "If any of you want to go home . . . ." He left the sentence hanging in the air, wondering if he would have to go on alone. For a moment he felt overwhelmed with the enormity of the task ahead. Then he forced his face to relax and watched as the younger children's eyes flickered doubtfully. "We must find out if there is a tunnel beneath our pond which can lead us to the sword. If there is, we must try to walk through it, irrespective of any danger." He coughed awkwardly and blurted out. "I might be able to manage on my own. In fact, I'm sure I can. So, I won't blame you if you would rather stay at home, you are free to return." He gave them a lopsided smile, but his gaze rested on Mark. He had to have Mark with him. Without Mark the desperate attempt to find the sword could not go ahead; the faun said Mark was the only one who could use the brass key to enter the castle. Timothy held his breath. What would Mark do? He remembered hearing once that if you tried to force something against its will it would always resist, but if you offered it freedom it would remain. He hoped the philosophy would work now. Silence. Time passed. They could hear the ice melting on the branches around them.

Diane kicked at a pile of muddy pine needles. Joan looked from one to the other. Everything hinged on Mark's reply. One second. Ten seconds. Nothing. Finally Mark nodded his head. "Okay, I'll go along with your plan. For now, anyway."

Timothy gave an exhausted sigh; he had been holding his breath. "Okay, let's get going." He turned and began running into the forest, the others hurrying behind.

But the tension between the two brothers had unsettled everyone and before they found the ivy-covered wall of the castle they were a rather grumpy group. Mark found it difficult to run so far and so fast and still have to carry the heavy key by himself, but within moments his good humour was restored when he used the key to open the secret door for everyone.

However, things had changed in the castle, and the children realised it as soon as they trooped inside.

"Ugh, that smell is disgusting," said Diane, covering her face with a handkerchief. "It smells like something rotting."

"Shh! The faun is coming," said Timothy, as Eorldormann came hurrying from the Guardian's Chamber and saw the familiar red hat bobbing furiously.

"Hello children," Eorldormann called, rushing forwards. "I'm so glad you decided to come back. I have been worried."

"You look exhausted," exclaimed Timothy, hardly believing how frail the faun had become in one day.

"We need your help," he blurted out, before quickly outlining his proposal. "We think we know where the sword is, but we can't get to it from above. Can you take us along the tunnels?"

"Oh, No!" Eorldormann gasped, cowering away. Even his red hat seemed to cringe. "You don't know what you are asking! The tunnels must be avoided at all cost. No one can enter them."

"We have to," Timothy said, not knowing what horrors the tunnels held. "It is our only chance. Assuming the sword was thrown into the lake, which is now our pond, we have worked out where the sword might be hidden. However, we can't get to it since the area is covered over by Dad's pig pens and he won't let us dig them up, *[pause]* even if we asked him," Timothy added belatedly. "We have to go into the tunnels because they may lead us underneath our farm, and we may find the sword there."

Eorldormann shook his head, looking ill. "I can't stop you from entering; I would go with you if I could, but I don't have any strength left. You need someone with you, to guide you; someone who is very strong."

"Can you think of anyone?" asked Timothy.

The faun hesitated; he had the perfect solution. He felt reluctant to tell the children what he knew, and what he had in fact been planning since the children left him the day before. Would it work?

A hoof scuffed somewhere within the tunnels. Mark blanched. He heard it again, and realised it was getting closer. A large animal was moving close by and he could feel a menacing presence coming from the darkness.

Timothy grabbed Eorldormann and shook him hard, fear making him rough as the sounds came nearer and nearer. "What is it? Tell me!"

Eorldormann shook his head; it was already too late to stop it happening.

A powerful voice boomed across the chamber, like some monstrous seal barking over foggy waters. Each word was separated from the other, unfriendly, and disembodied, as if from another world. "Who summons me? Who would call me from my duty? I am Caradon, last of my kind, and of ancient lineage. Show yourselves." The children held their breath. They could feel the beast waiting. Only the noise of its heavy hooves told that it came nearer as each step grew louder, and louder.

The children grabbed each other, instinctively making a tight protective group and watched, terrified, as an enormous mythological creature loomed into view. They had never seen its like before and could only gape, not realising this huge beast was an abath.

The abath was a creature of legend whose size, colour, and stature resembled a huge stag; the king of the forest. It looked magnificent.

And in the centre of its forehead gleamed a single horn of pure crystal shining like an opal. The beast twisted its head and the children saw that it was regal and strong, and its large nostrils were flaring, sending jets of hot vapour into the air. Its black eyes glittered angrily in the dull light, showing an aloofness, power and intelligence that challenged everyone, and made the children feel humble beneath its stare.

The abath stamped its hoof, abrupt, impatient, and angry. "I come here against my will, and only because my friend has asked it of me. I understand you need my help, though as children of men you do not deserve it." Its voice dripped with scorn and it shook his head vigorously like a dog shaking off water.

"Is it a unicorn?" whispered Joan.

"Don't be silly; it's not white," snapped Diane, feeling frightened and fascinated all at once.

Mark stepped forward. Immediately Timothy snatched him back. "Stay here. This creature might not be friendly."

The abath snorted loudly and bulging muscles rolled over its shoulders and down its belly. "If you don't want my help I will go back," it sneered. "I do not like the children of men, nor any of your kind. I have had dealings with you before. Many of my one-horned kind have been hunted and slaughtered for your pleasure; I have no love of you." Then it turned and began trotting away.

Timothy suddenly realised that the beast might be the only thing that could help them. He raced after it, hoping it was a friendly creature, but feeling nervously that he might be endangering all of them. "Wait! Don't go. Please! I don't know what you are, or where you're from, but we would never hurt you. We come from the farm, just down the hill from here; we care for animals. That's what we do on the farm. Please, stay. If you think you could help us we would be very grateful." Timothy looked across at Eorldormann, feeling utterly helpless.

The faun trotted over to the abath and began nudging it affectionately, like old friends meeting after a long time, and Timothy felt himself go weak with relief.

"Caradon is an abath; a special guardian like myself, from times long past. He is the one I was thinking of who might help you in your search for the sword. He is a special creature who knows everything about these tunnels, where each one goes, how long it takes to go there, if there are any lakes or rivers in them, and he can even help take you there," explained Eorldormann. "When you left yesterday I asked him for his help. I hope you don't mind. There was no one else you see. He's the only one left who can help you. Everyone else is dead. But, well, you see, Caradon is a rather unusual animal. He's not just an abath but is related to the unicorns, which were hunted to extinction by man."

Joan kicked Diane in the shin, her eyes gleaming. "I told you it was a unicorn," she mouthed. Diane pulled a face.

Eorldormann pretended not to notice. "Yes, his cousins, the unicorns were hunted to extinction by man, that's why he doesn't like you. He is also the giant's personal guard, and it is his duty to ensure the giant doesn't waken from his slumbers until danger is at hand. "

The giant's personal guard! The children gasped, mouths open, eyes moving from the faun to the abath, and then at each other. Mark staggered backwards, looking as if he had seen a ghost. There really was a giant nearby!

"Oh my goodness!" shrilled Joan. "The giant really does exist, and not just in my book!"

And then the enormity of what they had uncovered at the rifle range hit them. Everything was true. The ancient land of myth and mystery, where legendary creatures battled against Arthurian Knights of the Round Table, really existed. And finally they realised that Camelot was at Crewkerne!

Timothy gulped rapidly. "Will someone pinch me? Am I going crazy? Is a faun really telling me there is a giant living near our home? I always thought the giant was made from the trees of the forest!"

"I always believed in unicorns," whispered Joan.

"I'm afraid I'll wake up in a moment, and it will have been a dream," said Diane. "This is wonderful"

Mark said nothing, but a weird expression was flitting over his face, as though remembering things.

"Can this . . . abath . . . Caradon, . . . lead us through the tunnels? To the exact location where I believe the sword is?" Timothy nearly choked on the words. He would never have imagined himself speaking to a faun about legendary creatures such as giants and abaths. Whatever next?

They were soon to find out.

"Please!" chimed the girls, grabbing Eorldormann's sleeve. "We must go through the tunnels." Excitement overcame their worries about the unusual beast.

Timothy moved to the large creature with the single horn, though his knees were shaking and his hands trembled. "Will you help? Please. We don't have much time."

A groan rumbled overhead. Mark shrunk down into a tight ball, hiding his face in his arms. Joan gasped and ran to Diane. Timothy tightened his hand on his lance, ready to defend his little group.

"What's that? We heard it earlier."

"That is my master, the giant," explained Caradon, tossing his head and tail angrily as though swatting flies. "He is waking up. There is great trouble coming to us all because you interfered. Why did you come here upsetting things?"

"We're sorry. We didn't mean to," said Joan. "We only wanted a Christmas adventure."

"If you will help us find the sword, we'll go away and leave you alone. We got caught up in this against our will and now we have to tie up a dragon to protect our world. It's not our fault we're here. Won't you help us? Please!" Timothy's face dripped with beads of perspiration. He brushed them away impatiently.

The magnificent Caradon closed his eyes and began to rock to and fro, thinking deeply. Eorldormann appeared to be saying a prayer, and for once his little red hat lay motionless upon his head. Everyone waited for the abath to give his answer. Would he help them? Or would their adventure be doomed?

Chapter 16

Finding the sword

Eorldormann waved until the children disappeared into the tunnels and their voices grew weak and disjointed, then he did a curious thing for a faun; he brushed a tear away and blew his nose in a large red handkerchief. Though no one would believe it he had felt sick at heart when Caradon finally agreed to take the children into the tunnels, and such worry and anguish tore through his body that he didn't know if he would survive the day. Had he been right to entrust the children to the moody abath who disliked mankind so much? Would he see them alive again? Or would they disappear as other children had over the years? Surely Caradon would bring these back safely, wouldn't he? They seemed to be such good children and he had grown quite fond of them with their little spurts of loyalty for one another.

Eorldormann put away his handkerchief and gazed back at the towering dragon. It looked as if one small push would free it from its prison of rock. The beast was covered from head to tail with thick layers of garish green scales, each layer bristling and twitching like a fish caught on a hook. Its thick neck was flexed and arched like a monstrous viper about to strike, whilst its crocodile-like head hung with row upon row of cankerous fangs, yellow with age, slobbering and drooling venom. As Eorldormann looked up he saw the dragon's eyes glittering malevolently, unwavering, and blood red in the pale light.

Yet more horrible than the sight of the drooling fangs were the twelve murderous ciphers, impaled around the dragon's feet. These evil creatures were once the followers of Morgan le Fay, and known as the catoblepas. Each was the size and strength of a lion, but were like hideously scaly backed black beetles. They were one of the beasts most feared by man since one look from their pale pink gaze could turn a man into stone.

Eorldormann wrapped his arms around himself; the temperature had suddenly dropped. He wished he had never painted these creatures on the walls. Surely they couldn't come alive too. Could they? He had always believed that only the dragon might gain its freedom if the child failed to fulfil the prophecy. What if these ciphers of the dragon came to life also? How could the children deal with them? They were guarded by the strength of the dragon, and Eorldormann knew that only ancient powers could kill them, powers which the children did not have.

He walked nearer to the group of catoblepas, wondering if he could do something to delay the events which threatened to come soon. Then he froze. He looked. And looked again. Surely it couldn't be true. A tiny movement like the beating of a gnat's wing caught his eye. *No! It can't be!* He nearly shouted out loud; the dragon was coming to life. Eorldormann shook his head in disbelief. According to the prophecy the dragon could only burst free on a Christmas Day, the anniversary of Arthurian festivities. It wasn't Christmas yet. Then a chilling thought shook him, what if the prophecy were false? What if the dragon could break free at any time? How soon could the children return with the sword? What would happen if they didn't find it?

Eorldormann had to keep the dragon prisoner for a while longer; but he realised he was growing weaker each day as the dragon grew more powerful. How much more could he take before the dragon's strength overtook his own?

The faun snatched up a handful of the magic green thread. It seemed so flimsy. Was there enough here? Perhaps he ought to make more. And quickly. Of one thing he was certain; the dragon had to be bound; everything relied upon the children finding Excalibur. But as soon as his fingers touched the thread he felt his strength draining from him as the power of the dragon grew stronger.

Far underground, along the miles of deep, dark tunnels, Caradon trotted swiftly, leading the children down a maze of alleys without pause, confident of his route. Timothy ran hard, pushing himself to keep pace with the abath. Mark stumbled after, labouring with the weight of the key, yet determined not to part with it. Diane gritted her teeth, jogging for a few minutes and then walking, all the time struggling to keep the abath in view. Joan cried out that her side was hurting with the 'stitch', but the tunnels were full of darkness and none dared to stop. Time was running out.

Eventually they reached a large area where the roof of the tunnel disappeared upwards into a huge dome, and ancient waters ran in rivulets from the rocks above, blackening the sides of the tunnel to look like crystallised jet. The area looked like a central transept in a cathedral with tunnels running off of it in all directions. Here the abath stopped with a sharp thump on the ground. "This is the place you wanted on your map," he said abruptly.

Timothy threw a doubtful glance and pocketed his compass. *Are you sure,* he wanted to ask, realising the compass had been spinning uselessly for most of their dash through the tunnels. There was no north or south in the tunnels and each tunnel looked the same. *What makes this tunnel different?* "Okay," he mumbled, shrugging indifferently, struggling to give the impression he knew exactly where they were. "Thank you", and mentally kicked himself. How could they have got into this predicament so easily? They were completely lost, and what made him more furious with himself was the realisation they were all at the mercy of the miserable looking creature that looked like a dun coloured unicorn. What if it didn't lead them back out? They could be lost in the tunnels forever. Timothy dare not tell Joan they were lost or she would be frightened and start crying. His only hope of getting everyone out safely lay in pretending that his compass was working perfectly. He would tell a lie if he had to. "Okay, we're here. The abath has brought us to the exact spot. Let's start looking."

The heavy abath swung away ready to return into the dark tunnels. If the creature disappeared they would be lost, with no way of finding their way back out. He had to stop the abath. Now! He forced a bright smile on his face and called out. "If you wait for us, we can all go back, together." *Please!* His eyes narrowed, pleading. His breath caught in his throat. Would the abath wait for them? Would the beast lead them out?

Diane's girlish voice broke in, thin and nervous in the black gloom. "I don't see a sword here. Can we go now?"

"No! The faun said we have to find the sword. We can't return without it."

"Oh," drawled Mark with a strong dollop of sarcasm. "I suppose we find Arthur's sword just like that, do we?" He began rubbing his aching shoulders. "Perhaps you can tell us how you intend to find it. The sword was thrown into the lake almost fourteen hundred years ago! This is a bit like looking for a needle in a haystack. Except this haystack is made of rock!" He gulped back a lump in his throat. He couldn't cry now! That was the last thing he wanted. But their whole journey seemed to have been a waste of time; the abath had brought them to a place where every bit of the rock looked the same as every other bit. And of one thing he was certain; Timothy didn't know where they were and Mark realised they were both terrified.

"We're supposed to be looking for a lake, but where is the lake, Timothy? Can you tell me? Because I can't see it." He snatched a handkerchief from his pocket and blew his nose loudly. It was too awful for a ten year old to bear.

"Don't get upset Mark," said Diane. "Take a deep breath and count to ten. You know Mum always says arguing amongst ourselves won't help. And she's right." Diane, trying to be helpful as always, tried to soothe frayed tempers. Joan looked from one to the other and shifted towards Caradon who was rubbing his head disinterestedly against a sharp piece of rock, knocking his thick horn in a rhythmical manner. The creature was blowing softly, reminding her of their cows as they chewed their cud in the warm stalls on a cold winter's night. Feeling reassured she patted the creature on its head. It felt rough and thick, like the harsh curly head of their Devonshire bull. Feeling even more reassured Joan kept on patting it.

Timothy paced restlessly. Time was running out. They had to find the sword before the abath moved off, or else their journey into the dark place beneath the castle would have been for nothing. He had to at least try and find something while they were there. He began running his hands over the cold sides of the tunnel in a continuous sweeping motion. Beneath his fingers he could feel all the cracks and bumps. Perhaps the sword was hidden nearby on a ledge, and because of the gloom in the tunnel they couldn't see it. "The sword might be hidden, or behind something. Try looking with your hands, like I'm doing," he suggested to the others.

"Okay, but we'll only find it if all your co-ordinates and things are right," reminded Mark sourly.

Diane stumbled into a pile of boulders, grazing her knees, but soon began to copy what Timothy was doing. Joan dropped down beside her sister and the girls worked quickly together, sliding their hands around the rocks. After a few minutes Mark became infected by the same concerns. It was now or never, he thought, and gritting his teeth, put a plan into action that he had been thinking about for a few moments. He dragged the brass key out of his bag and pressed it up against the rock face, hoping the key might lead them to another secret passage.

In that way time passed. Hands and feet grew chilled so that after several hours they could scarcely feel them. The abath stamped restlessly. They were out of time.

"We may as well give in," Timothy said finally.

But just as he said it, hidden by shadows, Diane's hand knocked against something heavy. She gave a whoop of joy as if she had found the end of the rainbow. "I think I've found it! Over here! Quickly! This is it everyone!" And she gripped her fingers around a long, narrow object protruding from a crevice.

The object wouldn't move, as if it were caught on something. Diane gripped harder and her face worked with strain as she threw her whole strength and weight into pulling the object from its hole. Then they heard a dull sound of ripping.

"What's that?" said Diane, letting go the object and imagining some dreadful creature like a spider, wriggling up her arm.

"Don't let go, Diane. Be careful!" Timothy hurried to help.

"It's heavy, and very long!" Diane gave another tug, and found herself falling backwards. Suddenly all the children were beside her, grabbing and tugging at any bit of the object they could get their fingers around. It still wouldn't budge.

"Everyone catch hold, and pull on the count of three," said Timothy. "Two, three!"

One huge tug later and the dark object thumped on to the floor. The thud seemed to reverberate around their heads, echoing back and forth through the tunnel. It made a chilling sound.

The sword, for that was what it was, had a weak glimmering quality that sent faint rainbows bouncing off the walls of the tunnel. Joan exclaimed and reached out to touch it.

"Careful! It might be sharp," said Timothy.

He fumbled in his coat pocket, pulling on a pair of gloves and quickly ripped away some scraps of leather binding which still clung to the sword. Then he wiped it, running his hand down the length of the shaft and dragging the dirt off so they could see the object better.

The sword was unusual. It was ancient and very long and looked as if it were made of gold. Intricate engravings twined themselves around the blade, whilst large rubies, pearls and gemstones studded the hilt. But what made it even more unusual to the children was the shape of the handle. This was divided into two large moulded curves which reminded Timothy of a pair of ram's horns. It seemed as if it should be grasped by two hands. *Which might explain why it felt so heavy.* He slid one hand into each curve, so that the sword stood upright in front of him, relishing the perfect smoothness and the way his hands seemed to glide through and respond to the shape, so he found he was holding it in front of his face as though he were offering up a large flask.

"Excalibur!" he breathed. Then he grunted under a sudden surge in weight. "Ho! It is very heavy, Diane. Well done for finding it. This must be Arthur's sword; it even feels like magic." He let the tip stand in the ground and rested his aching arms. But once the tip of the sword touched the floor the air seemed to be sucked from the tunnel as if by a whirlwind. The children had been laughing in relief at having found the sword but now they stood transfixed.

"What was that?" whispered Mark. "I thought I was going to be sucked out."

"Me too," mouthed Diane. "Let's get out."

Timothy laid the sword down, then suddenly stepped back, expecting the sword to have caused the disturbance. "Did you see anything?"

No.

"Did you hear anything?"

Another shake of heads.

Behind them the abath snorted, tossing his head angrily like a frisky horse. He stamped. Once. Twice. Three times. He was leaving.

"Can we take the sword?" whispered Joan to Timothy. He hesitated. He had only touched it briefly but already he could feel its power. He had told the others the sword was magic, but he hadn't really thought about the implication of what he was saying. Well, what if the sword *were* magic? If only he could ask the faun for advice! Perhaps he should ask the abath, but he didn't feel like trusting that strange creature yet, so he had to rely on his own instinct.

Mark got nervous. "What are you waiting for, Timothy? Pick the sword up! Quickly! We've got to get back."

"He's right, Tim," said Diane. "Pick it up and run."

Timothy could feel himself sweating. If he agreed to take the sword back to the faun it would be used to cut the magic green thread to bind the dragon, but the thought of getting right up close to the dragon, to tie it with Eorldormann's thread, frightened him more than he liked to admit; in fact he was terrified. What was the dragon like? Was it asleep at the moment? Eorldormann had said it was injured, but had recovered, so how could they get near it? How big was it? If the real life dragon looked like the painting they saw on the wall then Timothy doubted his courage to go near it.

He tried to think positively; perhaps Eorldormann could tell them a simple way to do it. After all, wasn't the real dragon hidden behind the castle walls? Perhaps deep within a dungeon? With luck they might never have to see it. When Eorldormann told them the prophecy needed a child to bind the dragon, perhaps he meant it would be sufficient for a child to find the sword. Well, the children had found the sword. He would take it back, and tell Eorldormann they had achieved their part of the bargain. Then they could go home. He hoped so; he felt a really bad feeling wash over him.

Chapter 17

Dashed hopes

Diane and Joan looked at the sword in Timothy's hand, then at each other, and grinned. They couldn't see Timothy's terrified expression in the gloom and didn't understand his concerns. For them their adventure into Arthur's castle had been more fun than they could have expected, and they wanted to pinch themselves to wake up. What a lot they would have to tell their friends at school when term began in the new year! They chattered happily as they walked, no longer frightened by the darkness, and Joan had forgotten about her nightmares. Mark plodded behind Timothy, looking fierce, a deep line scarring his forehead.

Timothy swung the heavy sword from one shoulder to the other to ease his aching muscles, but he didn't join in his sister's chatter; he felt another sinister presence; something 'out there' but he wasn't sure where. He looked at the abath. Did the strange beast notice anything unusual, he wondered? But the abath kept up a determined pace, continually trotting ahead of them, then sometimes stopping impatiently if the children lagged behind. "Hurry!" Caradon barked. "We must move quickly."

The darkness thickened inside the tunnels, but the children were content with their trophy. They only had to get the sword back to Eorldormann and everything would be all right.

Suddenly a series of dreadful sounds filled the tunnels, like the clicking of giant needles. Snick. Snick. Snick. Caradon juddered to a stop, his body quivering, and bits of foam shot from its nostrils. Timothy stopped and held his breath. He had never heard anything so strange. Everyone listened. The noise stopped.

"What is it?" mouthed Diane.

"Shh!" Timothy waved her to silence.

Mark's face had turned the colour of ashes. "Something horrid is happening. I can feel it."

Caradon surged forwards. "Follow me," and the abath was gone.

"Wait for us!"

The children ran quickly, their rasping breaths burning their throats, and all dreading to hear a repeat of the snick snicking sounds.

After five minutes Caradon clattered to a halt. They were in a circular chamber with five tunnels leading from it, much like a spider's web. Each tunnel looked like the one they had come out of. Caradon pranced around in a wide circle, shaking his head and sniffing the air. Flecks of foam spluttered around his mouth.

He made up his mind. "Come," he barked to the children. "We haven't any time to lose." And he plunged into a tunnel.

Diane and Joan raced after. Mark started to run too, but Timothy stamped angrily, exhausted by the weight of carrying the sword. "I need a rest!" he shouted breathlessly. No one heard. They had disappeared into the gloom and Timothy was left alone. He gripped his fingers round the medieval sword to toss it onto his shoulder, but as he did so a bolt of electricity shot up his arm so unexpectedly he nearly dropped it. "Ouch!"

The sharp shock reminded him of the electric shock he sometimes got from touching the cattle fences on the farm and suddenly, thinking of home, a strange calm washed over him. It was with a new sense of peace that he took the ancient sword firmly in his hands, knowing that the strange current had disappeared, and that the sword was his friend. He lifted the powerful sword back onto his shoulder with a reverent movement, and as he stood there made a solemn vow. *If any of his family were threatened he wouldn't hesitate to use the sword.* With that vow made he grinned bravely; he would do battle with the dragon himself, even though he died in the attempt!

Mark came hurrying back, worried and cross. "Come on. The abath is taking us back another way. I think it's safer." He looked rather small and frail in the darkness.

"Are you sure?" demanded Timothy, drifting back slowly from the lofty heights of his imagination. "The beast could be leading us into a

trap. I've no idea where we are. These tunnels all look the same to me."
Until they turned another corner and saw a glow up ahead.

"We're back," Mark said, rushing forwards. Caradon shot Timothy a
long look before galloping into the tunnels.

Eorldormann trotted over as soon as he saw them and Diane and Joan
threw their arms around him grinning furiously, immediately forgetting
about their unusual helper and the fearful sounds they heard in the
tunnels. "Oh Eorldormann. We're so glad to see you again! And guess
what? We've found the sword!"

The long face beamed congratulations. "Well done. After all these
years of waiting. I can scarcely believe it. At last we can bind the dragon."
Not before time, he added, hurrying to take the sword from Timothy. As he
moved he stumbled, pitching forwards violently as if he had been pushed.
Everyone heard the horrible cracking sound like a dry twig breaking.
"Oohh," he cried, and clutched his left wrist.

Diane and Joan rushed to him. "What's wrong?" they cried, helping
Eorldormann upright. He quickly dusted himself off, carefully averting
his face from their gaze. He didn't want the children to see how upset he
was at the accident; he knew it was another sign of what was to come.
Abruptly he grabbed the sword with his good hand, giving a nod of thanks
to the girls. "Thank you for helping me. But see, there's nothing wrong,
just a little twist as I fell. I shouldn't be so careless. Silly me, rushing
around in all this wonderful excitement! Please, will you help me carry
the sword?" The faun gripped it with his good hand and moved towards
the Guardian's Chamber. This was the chamber with the painted dragon.
Timothy stood like a statue, his blood seeming to be turned to ice. For
all his brave vows he still didn't want to see the hateful dragon. He felt
sure he didn't believe in dragons, but he could feel a strange fearful
tension whipping through the air, coming towards them, gathering pace
with every moment, and it felt like it was bringing the dragon with it.

Diane and Joan fell silent, noticing the strange tension also. They
had been standing beside Eorldormann, but now they stood upright, as
pale as a little pair of ghosts. Mark seemed to shrink in front of them. *This
is it. This is where it all ends.*

"Do we say goodbye? Or shake hands?" said Diane, her voice tremulous.

"Hush. Not yet. If my plan works everything will be fine," said
Eorldormann.

And if it doesn't? The question hung in the air.

Eorldormann led them slowly into the Guardian's Chamber with the ancient sword balanced upon his shoulder. The children followed, with drooping heads as though they were following a funeral procession. Silent as lambs. Joan slipped her hand into Diane's, and for once Diane didn't jeer or call her 'baby'. They were just two sisters together, braving a dragon.

The green mound of thread lay before them. It seemed to be glowing in the half-light, and looked much larger now. It was clear Eorldormann had spent the last of his strength making more thread, worried that his plan wouldn't work after all. He was utterly exhausted and it showed in the translucent quality of his face and hands, as if he were dissolving with the effort it had taken.

The faun grabbed an armful of thread, with length after length cascading from his hands like giant skeins of wool, then raising the sword he gave the children a grateful smile and murmured a silent prayer. Within moments he knew they would be safe. He raised the sword high, but as it glinted aloft in the pale chamber light a screaming high-pitched sound reverberated around their heads. On and on it screamed, like a raging siren.

"Aaaaarghhhh!"

The children threw themselves to the floor, ramming their hands over their ears and screwing their eyes tightly shut. After a few moments Timothy peeped up. "What is it?" he shouted above the din. Eorldormann gave a terrified grimace, but kept his arm firmly raised, and the sword raised above the thread.

Diane and Joan tried pushing themselves into the ground, wishing it might open up and swallow them to save them from the terrible noise. Mark buried his face into his arms, seeming to get smaller as the awful sound jarred around their heads. Only the faun stood upright, his back straight and his voice bold and defiant. "You won't get free this time," he yelled, facing the back wall of the chamber. Then down he plunged the sword, down into the loop of magic, slicing downwards, down amongst the slithering fibres of green thread. "Now you are here forever. And ever!" He laughed and wheezed until tiny tears splashed down his face. "This is for my family! This is for my freedom!" And again the sword was thrust into the thread.

But as he drew it out his triumphant expression drained to one of bewilderment. For long moments he just stared at the mound of thread as if he couldn't believe what he was seeing. Nothing had happened; it was still intact. He raised the sword again, higher this time, grimacing with the pain from his broken wrist, and again he slammed the sword downwards. It should have sliced through the fibres as easily as slicing through ice cream, but the thread remained bewilderingly intact. His expression turned to despair, and finally fear. Every belief he had cherished over the centuries lay in tatters with the perfectly useless circle of thread. He dropped the sword to the floor, crumpled over and grabbed his sides, too exhausted and hurt to move.

Timothy snatched up the sword. "What's wrong with it? Can't you get it to cut? Here, let me try; you're tired."

He lifted it above his shoulders and, taking careful aim for the downwards thrust, struck the sword into the heart of the fibrous green mass.

"Ooff!" He moved back and stared. "Nothing has happened!" Yet it should have been sliced into a thousand shreds. He snatched up the sword again. He would cut the thread this time if it was the last thing he did! Then again, down into the green mass he drove the sword. But the thread remained stubbornly intact. He dropped the sword, confused and defeated.

"Leave it. It won't work." Eorldormann sounded weak with the failure of his plan.

Timothy slid to the ground in disbelief. "I thought the sword would cut it. What are we doing wrong?"

As he finished speaking everyone felt a powerful rumble swirling around the cavern. Then it became louder, then intermittent, almost as if someone were laughing. Eorldormann spun about, turning towards the painted dragon, his face white with terror. "No! Not yet. You can't break free. Not yet. It's not Christmas. We still have time!"

"Is that it?" Diane followed Eorldormann's pointing finger, then she began to shake and her voice ended on a shriek that pierced the awful rumbling noises. She realised the huge painted dragon on the wall wasn't a painting at all; it was the real thing. A great, hideous, drooling monster. And it looked much brighter than when they had last seen it. As they watched, dumb with fear, the thick yellowed talons on the dragon's front feet began to move, purposefully, one after the other; in a slow malevolent movement that seemed to mesmerise everyone. Then finally, after what seemed like five minutes but was only a few seconds, the girls screamed, releasing everyone from their awful trance. Timothy shook his head, breaking free from the mind numbing incapacity induced by the sight of the living, breathing dragon. He remembered the snick, snicking he had heard earlier and recalled how much it sounded like a cat sharpening its claws on a post, and when he looked at the painting again he could see how most of the talons were curled, crablike, raised and parted as if to strike. His worst nightmares were coming true. He scrabbled up, grabbed his brother and sisters and flung them out of the way. But Mark didn't want to be flung out of the way; shaking him off like a dog shaking off water he picked up the sword that Timothy had dropped and stood staring defiantly at the dragon.

"Let me try."

"No." Timothy grabbed at him again and pushed him backwards, then he snatched the sword out of Mark's hands.

Eorldormann braced himself, squaring his shoulders as if ready to do battle. He knew he had to recover his strength and shield the children from the evil that started filling the whole chamber. His face and voice grew wild as he stared at the dragon on the wall.

"You won't get out. You won't. We will bind you, as I promised centuries ago." But his words only drew mocking laughter.

'I will soon be free,' the rumbling sounds seemed to say.

"You said the sword would cut the thread to bind the dragon!" Timothy said, his voice a whiplash of anger, hurt and fear. Then he softened, realising his words were futile. They had tried and they had failed. It was as simple as that, and he had to accept it. "I don't understand why it didn't work."

Eorldormann looked wretched and then confessed the whole prophecy to the children. "The dragon of Camelot will break free at the time of the Christmas festivities, and destroy the world. The only one who can stop it is a child. But which child? We do not know. The chosen child will find Arthur's sword, and can ward off the evil from the dragon. I have created the magic thread as a way of binding the dragon forever, and I thought Arthur's sword would cut it. But," He looked at the pile of thread and shrank in despair. "I must have been wrong."

Timothy leapt up, thinking quickly. "You might not be wrong. This child you speak of, is it one of us? Do you know?"

Time was running out.

"Mark! You wanted to try to cut the thread, well, perhaps you're right. We all should have a go."

Mark, at ten years of age, was much smaller than Timothy but he managed to strike the sword into the fibres. Once again nothing happened. Timothy could feel his panic mounting. "Diane! Come here. Quickly! You try, and then Joan. Both of you. We haven't any time to lose. Hurry!"

The girls threw Timothy a white petrified glance then came across, clutching hands. Together they hefted the sword, grabbing it forcefully with both of their hands on one curved arc of the handle, and then letting the sword drop into the pile of green. But still the thread remained intact.

"There must be another way. I wish I knew what it was." Timothy looked at Diane. "How many days left before Christmas?"

"It's the 11th today; so, two weeks. Fourteen days," she replied.

Timothy flinched as if he had been hit. *Is that all?* Fourteen days to discover the secret of the legend. How could they do it?

He could feel waves of sickness wash over him as he tried to get his mind to focus on finding another solution. "When will the dragon break free?" he asked Eorldormann.

"On Christmas day, according to the prophecy. Until then it will be bound according to legend, but on Christmas Day the full horror of it will be unleashed."

"And the sleeping giant?" asked Joan, still clutching Diane's hand tightly. "Will that awaken on Christmas too?"

Eorldormann nodded. "They will both awaken on the same day: the giant and the dragon; good and evil. And the world will be destroyed in their fight for supremacy." His voice started to crack and his face fell; he remembered the time King Arthur's knightly Christian forces faced the treachery of his son Mordred, and the bloodiest battle ever known to man took place on the downs around Sarum. From Mordred's great treason sprung the roots of evil, and these gave the dragon strength. Only the slumbering giant offered hope. Eorldormann could feel the children's helplessness and fear washing around him. If only he could save them! But every passing moment heralded the dragon's return and his own demise. What else could he do? Then he thought of *Her*. It was a long shot but she was his only hope.

Chapter 18

An Arthurian Maiden

Eorldormann hustled the children through the tunnel and into the Outer Chamber, away from the you-know-what, only pausing to stop beneath a large painting of a beautiful lady with flowing golden hair. She stood like a tragic Grecian goddess, weeping gently beside King Arthur. Her skin was pale and tinged with green, like a perfect bird's egg.

"Welcome to the Maiden of Ascolot," stated Eorldormann. "A tragic lady who fell in love with Lancelot when he chanced to stay at her father's castle."

"Why tragic?" asked Joan who had discovered her voice again now they had moved away from the dragon's chamber.

"Because Lancelot had already given his love to Guinevere, Arthur's queen. So he said farewell to the maiden, and returned to Camelot, little realising how much she loved him. Later, during a tournament, he was severely injured and returned to the maiden's castle as a refuge where he might recover. However, the maiden was so in love with Lancelot that she fell ill through grief. Nothing anyone could do would save her, and she pined her life away. Just before she died she asked to be wrapped in a linen sheet and put into a boat with her most treasured items, then set upon the river to float away wherever the water would take her. The maiden clutched a note to King Arthur, Lancelot's lord and king, telling of her sorrow and her wish to die rather than live without the love of her one true knight."

"That is so sad," said Diane, noticing how Eorldormann's voice seemed to fade and pine as if he too had once loved as tragically as the Maiden of Ascolot. "What happened then?"

"The boat washed ashore at Camelot where the people of the city carried her body to the king. Some people believe that when she died a beautiful baby girl was born in Camelot and the Maiden's last breath found its way into that child. They also believe that through this child the Maiden of Ascolot lives forever."

"Oh, what a wonderful story," said Joan. "I especially like the last bit where the Maiden will live forever. I never read that in the books from the library."

"Not everything is written in books. Some things are left for us to imagine," said Eorldormann.

Timothy was pacing beneath the painting, impatient with his sister's chatter. "It's a nice story, but I don't see how this helps us."

"It is useful to have as much information as possible about something which puzzles us in order to discover the answers," said Eorldormann, giving Timothy a look.

"I realise that," said Joan sweetly, who actually didn't realise any such thing, but didn't want to admit it. She tossed Timothy a triumphant smile, receiving a glare in return.

"What were the treasured items?" asked Diane, thinking of romance and fine jewels.

"A key, and a turquoise locket. The key gave its owner access to all of King Arthur's castles." The faun humph-ed loudly, looking pointedly at Mark. "The key is in your possession young man,"

Mark winced, seeming to shrivel beneath his coat so that he looked like a tortoise peeping nervously out of its shell.

"After King Arthur's death the key found its way into the hands of that baby girl's family, where it passed through generation after generation, for hundreds of years. The last lady passed it to her daughter when she lay dying and shortly afterwards that daughter came to Henley Castle. There she fell and injured herself, and knowing of the prophecy she passed it to you, Mark, at the October Fair."

Mark spluttered, raising his head out of his shell. "Her! I didn't know who she was. I never met her again. It was as though she never existed; nobody could remember seeing her at the Fair. She looked so old."

Eorldormann chuckled at Mark's expression. "She could make herself young or old, at will, so no one would recognise her. That is part of her magic."

"She's magic too?" Joan said, and felt her eyes were popping out of her head.

"Does she exist now?" asked Diane.

"If only I knew," sighed Eorldormann heavily. "She might be able to help us. She was injured when she came here about ten years ago and I haven't heard of her since. Who can tell where she is now? Perhaps she disappeared forever when she passed on the key. However, if she exists still she might be the only one who can help you complete the prophecy." As he said the last words a loud groan sounded through the vaulted rocks above. "The giant!" he exclaimed. "We're running out of time!"

Timothy acted swiftly. "Right! Everyone, let's go back for a . . ." 'pow wow' seemed too childish an expression now; they had all grown up a great deal in the last few hours. "A . . . . meeting," he ended strongly. "Get your thinking caps on everyone. We need some answers." And they waved goodbye to Eorldormann before beginning their journey home and talking through everything they had discovered.

Diane said, "The thread that Eorldormann has been making looks like the stuff Mum gave me to mend my school bag with last week. It was ever so strong. I could only cut it with Mum's best and sharpest scissors; its unbreakable. Mum calls it her magic thread."

"Then next time perhaps we should take Mum's scissors to try to cut the *magical* thread in the castle," Timothy emphasised ungraciously. As soon as he said it he was sorry; Diane was trying to help, and just because they were all worried and in danger was no reason to be unkind. He smiled, hoping to take the sting out of his words. "Mum's thread is special isn't it? I used it to tie my model aircraft on to the ceiling." He stopped, thought for a moment, then burst out loudly, "You're right! Why did I miss it? We have been told that the thread can only be cut by King Arthur's sword, but, what if something else can cut it? Perhaps we need to look for other things!" Having decided upon that solution the children hurried home with more purpose. Their next problem was to find the 'what' which would cut the thread?

Mark trudged along as fast as he could. The weight of the brass key which he carried in his school bag appeared to be getting heavier and heavier each time he held it. Joan hurried behind, not wanting to let the others out of her sight. She slipped her hand into Timothy's larger, more comforting, one. "I'll be glad to get home," she whispered.

Their mother was looking out for them from the garden. "There's been a telephone call for you, from Betty Vanstone. She wants you to see her now. It's urgent, she said." Adding, "Here's some lunch," and passed Timothy a large canvas bag. "You can eat it when you get there."

Lunch? Was it only lunchtime? So much had happened they thought they had been in the castle chambers for days.

Betty was outside waiting. As soon as they saw her they realised things were more serious than before. She hurried them into her kitchen, manoeuvring her wheelchair easily and watching them eat their sandwiches as she brought them up to date with everything. But first she wanted them to tell her all they had seen and done.

Timothy kept explanations brief, explaining how they had gained entrance into King Arthur's ancient castle, how they had found the outer chamber covered in paintings, and how Mark had put his hand onto the hand of a young knight in silver armour on the wall and it had opened to another chamber. "Sir Galahad," explained Betty Vanstone softly. "Son of Lancelot."

Diane took up the explanations, telling about Eorldormann the sole surviving faun and keeper of the Guardian's Chamber, and the great pile of magical thread he had been spinning for centuries with which to bind the dragon. Joan mentioned the magnificent abath, Caradon, the descendant to the ancient unicorn and how he had led them through the tunnels. Mark showed her the brass key, and said very little else. When Timothy told her about finding the sword she was delighted. However, when they told her the sword had not cut the thread she grew serious. They were too scared to tell her of the dragon encased in the chamber walls.

"I have been thinking about the 'treasure' mentioned in the original sleeping giant legend, and also reading the Arthurian legends again," said Betty. "If the sword didn't cut the thread then perhaps we are looking for other treasure, and that we should be looking for the Holy Grail."

So softly did she say the two words that the children felt a gentle sigh of winter wind come slipping through the windows. "I never thought there would be a link to the Grail, but now you have seen a painting of Sir Galahad the possibility is greater. You see, Sir Galahad was the only perfect knight in Arthurian times, and he was the only one who could finally reach the Holy Grail itself."

"What is the Holy Grail?" asked Timothy.

"A chalice that is said to contain some of the blood of Christ," replied Betty. "I wonder if you should have been looking for the Grail, rather than the sword of King Arthur. It is unusual, but it would explain why the sword did not cut the thread."

"But Eorldormann, the faun, said the prophecy refers to a sword, found by a child, and used by the child to cut the thread," said Joan. Betty looked perplexed.

"Then it must be the sword and not the Holy Grail; the faun would know. He is a creature from a magical kingdom and his knowledge would far outweigh my own. Oh, I really need to look at those paintings on the walls, to see if there is anything there you have not noticed," she said, a tiny frown marking her face.

"I made lots of drawings," explained Mark, trying not to stare at Betty's wheelchair. He didn't see how they could hope to get her and the wheelchair to the castle. "I have tried to put in most of the details." He passed his pencilled drawings to Betty and at the same time noticed a brown mole on the back of her hand, which made him gasp. "I saw a mark like that on an old lady's hand once. Are you . . . ? Did you . . . ? Did you give me the brass key at the October Fair?" he asked.

Betty touched his cheek. "No, my dear, that would have been my mother. The mole on my hand is something worn by all females in my family. It was my mother who gave you the key. I wanted her to give it to me when I was growing up, because I was her daughter and it had always been passed down in my family through the daughters, but she never would. She said it didn't belong to me. I didn't understand the prophecy then. At first I was upset with her because I thought the key was mine, until I realised I had more important work to do. One of which is to help the child who is entrusted with the key. That is why I must go to the castle with you, and look at the paintings." Betty's face grew very white as her voice grew more determined, and then she spoke some ancient words *"Ihruim bachran megroed hanc guith thyn"* and some mystical apparition flickered in her eyes. "It is my duty; I must try." She turned the pages of Mark's notebook and carefully noted all the symbols, characters and items he had drawn. A tiny frown grew between her brows and at length she handed the notebook back to Mark. "These drawings are good, but I feel some vital clue is missing. It's not your fault, Mark, you don't know what you're looking for, but I'm sure I can help if I go to the castle."

"Because you are descended from the Maiden of Ascolot." Joan waited for a reply.

Silence.

Somewhere nearby a dark cloud began to gather, and above Henley Forest a flash of vivid brutal lightning snaked across the sky, making Betty's house shake with a gigantic clap. The children dived beneath the kitchen table.

"What was that?" Timothy asked, peering around at Betty who seemed unperturbed by the noise.

"It is a warning. For me. I have had them before. Come, I will tell you a little more of my story, and tell you of the end of Arthur and Camelot. Then you will understand more about what is expected of you, and why you have to be brave." She motioned them back to the stools and proceeded to nod her head backwards and forwards, talking slowly and quietly until eventually she fell into a trance.

"You asked about the Maiden of Ascolot. Yes, I am one of her daughters; one of an endless line of daughters that has existed throughout the centuries. Each maiden has been waiting, forever waiting, until the child comes to fulfil the legend. I hope one of you will make the prophecy come true since you already have the key and have used it. I therefore must accept my time has come to help remedy the evil done through my ancestor, the first Maiden of Ascolot, because of her unrequited love for Lancelot. We must all try to bring good out of evil." She repeated it more softly until it sounded like a mantra said many times before. "We must all try to bring good out of evil. We must all try to bring good out of evil."

Her voice suddenly grew sharp and she barked out an order full of warning. "Listen! Can you hear them? They are here."

Wraith-like figures of blues, purples and greens danced through the air of the kitchen, seeming to surround the children with scenes of the past, of men in armour, charging horses, and bloody battle.

And after these came images of the present.

Chapter 19

Arthur's last battle

The brave knights of the Round Table were losing the battle. Surrounding them the enemy, like rapacious devouring ants, poured through their lines, destroying and killing everything in their path. The knights fought on, outnumbered and exhausted; they all knew they couldn't hold out much longer.

In the heat of battle up went a shout. "The king is down! To the king! The king!" shouted Sir Bedivere, and he struck his heavy gauntlets on his horse's reins ignoring the shooting agony from his blistered and bleeding hands. His heavy charger pawed the air and screamed in surprise before the faithful knight turned it around and galloped off to where Arthur lay.

The dead and the dying lay everywhere; the day had seen a glut of killing such as never had been seen before. Now Sir Bedivere hacked and picked his way through this bloody melee until he came to Arthur, his poor bleeding and broken king. All around were the remnants of the enemy, and if he looked closely he could still recognise a few friends gasping out the last of their strength, desperate to win the day and triumph over Mordred.

King Arthur raised his head, his tortured expression showing that every movement was a struggle, and his grimy red rimmed eyes peered bleakly from behind the visor. Sir Bedivere felt a quiver so deep in the pit of his stomach that he understood what Arthur himself knew, the knights of the Round Table were beaten.

Arthur began to struggle to sit upright. He looked grey with fatigue and crimson blood poured from a wound, spilling through his armour and soaking his shirt.

"Wait, Sire. I will help you." Sir Bedivere whipped a piece of torn cloth from a discarded pennant and made to staunch the flow, but Arthur waved him away. "No matter about me, my gallant knight, I am no longer for this world. Save yourselves!" Arthur fell back, "I fear the day is lost!"

"Never!" faithful Sir Bedivere shouted, and planted his feet squarely beside the king, determined to enter the fray again. "The enemy are retreating Sire. Even now they are scurrying back across the plains with their tails behind them. Take my arm, my lord," said Sir Bedivere, spitting out a mouthful of dust and blood and feeling a tooth wobble loose in his mouth. "See, here is your banner, rescued from the battle. Our kingly return and rightful claim to the throne of Camelot will rally the knights of the Round Table once again. The day is not lost."

"Loyal knight, how well you have deserved my love, and how I would wish I might believe you. But I have been plagued of late with evil dreams, and I fear my time here on earth has ended." Bitterness and regret laced his voice, recalling the joy of reigning over Camelot, remembering the love and beauty of Guinevere his queen, and the bravery and skill of his gallant knights. Most of all he remembered the chivalric deeds and heroism of those who aspired to join his elite group of knights in arms, to become a Knight of the Round Table. His lined face grew sad and grey. "This day on Sarum fields we face our mortal enemy."

"Mordred! A treasonous thief!" the knight spat. Then remembering he spoke of the king's son he added a hasty apology. "I am sorry my lord," then with energy, "We may face our mortal enemy, but twenty times two hundred brave men will gladly give their lives for you at Sarum this day, Sire. We will not die without letting his blood first, I think. And remember my king, you still have Excalibur on your side. Never have you lost a battle whilst wielding the sword of the ancients."

King Arthur acknowledged it with a nod. He removed his helm to wipe the blood from his face and eyes, then took Sir Bedivere's arm and forced himself to stand, wincing at the pain and pushing a wad of leather under his armour to stem the crimson tide that gushed forth with each movement. The knights of the Round Table fighting nearby saw him rise and gave a cheer.

"Hurrah for the king! The king! King Arthur of Camelot!"

"Camelot, and the king!"

Arthur waved his thanks before carefully cleaning the cold blood from Excalibur, then drawing it across his leather gauntlets in one determined movement. "Let's to battle, my knights!" With a thundering cry he called, "Mordred, where are you? Ill-begotten son. May Heaven forgive me for giving you life!"

A black knight swung close by the wounded king and swept a mocking bow but his eyes were hard as flint behind the visor. "Heaven may forgive you, dear father, but I do not!" Arthur whirled at the hated voice coming face to face with the son he once loved but now despised.

Mordred was dressed in black with tiny black pennants flying from a black helm. Pictures of vultures, with their vicious claws and beaks gorged in blood, adorned his shield. "Sire! I hope you come prepared to meet your death." Mordred boasted, and the last word was a deliberate taunt. "No quarter will be given."

"Nor will it be asked from such as you!" came the bitter response.

Arthur had been the greatest knight in Camelot, but now he had grown old. The best he could hope for in the coming fight was to use his experience gained over many years of campaigning. But Mordred had the skill and lust of youth on his side. The fight would not end until one of them lay dead on the ground.

Those knights nearby who saw the black knight threaten the king picked up the shout, eager to spur on their champion. "No quarter. A fight to the death!"

At that moment Mordred sprang, his sword raised, and drove with all his might towards Arthur. The fight began. Those standing nearby surged forwards to get a better view when all at once the knights began to feel the hatred between the two assailants and the blood lust rose. Soon everyone engaged the enemy again and once more the screaming of battle filled the air as swords stabbed into shields and maces sawed the air.

Suddenly a cruel stab on the left saw a knight in Mordred's group fall to his knees, blood gushing from beneath his coat of armoured links. Sir Bedivere smiled sadly, then stepping aside avoided the blow from a careering mace before darting under the lance of a charging knight and jabbing hard up into the belly of the oncoming horse. Instantly it came crashing down, screaming, legs thrashing in its death throes and unseating his rider in a rolling mass of broken metal and tumbling weapons. Sir Bedivere brought his razor edged sword downwards over the body of the knight and the enemy was despatched. Quickly he whirled away, lifting his sword and anxious for his next victim. There were so many to choose from, the field was full of hired mercenaries, assassins and murderers, common criminals who had been set free and then bribed with the promise of gold to fight against King Arthur.

And so the last battle of Camelot raged throughout the long day. At the centre Arthur and Mordred circled each other, one weary and sad, the other full of jealousy and venom. "Well, father, how pleasant to see you! What, back from the wars so soon? What a pity."

"I entrusted Camelot into your keeping, my son, whilst I went to fight across the seas. Is this how you repay my trust?" growled Arthur, whilst pain and grief tore at his heart.

"I have kept Camelot very well. We have been very happy whilst you have been off waging war, and I have placed my own friends around your precious Round Table." His lip curled in a sneer of contempt.

"Murderers, all of them."

"As you will," Mordred said, loping out of Arthur's reach. "I have been keeping your lovely queen company too, whilst you and your pretty knights have caroused the lands of Rome."

Arthur flinched and felt his blood rushing so quickly to his head he felt dizzy with it.

"Let us finish it. Here. Now," he raged, choking on the ugly images which spilled through his brain.

Mordred smirked. "Do you recognise this?" He stretched up his right arm until the thin winter sunlight fell upon his sword.

Arthur gasped in recognition. "Clarent! How dare you despoil the sword of chivalry with blood! It is the sword of all knightly virtues and should never be taken into battle."

"Spite to your knightly virtues, father. The sword has been good to me, and enjoys tasting blood, I think. I am sure it will enjoy tasting your blood most of all!" Mordred spun away as he uttered the last taunt and prepared to lunge forward, sword at the ready. He let out a chilling yell which ricocheted across the plains, and a few watching knights looked on aghast as father and son charged at each other, hatred twisting their features whilst splinters flew from their heavy shields as they locked together, and the open hills rang with the smashing of their swords. They fought on until the sun began to set, and their strengths began to fail. No quarter would be given.

One by one the wounded and bedraggled knights of Camelot overcame their opponents and silently, respectfully, gathered in a close circle around the last two fighters, willing their king to victory.

Moments later Arthur caught his son off guard and with one swift stroke sliced through the black chain mail, leaving him drenched with blood and reeling in the dirt. Mordred howled in despair, he was dying. Struggling to fend off his death for a few moments more he made a desperate lunge at his father who had for a moment lost his concentration. Mordred's sword went raking viciously into his father's flesh. The sharp steel of Clarent, the magnificent sword of the knighthood of Camelot, sliced through the kingly neck, severing the full rich artery, to leave a fountain of bright red blood gushing after. Arthur reeled drunkenly just as Sir Bedivere sprang forward, catching the king in his arms.

"I am done for," Arthur cried. "My life has ended as foretold by Fortune in my dreams. Quickly, Sir Bedivere, help me! I must make the offering to the Maidens of the Lake, before I die. I made this promise when first I held Excalibur"

"Yes, Sire. Anything."

"Take the sword, make your way to the hidden vales of Avalon and there throw it into the deepest part of the lake."

"But, Sire . . . ."

"Go! I command you, while there is still time! Make haste."

Sir Bedivere hesitated, unsure of what to do. To throw such a magnificent sword into a lake seemed madness to him. He wanted the king to take the sword with him, when he made his final journey into the land of gods. "I cannot Sire; the sword belongs to you."

"Do as I ask, to appease the Maidens, while I still live. Promise me . . ." Grey mists of death began to wash over Arthur's eyes.

Sir Bedivere bowed his head to the inevitable. He had always obeyed his king and he would continue to do so, even in death. He turned to those knights who stood around, quiet now except for sounds of weeping to see their beloved king brought so low. "Come, help me take the king back to Camelot. We must hurry."

Carefully they wrapped their king in thick furs, bandaged his bleeding neck and placed him in a boat bound for Camelot. By now the king was nearly dead. Sir Bedivere cradled Arthur's head on his lap and slowly began the journey into the Isle of Avalon where he would throw the sword into the lake and send the boat off on its own with its grisly and sorrowful load. Meanwhile the boat drifted down the long winding ancient rivers, heading west, passing Arthur's castle at Crocern, until finally, brushing into thick bracken which lined the edge, and set amongst emerald waters, Sir Bedivere entered the land of the hallowed lake.

Along the banks strange trees grew like twisted, willowy giants and a gnarled monster splashed angrily on the far shore and gazed balefully at the passing vessel. It had been waiting nearly forty years for the return of the sword. Sir Bedivere brought the boat to a small wooden jetty where he stepped out carefully, and taking up the sword he flung it with all his might into the centre of the lake. At once a great splash echoed from the far bank and the gnarled monster disappeared into the deep. Sir Bedivere took a sorrowful glance at the boat and shoved it hard back into the waters. This last deed would send the king on his final journey, into the land of dreams.

In the kitchen the children saw the picture fade. The softly lapping water around the lake fell away and the wooden boat with its sad load rocked slowly out of view.

Within moment other images filled the kitchen. Newer images, not yet of the things what had been but images of what would be tomorrow.

They were more terrifying than anything they had just seen.

The children saw themselves. They were beneath Henley Castle in Henley Forest. Eorldormann appeared to be rushing round in an agitated manner, hearing the crashing of falling stones growing louder and more persistent as the dragon began to swish its tail in growing frustration. Already a group of wild boar which had been painted along the walls in the outer chamber had burst free, broken out of the castle and were roaming the forest. Another group of monsters, more aggressive and cruel than the boar, the catoblepas, familiars of Morgan le Faye, mother of Mordred, were wrestling to get out of the walls. Eorldormann covered his ears to shut out their awful screams as the catoblepas writhed to freedom.

The faun bunched his shoulders up, haunted by memories. *I'm getting old,* and realised he was about to die. But he couldn't. Not yet. There was something he had to do first. Quickly he ran through his options. There weren't many. Then it came to him in a flash. It would endanger his life but he didn't consider that now, the most important thing was to buy more time for the children; they were his only hope.

Rushing around he gathered the circle of green thread into a huge mound, then carefully he started to drag it across the stone floor. It bumped and dragged after him like an enormous skein of green candy floss. And as he walked he found himself praying for the children to return quickly. If only they could get back before the evil creatures around him broke free from the walls, but time was slipping by, and soon it would be too late.

The image faded.

For long moments no one around Betty's table spoke, then Joan asked, "How will you be able to help us Betty? How can we get your wheelchair to the castle?"

Chapter 20

Mother's plan

Excited and afraid by the events in Betty's kitchen the children raced home. They understood they had seen magical apparitions, conjured by Betty, and were reluctant to look each other in the face in case their own fear was reflected there. Within minutes they arrived home and instantly knew they were in trouble; mother had that look on her face that always boded ill.

She was sitting at the large pine table surrounded by another fresh batch of buns and pies. The children sniffed appreciatively as the smell wafted through the room, but mother's expression was grim so they bit back their usual request of 'a taster please' and kept their eyes averted. Everyone knew that no cakes from the shops tasted as good as Mum's cooking, especially when eaten straight from the oven and usually they were offered a dainty jam tart, with hot flaking pastry, or a huge slab of fruit cake as soon as one of them appeared in the house. But not today. They were in trouble for doing things they shouldn't have been and mother looked forbidding.

"It's time you told me what's going on," she said, eyeing each one in turn and wondering which of her children would weaken first and tell her. Their eyes flickered at each other daring anyone to break the secret of their adventure. What they wanted to know was how much did mother know, and how much had she guessed? They knew instinctively that to tell her about the apparitions of King Arthur fighting Mordred would be a 'no-go-area', because she would either call the doctor, believing them ill, or worse still, think they were telling lies.

Timothy moved in front of Joan hoping he could stop her blurting out everything and frowned hard at Diane and Mark. *I will do the talking*, he seemed to be saying. But where should he start? How much should he tell?

For a while he had been wondering what to believe in, and what not, and he still felt unsure. He did realise however that it was a matter of honour within the family to tell the truth, even when it was difficult, and a lot of his worries recently had been about keeping Diane, Mark and Joan safe. Well, now he needed to face his fears and secrets and get them off his chest by telling mother. He took a deep breath, slung his arm around her shoulders to give her a gentle hug, and began. Or tried to begin, because as soon as he started talking his words became jumbled up.

"We've found an Arthurian castle, behind the rifle range, in Henley Forest. It's like walking into our own Arthurian legend," Timothy gabbled. "Mark's got a magical key which opens rock and I found a medieval lance. Mark can open the castle walls . . . And there's a silver knight at the beginning of another secret entrance." Timothy's eyes rolled around in dismay. He was explaining everything very badly but his mind felt numb and he couldn't get his mouth to say the words he wanted to. Finally he took a deep breath and blurted out, "We're trying to find King Arthur's sword to cut some magical thread. Though when we did find it, it wouldn't actually cut the thread. But we tried many times . . . . so we'll have to try again. With something else." He could see the others giving him strange looks and clamped his mouth shut, fully expecting mother to stop them investigating the prophecy of the sleeping giant.

But a strange thing happened. She studied his face carefully and then her expression changed from amazement, to disbelief, and finally to laughter.

"Timothy, that's fabulous! What wonderful imaginations you all have. This must be your best adventure yet! I remember when I used to create stories of make-believe as a child, and loved every minute of it. Well done all of you. This Arthurian adventure will be absolutely perfect for Christmas."

Diane blinked. "Don't you believe us?"

Mother hugged her children in turn. "Of course I do! If I didn't it wouldn't make the adventure very exciting for you, would it? Sometimes your imaginary world can feel very real. That's when the best adventures take place." She handed each of them a warm fruit pie and set about making a batch of fairy cakes.

Timothy was staggered. Obviously his chaotic explanation had somehow reassured her.

Mother pushed a wisp of hair back from her face with a floury hand and picked up a slab of butter for her baking. "I am so relieved! I thought that you were . . . Well, I don't know what I thought, but if you've made up such a great adventure for your holidays then I couldn't be more pleased for you."

"It's all true," Mark broke in noisily and blinking owlishly as if awoken from a trance, then began feeling cross with everyone and stomped off to get his bag. He would convince mother once and for all, he reasoned; he would show her the brass key. *His* key. Then she would have to believe them. A few clatterings of his feet on the stairs and a few moments later he dropped the key into her hands, giving her a satisfied smirk at the same time. *There,* he seemed to say.

However his plan failed because the brass key suddenly looked different. Ordinary.

Mother smiled absently. "Mmm, what a large key you have here."

Mark gaped. She had realised it was a key, which was odd because he knew the brass object had looked nothing like a key he had seen before.

"It needs a good clean," said mother. "I'll polish it if you like." Her words acted like a cold shower, and he felt as if their fabulous adventures hadn't happened at all. Mark took the key back, feeling upset. For an instant, when mother had held it, it looked like an ordinary key. *Which of course it wasn't. It was a magic key. Everyone knew that!* Then a ball of fear gripped his stomach as he remembered Eorldormann's words; the key's magic powers would be lost if someone else touched it, What if it wouldn't open up the castle wall and lead them to Arthur's world again? How would they get back and help Eorldormann? Mark dropped it back inside his bag and tucked in the top edges so that it was out of sight. If he tried not to think about it and didn't touch it for a few hours it might get its magic back.

Joan was telling mother about a huge beast, the paintings, and a faun called Eorldormann; her small voice full of excitement and her mouth full of pie. Mother burst out laughing and planted a kiss on each of their foreheads. Thank goodness she had thought to buy Joan more storybooks for her Christmas gifts. What a vivid imagination!

Timothy stood sentinel like and silent, a happier but fierce determination on his face, realising that now they had all tried telling mother the truth, even though she didn't believe them. Now they could return to the castle with a clear conscience, just like they promised Eorldormann. He knew there would be more dangers for them ahead and he would prepare for them accordingly. They also had one clue they could follow up, the Maiden of Ascolot. If she did live forever, and if Betty Vanstone was a descendant, then perhaps Betty could help them. They needed to follow it up quickly.

"Mum, would you mind if we went to the castle again?" Timothy asked. "We were thinking of taking Miss Vanstone with us. As a Christmas treat."

Mother looked up, startled, and stopped filling a cake case with a soft creamy mixture. "You want to take Betty to the rifle range?"

Timothy shrugged indifferently, knowing he had to play his next part casually to avoid frightening mother. "She happened to mention she wanted to go there, when we talked about the legend. So, we offered to take her."

Mother popped the cake tin into the oven before replying, and took some pastry from the fridge which had been cooling prior to being rolled out for an apple strudel. "Fancy Betty wanting to go back again, after having had her dreadful accident up there. She had been calling for help for nearly eight hours before she was found," she explained. "She could have died! Oh, well, I expect she dislikes being limited to that wheelchair most of the time." Then she said, "It'll be a very difficult journey for you with Betty in her wheelchair. Do you think you can manage it?"

"Yes, easily," the children nodded.

"You might ask your father for some help, you know. He could drive the Fergy tractor to the edge of the forest, and then you can use the paths through the trees."

"Good idea," said Diane.

"Perhaps he could even fit Betty's wheelchair onto the front forks, and attach it with a wooden frame or some such." Mother started warming to the idea.

Mark brightened and said. "I'll get on to it right away. I could design some box thing; there are lots of old wooden planks hanging about in the barns, and Father's tractor will drive up the hills easily enough, and get her wheelchair over the streams and things."

"You can ask Father tonight, when he comes in from milking the cows," said mother. Then she chuckled as a thought struck her. "You'll have to be quick if you want to get Betty there for the true Arthurian festival of Christmas."

"We've got nearly two weeks," said Diane munching happily and unaware of impending disaster.

"Not if you're planning to celebrate it according to Arthurian time. The Arthurian Christmas was celebrated according to a calendar we no longer use; the Julian calendar. Our present calendar, the Gregorian calendar, runs eleven days later. So, if you want to celebrate in true Arthurian style you will need to do so eleven days before Christmas. In fact, in a few days time, the 14th of December!"

"It can't be!" Diane choked on a cake crumb. "'Scuse me! Sorry Mum," she gulped. "But, we won't have time to get everything solved!"

"Don't worry, Diane. If you manage to take Betty to the forest for our own Christmas celebrations I expect she'll be just as pleased. She enjoys visiting historical sites because of her teaching career. What fun you will all have pretending to look for Arthur's sword and playing at knights and damsels in the old rifle range! And you can celebrate a real Arthurian Christmas!"

"In two days?" The children could only focus on the impossibility of the problems ahead. How could they hope to cut the magical thread and bind the evil dragon in two days? No wonder Eorldormann had said they needed to hurry. Everything was becoming more frightening than they had imagined. Timothy frantically tried to get his mind around what they ought to be doing next, but his brain seemed to be spinning in confusion with no coherent thoughts forming. The only idea he managed to grasp was that Betty felt she might be able to see a clue or something in the Arthurian paintings on the walls. Perhaps her relationship with the Maiden of Ascolot was deeper than she led them to believe. Could she come up with the answers they needed? Then another thought began to worry him. If she knew the solution to the legend why hadn't she managed to bind the dragon herself? Timothy tried to recall how the prophecy spoke of a child breaking the evil legend, and the finding of Arthur's sword.

Again and again his mind kept whirring, like a troublesome toothache. Why hadn't Betty solved the legend when she had been a child?

He groaned aloud, feeling his stomach knot with worry; nothing was as it seemed. All he knew for certain was they had to get Betty to the castle, with or without her wheelchair, and within two days.

"Thanks, Mum," he said, before quickly herding Mark, Diane and Joan upstairs to plan their next move.

Once inside his bedroom everyone immediately agreed *time* was the most important factor.

"Well, lack of it," commented Mark wryly. "Mum's scheme to put Betty's wheelchair on Father's tractor is a good one, but I'm not sure about hoisting the box up onto the forks. I'm worried it might topple forwards and fall off. Perhaps there is something I can design for the back of the tractor instead.

"You're the engineer and designer around here, so go to it, Mark," agreed Timothy. "Have a word with . . . ."

A loud sound exploded in the sky over their heads. The children rushed to the window in time to see a dark cloud billowing over Henley Forest, smothering all the daylight.

Joan gulped. "What's that?"

"Sounds like a bomb," said Diane

Timothy pulled them back from the window. "Don't look," and he swished the heavy curtains across before flicking on the light to disperse the gloom.

"We must plan something, and Fast!"

Mother called up the stairs. "There's a huge storm brewing. I hope you haven't planned to go to Henley Forest today. I think your knightly adventures will have to wait until after the storm has passed."

"Okay. Thanks Mum," Timothy said coolly, before giving a slow whistle and turning to the others. But his face looked grim. "I think you know what made that noise."

"The giant?" guessed Diane.

"Or the dragon," breathed Joan her eyes popping open.

"Eorldormann says it will awaken at Christmas," said Mark. "That means *they're both* nearly awake!" and he slumped down upon the bed covers while Timothy took over, his voice calm, clear, and decisive, but his brain working furiously.

"Yes, they will be awake at Christmas. Remember what the prophecy said; both will awaken at the same time and then they will fight, and our world will be destroyed. But not until Christmas. We have two days left to stop it. We have to ignore the noises and concentrate on what we can do to prevent it happening." Timothy jabbed the large sheets of paper stuck around his walls. "Our first problem is: How to cut the magical thread since the sword didn't do it. We must try something else. To do that we have to look for the clue which Eorldormann spoke of. Does everyone agree with me that we enlist the help of Betty Vanstone?" They nodded. "Then our first task is to get Betty into the castle to look at those paintings. Mark, since you like carpentry and design at school you can be in charge of the 'How', and the making of whatever you think will work. Don't forget to ask father if he will help as it may save a lot of time. Also, ask Dad if he has any useful ideas about getting the wheelchair through the narrow forest tracks, where the tractor can't go. You had better do it now, before it gets dark. But, whatever you decide on, it must be sorted and built by tonight. We leave first thing in the morning."

Mark dashed out to the milking parlour to speak to father.

"What about me and Joanie?" asked Diane. "We want to help if we can. I can pack a picnic for tomorrow, but what can we do tonight?"

"Hmm. I've been thinking about that. Earlier you mentioned Mum's special unbreakable thread, and I didn't see how it might help, but now I have an idea. Have you noticed that when Mark carried the brass key up to the castle it gets more difficult?"

"Yes. When we came back earlier today he fell down," said Joan. "I think it hurt his arm."

"It did," agreed Diane. "I rubbed some witch hazel into it to stop the bruising."

"He looked very white," said Joan." Like the key made him feel sick or something."

"I want you to find a way of helping him to carry it, Diane. You're good at making things at school in needlework class. Could you make Mark a special rucksack, using Mum's thread, so it doesn't break? Perhaps the bag might be something he could slip over his head and shoulders."

"I'm sure I could. I could sew the bottom of it on to a belt, so he could tie around his waist to help take the weight."

"That's a great idea. It sounds just like the sort of thing you see mountaineers wear. I wonder also if perhaps you could paint a red cross on it, pretend it was a medical bag." Timothy's voice was casual but a bright spark glinted in his eyes, which it always did when he was thinking hard.

Joan touched the cross at her neck. "And as well as the red painted cross I could tie one of those wooden crosses Mark made earlier onto the bag; to keep away evil."

The mood in the room became sombre.

"I'll make all the stitches *cross* stitch," said Diane seriously, and rushed out to begin.

Timothy called Joan back and gave her some special instructions. It was a long shot, he knew, but they were in such a desperate situation with only two days left that they had to try anything, and they needed to prepare as much as they could before they went to bed.

Chapter 21

The maiden's return

It was a cruel winter's evening; a heavy mantle of black smog hung above Henley Forest and smothered the landscape as it moved towards Crewkerne. Eventually it filled the streets and the householders went indoors with a worried frown. No one had seen anything like this before, and none dared venture out, not even the dogs.

Mark spoke in hushed tones, telling father about their plans, and was relieved when he suggested a wooden box like one of the calf crates, with runners for the chair wheels. But it would have to be specially built. When Mark said he wanted to build the crate straight away so they could take Betty up first thing in the morning their father was rather confused.

"There's no need to hurry, son; you've got the rest of the holidays to do it." Then seeing his son's anxious face he added, "Well, if you want to do it before Christmas, we'll get on to it tomorrow morning, after breakfast."

"Tomorrow! But . . . we have to take her up to the castle tomorrow morning, at the latest!"

It was unusual for any of the children to contradict their parents, and father looked at Mark rather strangely now. In the last few days Mark's face had begun to look translucent, almost as if he were going down with 'flu. Perhaps Mark ought to stay in bed for a few days, he reasoned; he looked quite drawn and tired.

Father unlatched the door, turning to go indoors for a cup of tea. "I don't like the look of that sky," he muttered. "Bodes no good for anyone, I'll bet.

"Please, Dad," said Mark, running to catch up and feeling weak. "I need to make it tonight. I've already worked on some plans. I could make it fairly quickly . . . . if you would let me have planks and things. And you needn't worry about me being up late, I'll work fast, and make sure the crate is ready by my usual bedtime."

Father strode towards the house deeply troubled. Mark's behaviour had been rather odd lately, and there were several things puzzling him about his other children's recent activities, especially the reference to a 'castle'. Perhaps he needed a rest himself, he thought. Later, after a cup of tea and a talk to mother about Mark's unusual behaviour, he was left chuckling and much happier, and dozed off in the chair, dreaming of Arthurian castles.

An hour later loud banging and drilling noises came from the barn and finally woke father up. "Plucky kid," he chortled, wondering if the crate had already been made, and putting on his Wellington boots strode out to help.

"Thought you might need a bit of a hand, old thing," he said by way of greeting. Mark smiled in relief, wiping away a lock of damp hair with a hand covered in saw dust, and together in a companionable silence they made the crate and fitted it on to the back of the little grey Ferguson tractor. Strong planks of wood formed the base and sides whilst the front and back could be opened for easy access and allow for Betty to 'drive through' the crate.

Mark even managed to find some old seat belts in a disused van at the back of one of their red brick barns, and with a few stout bolts they attached these to the sides of the crate. Then they made up several runners to act as a ramp so they could push Betty and her wheelchair into the crate, and these they laid on the crate floor. Father looked up thoughtfully. "There's nasty weather forecast for tomorrow," he said. "We'll fit a tarpaulin for the top, so if it rains Betty will keep dry." When all was finished the two of them looked at the strange wooden box now soundly attached to the back of the grey tractor as a crack of thunder ripped overhead. Mark felt the first twinges of light-headedness and grabbed the door for support.

"You poor thing; you look all in," said father, and swinging him up in his arms took him straight to bed.

Neither of them noticed the sturdy bag on Mark's bedroom floor made of hessian sacking and into which Diane had carefully placed Mark's special key. On the front of it was painted a large red cross and there was a wooden cross tucked into the top. Diane made up a shoulder bag for herself, and into this she slipped her first aid bag, mother's very sharp scissors, and everyone's lunch. She yawned as she made her way to bed; she was all ready for their trip to the castle on the following morning.

Joan was tucked up in bed and the floor of her bedroom was littered with every pot, tube, pen, paint and colorant she possessed. But in the middle of the floor was a new pot of mixture and a small paper bag; and on her sleeping face a pleased smile, as well as a few green finger marks. She too was ready for their trip in the morning.

Only one child paced restlessly around his room, scanning all his notes, writing up a few ideas and then screwing them up into a ball to hurl them into the waste paper basket. Timothy was struggling with plans of what might happen on the following day. Would they be able to get Betty up to the castle on the tractor? He knew Mark and father had worked all through the evening to make the crate, but would the wheelchair fit inside? And if they did get to the castle, how could Betty be wheeled inside as the ground was made of broken rock? The more Timothy thought over things the more he realised he was getting out of his depth, he had to tell father the truth about everything. As he thought about how he would tell father he remembered the prophecy stipulated only a child could save the world; they couldn't get anyone else to do it, they had to do it on their own. *But, Betty is an adult*, he thought, and wondered if she could help them after all. The whole problem was like a conundrum, with too many problems to solve. How could they take Betty to the castle? And what would Eorldormann say when he saw her?

With an exhausted yawn Timothy got into bed. His last thought before he fell asleep was, why didn't the sword cut the thread?

The lightness of a winter's dawn did not appear the following morning. The sky still had that thunderous black colour verging on a raging storm, and a bitter coldness seeped into everyone's bones, sapping their energy. Throughout the town of Crewkerne residents found numerous excuses to stay in bed rather than to get up and begin their chores. Milk was delivered late; bakers were slow in baking the day's bread, and lorry drivers grumbled at each other, thumping their arms in an effort to bring some warmth into them. But on the farm the children were alert and dressed. Today they were taking Betty to the castle and there was only two days left to solve the riddle; soon it would be Christmas according to Arthurian times. With every grumble of thunder they recognised the sound of the dragon getting stronger and in amongst the thunderous rumbles they heard the softer, warmer rumblings of the giant. Both monsters were awakening together.

"What was that?" asked Diane as a car door slammed shut outside and she hurried into the kitchen for a warming bowl of porridge.

"Betty's here," replied mother, and slapped another bowl of porridge onto the table as the doorbell rang. "She'll be cold and hungry I expect. Let her in please, Timothy. Mark, move that chair out of the way so Betty can get her wheelchair there." Within moments Betty had wheeled herself into the large kitchen and everyone was tucking into breakfast. The children avoided looking at each other, not certain whether to laugh or cry at the drama they were in. Father came into the kitchen from the milking parlour. "The milking is all finished," he said, looking steadily at Mark and noting the vivid red flushes across his son's cheek. "Are you still determined to go to the forest this morning?"

All eyes looked to Betty who nodded quickly.

"Well, make sure you all wrap up warm," said Father, with a finality in his voice that boded no objections. He sat down and proceeded to eat his breakfast. When he had finished he laid down his spoon and pushed aside his empty bowl. Then he pushed back on the arms of his Victorian carver chair and moved it backwards from the table as if implying that the niceties of the meal time were over and now it was down to business. The children held their breath, knowing that when he spoke their worst fears would be realised. They didn't have long to wait.

"I had a talk with your mother last night," he began. A silence fell over the breakfast eaters, spoons were poised, mouths stopped eating. Everyone waited, wondering what he would say.

"At first I couldn't make head nor tail of all this nonsense about King Arthur and his castle and things, until later, when Betty here telephoned me. It seems as if you have all got yourselves involved in some rather peculiar goings on. I can't say I approve of my children rushing into strange places and getting involved in legends and prophecies and such like, but Betty here assures me none of this was of your making, but you are all trying to help solve a problem. Is that right?" The children nodded quickly, hearts in their mouths, wondering what would come next, until he added, "I want you to know that if you need any help, my help more specifically, just make sure you ask."

Timothy felt tears bite at the back of his eyes and he blinked rapidly. Elsewhere raised eyebrows met across the table with some pleased grinning and nudges of elbows.

"Thanks, Dad," Timothy muttered, and hastily thrust the last bit of bread and butter into his mouth to stop him blurting out anything more.

"Right, let's get the tractor loaded," said father, and pushing his chair all the way back hurried outside, talking rapidly as the children followed in his footsteps. "We've got Betty's chair to fit into the crate first. Have you got a walking stick, Betty?" he asked, watching as she wheeled herself out of the kitchen, around the side of the house and then manoeuvred it behind the tractor.

"Of course."

"You can walk?" Timothy asked, hardly believing his luck.

"We'll see," she replied lightly. Then waving her walking stick at him he put it safely into a bracket on the side of the tractor. Between them the children opened doors, put down ramps, and within minutes helped Betty up the ramp, and into the crate so that it looked like a mobile hen house. Father helped Mark tighten all the straps and check the securing bolts and gave a thumbs up sign; Betty would be completely safe inside her special crate. Joan dashed into the house and came out carrying one of the wooden crosses Mark had made.

"For you. For good luck," she said, pushing it into Betty's hands through the bars of the crate.

"What a kind thought. Thank you. As it happens I have brought a charm of my own, not a cross, but an amulet, passed down from my mother. It wards off evil," she said, making a face, her eyes laughing. She held up a rose shaped amulet which nearly filled her hand. It was obviously very precious and made of heavy beaten gold with ivy leaves engraved around the edges. But the object which drew Joan's gaze was the large single stone of perfect turquoise blue, fitted at the amulet's centre like a perfect bud.

"It's beautiful," gasped Joan. "But I think I've seen it before . . . it . . . looks familiar, though I don't know how . . ." At that moment she gave Betty a quick look, remembering just where she has seen it before, or one like it. It had been in one of the paintings on the castle walls, hanging from the neck of an Arthurian lady. Betty quickly slipped the amulet back into her pocket.

"I hope you'll be all right in there," called father, checking the bolts and straps one last time. He took off his cap and scratched his head in a puzzled fashion; it was clear he was confused why his children were so intent on this adventure, and why Miss Vanstone had spoken to him about an old legend concerning the old rifle range. And why they all insisted they call it a castle. But shrugging his shoulders he was happy to humour them and his wife in their pre Christmas adventure.

Timothy checked Diane had her scissors, and that Joan had her pot of special mixture. Meanwhile Mark was struggling to put his arms into his new haversack. It was clear the brass key was becoming more troublesome. Timothy called. "Are you sure you want to carry that key? I can help you."

Mark glared, his face tired and lined, and not fresh faced as it should have been after a good night's sleep. He shook his head angrily, as if speaking was too much effort.

Timothy felt worried. *I hope Mark isn't going to be ill.* "I could carry it to the forest for you. I won't use it or anything."

Mark snarled at him. "I can manage," and stomped off. Father gave him a searching look, then shrugged. Children's arguments, he seemed to say. "It's time we began."

"Okay Dad," said Timothy. "The tractor can go first, and we'll walk behind." He slung his new lance over his shoulder, grabbing a useful bag of objects he had collected. He too had been busy last night, stripping a hazel stick to fit the medieval spearhead and he could tell it was weighted perfectly by the way it balanced as he walked. Joan tucked her precious few objects into her pocket and Diane carried their first aid supplies and food.

The black cloud that had hung over the land since the previous evening seemed to drag heavy pillars of dense matter over the little group as it trudged towards the forest. Diane pointed at it in awe, feeling unnerved. Then she froze as a series of screeching sounds ricocheted down the hill towards them and forks of lightning ripped into the tree line of the sleeping giant.

Diane gasped as she looked up and what she saw sent a wave of terror thumping through her chest. "It's altered! The giant has changed shape! It's not lying down any longer . . . . It's . . . . it's . . . ."

"It's getting up," screamed Joan.

Betty called out from her chair inside the crate. "Don't worry girls, we still have two days until Christmas." They fell silent.

Father heard nothing, his ears full of the chugging noises from the tractor as it kicked puffs of smoke from its exhaust, and he whistled tunelessly, happy to be taking his children on an adventure.

Timothy felt alarmed. If the tree shaped giant had moved, was the dragon moving?

Chapter 22

No way in

"Keep together," warned Timothy, entering the forest and gripping his lance firmly. "Something awful is happening."

"What?" asked Diane, running to his side.

"I feel we're being watched."

"So do I," agreed Joan.

"Then we must show whatever it is that we're not afraid," said Mark, adding excitedly and pointing ahead. "There's the path to the castle wall! At least I think it is . . ." His voice trailed off. "I'm not sure . . . and this key is really heavy today; I could do with a rest," and slung his offending bag with its precious cargo to the ground. The girls dropped their bags beside him and Father stopped the tractor, pushing in the throttle until it settled into a soft idling purr.

At that moment a thundering crack sounded nearby, as if a ton of fireworks had exploded all at once. Behind the tractor a heavy bough came crashing down, landing at the back of the group, its vast branches thumping across the path they had been standing on a few moments before. Betty screamed, remembering her accident years before. But it narrowly missed the crate on the forks at the back of the tractor, and only a few twigs fell inside. The hydraulic lever on the tractor bar was jolted downwards by the force of the thump and the thick iron bar at the back of the tractor dropped like a stone sending the crate smashing to the floor. The door of the crate burst open showing Betty frightened, wide eyed and staring owlishly. Timothy raced across, pushing the heavy branches aside. "Are you all right?"

Father leapt down, hurrying to check for damage. "Is everyone okay?" he barked.

Diane and Joan clambered off the ground, pulling twigs and leaves from their hair. "All okay, Dad. We're fine."

"The branch must have cracked with all the frost we've been having. Hey! Where's Mark? Is he all right?" Father's voice sounded sharp. Mark was nowhere to be seen.

"Mark!" called everyone, pushing amongst the fallen branches and growing more and more alarmed.

"I'm coming, don't panic." Mark appeared further along the path rubbing his head. "I fell into a pile of bracken."

"The branch was meant for me," explained Betty grimly, deathly white beneath the tarpaulin. "I should have realised I would be noticed."

She pushed aside the seat belt, grasped the wheels of her chair and propelled herself out of the crate until she reached the children who were knotted in a group, looking extremely worried. "This journey might be more dangerous than I thought, I shouldn't have got you into this. I will go on alone."

"You can't," objected Timothy, steadying her chair which had got tangled amongst the fallen branch. "You'll need someone to push you along this path."

"I'll manage," said Betty. "It's not far from here. I remember how I found a short cut to the castle many years ago. That was when I had my accident." She grabbed her walking stick from the hook near the back of the chair, and with painful slowness prised herself out of the chair. One step, then another, and moving along the path slowly pushed into a thick clump of trees, with Timothy, Mark and the girls following.

Joan blurted, "It was you who came to the castle all those years ago! You are the one Eorldormann spoke of when he said someone tried to enter the castle."

Betty paused, her face splitting into a beaming smile as she wrestled with the pain of walking. "Eorldormann!" she exclaimed. "My friend! Such memories! I shall be pleased to see him. Perhaps, no, I'm sure it won't work," she finished cryptically.

Father had been repairing the broken hydraulic lever on the tractor, and as soon as he finished he hurried to catch the others up, just overhearing Betty's last words. "What won't work?" he asked.

"An idea I have." replied Betty lightly, striking forwards again with her walking stick, and dragging herself slowly towards it.

Mark was looking increasingly nervous. "Where's the entrance?"

"It must be here," countered Timothy. "I'm sure I recognised some trees just now."

"I can't see it," snapped Mark. "The entrance has disappeared."

Father pushed into the trees and wrapped an arm around both of his sons, looking as if he was beginning to enjoy himself and the children's new adventure. "Oh ho, can't you get into the castle?" he teased. "Have the fauns locked you out?" and he banged his hands together, rocking with laughter.

Mark twisted himself away, angry that no one was taking him seriously, and as he did so his hand struck something. A stone wall. Ripping aside the ivy Mark felt a deep sense of relief. "Here it is! I've found it at last! Come on, quickly, we have to get in and face the dragon." He pulled the brass key from his bag and dragged it against the rock face.

Father nearly fell back choking with shock. "Dragon!" His head shot up and he begun spluttering, all trace of humour gone. "What are you talking about? Betty what nonsense is this?" He glared at her, his face like a ghost. "No one said anything to me about dragons." For some reason his fear shocked his children more than anything they had come across and he stomped back through the trees to the tractor, his back rigid with disapproval, grumbling over his shoulder. "I thought this was a bit of Christmas fun. An adventure. It's time to stop before it gets out of hand. Come on, I'm taking you home. Right now."

Betty started hobbling after him, moving her sticks as quickly as she could without falling. "Wait! Let me explain." But father wouldn't listen he leaped into the tractor seat, pressing the starter and instantly the tractor burst into life.

Timothy's mind raced; they couldn't go back home. It was up to them to solve the prophecy, even though they didn't know how to do it.

Diane and Joan hurried to help Mark, scrabbling with the key between them, pushing it to the rock wall, and praying the castle would open.

Timothy heard something. He cocked his head, instantly alert, his heart pounding and afraid. "Dad! Listen! I can hear odd noises coming from behind the rock."

But father's ears were filled with the chug chugging of the tractor as he swung the tractor into reverse.

A moment later a large section of rock came toppling right in front of them. "Watch out!" yelled Timothy.

"Run," screamed Mark.

"Help!" Diane shrieked leaping into a covering of ivy.

Falling rock tumbled into a huge heap of billowing dust, stone and vegetation, completely blocking the path where they had stood moments before. The wall had disappeared. And so had father.

"Dad!" shouted Timothy, panic filling his voice. "Dad? Where are you?" He grabbed the two girls, clutching them close to him for safety and noticed Mark retching nearby. "Dad's missing," he croaked, wondering what he was supposed to do now. But as the dust settled he could hear some movement coming from nearby. Father had been cut off from the others by a huge pile of rock.

"I'm all right." Father's voice sounded thin. Alarm bells immediately began going off in Timothy's head. He had to get to his father and see if he was injured.

"I'm coming over the rocks," and began looking for firm foot holes across the rocks.

"No, son. Stay where you are. I'm fine, just covered in dust. I think I am beginning to understand a little of what you've been saying. I'm sorry I didn't believe you." They could hear him coughing and wheezing, then using his inhaler. He called again. "There's too much rock here for me to get through to you, but I'll be back later to clear all this, when I've fitted the large shovel on the tractor." His voice changed, defiant, concerned and authoritative. "Betty! I don't know everything that is going on here, but take care of them. I'll get help."

The children could hear him moving on the other side of the rocks, then the chugging of the tractor as he tried to untangle it from the branch. The sounds grew more faint. Father had gone.

Joan sniffed. "I'm scared."

"He'll be all right," said Diane, giving Joan a comforting squeeze. "I'm sure of it. I sometimes feel someone is watching over us, a bit like a guardian angel. We could have been killed just then by the branch, or by the fall of rocks, but we haven't even got a scratch! It's only Dad who has been cut off. I think it means we're allowed inside the castle, but Dad isn't."

"Then why doesn't my key fit?" grumbled Mark, shaking the dust from his hair.

"I can answer that," said Betty. "You've brought an adult with you; me, and the key will only work for a child. My presence has upset the balance of magic." She dug inside her pocket and brought out a soft chamois bag. "We need some Arthurian help to make the key work again."

Deftly she unwrapped her sacred golden amulet and lifted it high in the air where it looked like a shining turquoise star. It grew brighter and brighter; the centre of the amulet pulsing with a life force and radiating powerful turquoise rays that spilled over Betty and moved through the trees.

No one spoke. The children were dumbstruck. What powerful magic was this? They had never imagined anything like this could happen. Betty lowered her arm, popped the amulet out of sight and the forest returned to silence and the sharp scent of winter pine.

But it only lasted a moment. An icy blast came whipping through the trees followed by a host of shrieking, snarling wild boar, bursting through the undergrowth, rampaging amongst the trees and heading straight for the children. The beasts came from all sides. They were huge, three times larger than the pigs on the farm and covered in long cruel spines so they looked like angry porcupines. Timothy judged there were twenty snuffling, frothing animals charging closer and closer. The children were frozen in sheer terror and just when it seemed as if the boar would leap Betty managed to yell "Move!" which made them jump out of their terrified trance and race to safety. Diane held her cross in front of her as she ran, Joan backed up hard against the rock face and tried to burrow in amongst the ivy, whilst Timothy brandished his newly made lance at the hideous creatures. He looked like a titan, ready to hurl his weapon, as if he were one of the knights he had read so much about. His nerve never wavered. He would kill one of the beasts at least, he thought.

Betty rushed to the knot of terrified children, quickly taking charge of their desperate situation. "Mark! The key. Use it! Now! Concentrate on opening the door. Quickly!" Betty's voice snapped Mark into action. Snatching up the key he rammed it against the rock face and this time, as if by magic, the secret entrance slid open and immediately the three children raced towards it, with Betty limping behind.

The boar-like creatures were closing fast, less than ten paces away and bunching their powerful legs ready to spring.

"Timothy!" Joan yelled, as her brother stood, defiant, lance poised, but not noticing a beast attacking from the side. He whirled just in time and raced after the others through the castle entrance.

Mark thrust the key against the inner edge of the doorway and stood back as the rock face closed upon the charging boar. At least they were safe. Phew!

Blessed silence. Then they heard one, two, three, four, thump, thump, thumping noises pounding against the outside of the rock as the hideous creatures hurled themselves uselessly against the entrance.

Inside the castle the children stood panting in relief, clutching their sides and trying to calm down before they began to look around. But things had altered. The thin light they had noticed before had gone, now they found themselves in a thick blanket of nothingness. There was also a dank smell of rotting vegetation that filled their nostrils, reminding them of something primeval. Betty made a movement and for the second time took out her turquoise amulet and held it high. She knew she shouldn't burn up the amulet's power too quickly; she didn't know what to expect.

"Oh," breathed Mark, as the magnificent stone began to glow, at first gently, and then more strongly, searching out the farthest, darkest corners of the castle chamber and filling it with a beautiful blue light.

Diane let out a pent up breath. "We're safe," she said, and felt that she had never run so fast before in her life.

Joan turned a white face to Betty. "My legs feel all funny," then "I feel sick," before bursting into tears.

Timothy felt as if his insides were being rung through a mangle. "What were those dreadful things?" he asked, knowing Betty had somehow seen them before, but not knowing why he was so sure.

"Those beasts are wild boar from Arthur's forests. In previous centuries they were hunted and killed by Arthur's knights. They must have been called back to life by the dragon," explained Betty, trying to keep her voice matter-of-fact so as not to scare the children.

It nearly worked until Diane said, pointing out, "I remember seeing them in the paintings over there," and turning behind her suddenly let out a loud scream. Everyone followed her pointing finger. At the far end of the chamber, leading down to the tunnels, the whole side of the wall had been shredded as though a giant scraper had ripped across it. None of the wall paintings were intact and some had completely disappeared. "The boar! They've gone from the wall! The wall has crumbled! Did they come to life?"

No one wanted to answer though it was clear they all had the next dreadful thought in their heads; if the wild boar could come to life what might happen to the other painted creatures upon the walls of the guardian's chamber? Could they come alive too? What about the dragon?

Mark let out an agonised cry. "Dad! He's left outside, with those creatures! We must help him." He whirled back to the rock entrance.

Betty grabbed his arm. "It's too late; you can't help him now. Besides, your father is quite safe. The wild boar knows he can't stop the prophecy. No, they are not after him, but us. One of us here pose the threat to their master and that is the one they want."

Timothy nodded, emotionally drained. He felt heady, yet calm and strangely powerful, as if he had imbibed some of the courage from those medieval knights who had once fought in the forests above. "Mark, put your key away. We must trust what Betty says; father is safe. It cannot help us to think otherwise. We must focus on why we are here and do what we have to do."

Betty gave Timothy a reassuring squeeze on his shoulder. "If I see any sign or clue in the paintings I will call you."

"You must keep away from the tunnels where the . . ." Timothy bit his lip. He would try to forget the wild boar that had chased them earlier, and which had been merely paintings when they last saw them, a few hours previously. "Diane, can you help Betty get around to see all the paintings?"

She nodded.

"And," Timothy called, a queer break in his voice, "Could you leave Mum's scissors with Joanie?" To Joan he said, "Can you do what we talked about last night? It's a lot to ask, but it may help us . . ."

Joan gulped, managing a little nod even though she didn't know quite how to do *it*. She took the scissors from Diane, gripped her own tiny bag with its precious pot and moved to one side of the great entrance chamber. She needed to find a secretive place where she couldn't be seen.

Timothy felt very grim indeed. Would this crazy scheme give them some breathing space? Turning to Mark his expression changed; his brother had collapsed. Was he sick? Quickly Timothy draped his coat over Mark, doing up the buttons even though his fingers felt paralysed with fear. "Keep warm, Mark. Stay here and don't try to move. There's nothing to do at present." But as he said the words Timothy knew he was lying. There was everything. They needed to have another try at cutting the thread with the sword. And then there was Betty. Even though she said she could help she presented a problem of her own since she could hardly move without her wheelchair, and this had been left outside. If Mark was ill then Timothy knew he and the girls would have to manage on their own. Then Timothy had an idea. Was Mark's illness something to do with the strange key he had found? He wished he felt more grown up and able to cope. But before he could make any plans on what to do next he suddenly heard three loud bangs above his head. His eyes flew open, there was no more time for delay; their time was running out.

Thump! Grumble! Groan! They all heard it.

"The giant!" shouted Diane, turning desperate eyes to Timothy.

"It's waking up; we know that," Betty said flatly. "Come on, Diane, let's see the rest of the paintings." Hobbling as best she could, stick tapping unevenly over the floor, they moved to the back of the chamber, all the while her eyes devouring the fabulous Arthurian paintings. So many familiar faces: Arthur, Guinevere, Gawain, Sir Kay, Sir Agravain, Sir Bors; every one an old friend, making her smile with pleasure, until she saw the one that made her blood shrivel in her veins. She recognised the knight instantly, the blood red coat of arms with three hornets diving in formation, as if they were attacking. *Mordred!* Here was the bastard son and stepson of Arthur's unknowing relationship with Morgan le Fay, his sister, and the most treacherous knight in Camelot. He was responsible for the destruction of Camelot. Betty cringed; even now his face seemed full of evil, twisted in a vicious leer, contemptuous and arrogant. And beside him, his mother, Morgan le Fay, black, forbidding, sinister, and filled with the blood lust of life that eventually drove her insane.

Betty tore her gaze away; she had to move on, they were running out of time.

Swiftly she scanned the rest of the paintings, admitting to herself she was looking for one person in particular. Finally she found him. *Lancelot.* Her face glowed with light, and something else. "I've found you again," she said softly, and smiled as she saw in his outstretched hand a glimmer of gold and turquoise; a rose shaped amulet. "I've brought it back."

"That's your amulet, Miss Vanstone," Timothy caught her and Diane up, breaking into her thoughts, and bringing her back to the present. "A good job you brought it."

"Yes." Her eyes flew away from Timothy's searching look, upwards, embarrassed, saddened and cramming her mind with emotions that were centuries old. She pushed them away; no time for that now.

A few more steps took her beneath the painting of Sir Galahad. Youthful, almost the age of Timothy, she thought. And Lancelot's son. This was where she hoped to find the answer to the prophecy, as once Lancelot's son had found the Holy Grail, but there was nothing. The paintings told the tale of Arthur's last battles, his victory over the Emperor and his meeting with Mordred. Each painting became a scene, and moving along the wall they became one continuous story, like a comic book. Reaching the end she turned back upon herself and suddenly she was staring up at the great central wall. "Clarent!" Her anguished cry made her catch her breath; she could almost feel the ancient sword beneath her fingers.

Timothy stopped, shocked and excited. He had an inkling that something wasn't right, but couldn't put his finger on it. He rushed over. "What did you call that sword just now? Clarent? We thought it was Excalibur."

"That sword is Clarent, and it is Arthur's ceremonial sword," she agreed. "It is such a magnificent weapon you might think it is Excalibur, but this is a special sword, of peace and honour. Arthur never used it in anger, only for knighting brave men after a battle, and for ceremonies He loved it. After Excalibur it was his favourite sword." Then her voice grew deep and angry. "When he left Camelot to fight the emperor he gave this sword to Guinevere for safe keeping, but she gave it to Mordred. And he used it in his final battle against Arthur. This is the sword that killed Arthur." A wave of sadness caught at her voice.

Diane touched her gently. "Come Miss Vanstone, there are more paintings to look at through this tunnel." Adding, "I hope we can meet up with Eorldormann," before her voice faltered, feeling the enormity of what they were trying to achieve, two boys, two girls, and one woman in a wheelchair.

They moved across the chamber to the picture of Sir Galahad. "This entrance leads to the Guardian's Chamber," Timothy explained, as Mark touch his hand upon the hand of the young, flaxen haired knight, then Whoosh, and the door swung open. "We found it by accident."

The children bunched up, anxious now to get through the tunnel and into the next chamber, but as their eyes got used to the light they stopped abruptly, their mouths gaping open. They scarcely recognised what they saw.

Chapter 23

Eorldormann dies

The faun clung desperately to the thought that the children were returning tomorrow. He had to work quickly. He dragged the mass of green fibrous thread across the Guardian's Chamber until it formed a gigantic heap at the feet of the dragon. The strange bundle crackled with magic beneath the beast's wary gaze. Eorldormann glanced up as he had done for the last fourteen hundred years, and froze in fear. The dragon seemed to be smiling malevolently at him beneath its hooded eyelids. Was it a trick of light? Eorldormann shook his head, No! Christmas was still two days away. Yet the dragon seemed to be staring at him, noticing everything.

As the faun watched the wall became distorted, the monstrous dragon was pushing forwards as if at any moment the creature would walk free. Everything about the creature glowed with vibrancy, its back glistened like liquid oil, rippling over dark green scales that hung with razor sharpness, while a glutinous drop of venom oozed from the corners of its gaping mouth. Plop. Plop. Plop. Fat gelatinous globules rolled like opaque marbles down the side of the gaping lips before slithering along the edge of its tongue to fall in a thick congealing mess on the chamber floor. Eorldormann caught his breath, panic rattling his throat as he saw a translucent quality to the implacable eye fixed upon him. He couldn't deny it any longer, the dragon was coming back to life.

"It's not Christmas yet. There is still time left," the frail faun shouted.

"Not for you," the dragon gloated, its harsh rasping noise vibrating upon every wall.

Eorldormann clamped his hands over his ears but the sound grew louder and louder.

"I am nearly free. Nearly free," it continued.

The scaly lips started slathering, followed by a flake of paint which peeled off the rock and slid over the creature's cheeks, moving slowly downwards as the dragon's mouth twitched and grimaced in its desire to be free. Eorldormann knew the end of the world was coming.

Eorldormann inched away from the dragon, his hand behind him feeling for the bright green thread, endeavouring to keep what he was doing hidden from the dragon's watchful eyes. He needed to touch it to reassure himself it was still there, waiting to be used. So much of it! But why couldn't Arthur's sword cut it? He blamed himself for the mess he had got the children in, and he needed to help them if he could. That was what he was doing here now, trying to gain time for the children to come up with an answer to the prophecy and cut the thread. But time was running out.

Grabbing the green thread Eorldormann thrust it towards the dragon.

"Look what I have here! I made it especially to tie you up! Forever! This thread is indestructible and everlasting and it will bind you forever. You will never be able to terrorise the world again. You will remain down here as a perpetual legend, trussed up like a chicken!"

Roarrr! Aarghh! The dragon bellowed loudly, its powerful voice swelling like thunder, then it fell silent, wondering what power the thread had over him. The beast paused in breaking free. It wasn't prepared to risk the power of the thread until his own powers were complete and he could be sure of victory. How he wished he had killed *all* the fauns when he awoke many years ago. Well, one still lived, but not for much longer! His eyes glittered, he would soon be free. Yet, at the back of the creature's mind lay a feeling all was not as it appeared to be. The thread appeared ominous, yes. It threatened him, yes. But something was not quite right. Well, he could wait to find out, after all there were only two days left before he was free. He growled softly, the first thing he did would be to make sure the faun died. It was a delicious thought. The beast almost laughed, freedom sounded so deliciously close.

Eorldormann couldn't breathe. He kept his back against the thread, every bit of his body aching with fear until he noticed the dragon's eyes closing. Good. The dragon appeared to be sleeping again, it would give more time for the children to get here. And they were bringing Betty Vanstone with them. He knew. He felt it last night. It was the first time he had allowed himself to think of her in years and suddenly all the old longings came bubbling up inside. He grinned, he smirked, he skipped around; the Maiden of Ascolot! She was coming back! He could almost felt the nearness of her. Would she bring the golden amulet? Would she invite its chequered history into their world once again? Guinevere had given it to Lancelot as a love token and he in turn had given it to the Maiden of Ascolot to thank her for her hospitality. The amulet had powers beyond anything in Camelot. Except for Excalibur.

Eorldormann touched the sword, wondering at the blood flowing from his fingers; it was as sharp as the day Arthur had died! Then why hadn't it cut the thread? He sat on his haunches for a moment, thinking hard, exhaustion making his head droop.

An unnatural whoosh like a slithering train woke him. He jumped guiltily, wondering how long he had slept. His focus rushed to the dragon, was it showing more signs of life? His worst fears were realised. The dragon was no longer a painting flickering into life but a living, breathing being. And, something else caught the faun's eye, the twelve catoblepas, the evil black familiars of Morgan le Faye which had been gathered around the beast's feet were also coming awake. It was more than he could bear. Snap! Snap! Snap! Everywhere he looked black serrated teeth were tearing into the imprisoning wall and crushing it like dust in their effort to be free.

If he hadn't realised it before time was passing very quickly and Christmas day loomed ahead. What could he do? If the children arrived now they would be killed by the catoblepas. He had to do something to stop the beasts from escaping the wall, and quickly.

Picking up Arthur's sword Eorldormann sprang to his feet, the white flag of his beard streaming behind. He swung the sword at the catoblepas with all his might. First he sliced one of the creatures' face following it with a quick thrust up into its belly. The catoblepas let out an agonised scream as it tore itself from the last bit of wall, but the creature was already dying. Beside the writhing dying body another creature leaped to kill the faun, but again Eorldormann struck with the sword and again the catoblepas fell dead at the faun's feet. All around the catoblepas were breaking free of the rock and rushing forwards like a pack of vicious wolves, attacking from all sides at once.

Inevitably Eorldormann knew he was outnumbered, and when he heard the fatal snap, snapping sound behind him he spun round, sword raised and met the biggest hideous creature hurtling straight towards him. There was no where to go, no time to protect himself, and Eorldormann felt all his actions turning into slow motion. He would die, and could only watch helplessly as the beast leapt, powering forwards, and swiped its ugly claws at his face. But, unbelievably, it missed. Eorldormann had a chance! Once more he fell back, swinging the Arthurian sword high above his head to bring it slashing down on the hard back of the beetle-like creature. But the blade jarred in his hands, bouncing harmlessly off. Immediately the catoblepas turned fiercely about, twisting its tail, and lifting itself high upon its legs. Eorldormann shut his eyes in fear and stumbled against some fallen rubble. The catoblepas sprung upon him in a flash. It ripped its claws at Eorldormann's face, but they were caught in the tangle of hair and beard and instead of sinking deep into flesh merely slid over the skin, grazing it like a sharp razor. Back and forth went the fight.

The catoblepas was swift and strong, whereas Eorldormann was old and tiring fast. He struggled to lift the heavy sword once more and brought it down upon the back of the scaly creature. It found its mark. Crack! The black beetle shell snapped. Eorldormann jumped back but lost his footing again and stumbled as the pack of catoblepas surged towards him. He knew it was the end.

At that moment the children came rushing through the tunnel to stand there gaping in amazement at the carnage in front of them.

Diane began screaming. Timothy gulped, straightened his back and stepped forward, raising his lance instantly. Everywhere was chaos. The black beetle like creatures were racing towards the faun, mouths eager to rip him to pieces. Timothy didn't blanch. He felt Mark beside him and knew he had to protect him. Breathing deeply he focussed all of his strength into his right hand before balancing the lance and throwing it at one of the hideous catoblepas.

It was a good throw. The medieval spearhead bit deep into the creature's flesh and it shrieked in agony, writhing horribly before dying at Timothy's feet.

Betty hurried across, working her stick furiously and raging at her helplessness to move faster. Yet with one hand on her stick she used the other to raise the golden rose amulet. This was her chance to help the children; this was why she had come. But she had to move quickly. She had to get rid of the catoblepas to give the children a chance to solve the prophecy.

Desperately punching her arm high into the air she let the bright rays of the amulet come streaming forth to spill throughout the chamber and bathe the scene with its powerful magic. For a moment the catoblepas were halted in their headlong attack, and for one moment the chaos stilled to let the brilliant blue rays race through the air towards the dragon. Here they bored deep into the beast's mind sending horror and dismay and leaving it temporarily powerless.

But around them other catoblepas were charging into life. One after another they turned to face the children and bunched their muscles ready to spring upon the tiny group. Timothy yanked his lance from the beast he had just killed, took careful aim and fired it again with all his fear and strength, straight into the heart of the deadly creature. Once more black blood splattered the floor and the creature fell silent. Mark cheered, but his voice quickly changed to one of alarm as he saw another catoblepas behind Timothy ready to spring.

"Look out!" he called, before crumpling in a swoon.

Joan ran to his side, she would protect him, she thought.

Diane picked up fallen stones and began hurling them at the awful creatures.

"Leave him alone!"

The children were trapped, only Timothy seemed able to kill any of the creatures and it took long seconds for him to retrieve his lance each time he hurled it. Yet beside him Betty stood erect, continuing to hold the turquoise amulet in her hands.

Just as the children felt they were bound to die they heard Betty murmur a few words. This time when she held the amulet aloft she moved to each side, side stepping to let the powerful rays from the amulet glide brightly over the awful creatures. Each time a creature was caught by the rays it was stunned and staggered helplessly around the chamber floor.

"Now!" called Betty.

Timothy needed no second bidding. He raced over to one of the beasts, took careful aim and fired his lance into it, throwing every bit of his strength behind it as he did so. The ancient lance struck deep, killing the creature instantly. He ran to the next beast and hurled his lance again. And again it felled a terrible foe. Time after time he did this until the floor around him resembled a sea of carnage. Now the chamber fell silent, and Timothy could finally lower the faithful lance and rest. But, hiding amongst the shadows, the last of the catoblepas crouched and watched, unsmiling.

Seeing the lowered weapon the creature leapt out, racing towards Betty, its cavernous jaws ready to snatch the amulet. Eorldormann, weakened, exhausted and losing blood, had been making his way across to her. Now he glanced up and saw the catoblepas, and knew in that instant that he would die before he got to her. But he didn't care. He had known all along how it would be and had been willing to pay the price. He would pay it now.

Snatching up Arthur's sword Eorldormann leapt between the beast and her, slashing wildly at the creature's unprotected belly as if it were a melon. The creature screamed, but it wasn't finished. Some lasting dregs of strength twisted together for one last attack. It eyed Eorldormann, malice twisting its face, and with a hideous noise of triumph sunk its teeth into the faun's unprotected flesh, before falling dead at his feet. Eorldormann kicked the beast away, knowing he was fatally wounded; already he could feel the creature's venom coursing through his body, and a few moments later Eorldormann also collapsed.

"Aahh!" Betty cried, her eyes black pools of despair.

For a moment the whole chamber fell silent; the dead catoblepas littered the chamber floor; the children mesmerised by fear and wonder. It felt as if they were spectators in a secret world. Then Diane noticed a strange shimmering light filling the chamber and radiating outwards as if it came from Betty. She shook her head; it couldn't be true. After a moment the light converged into one large beam of light before moving across to where Eorldormann lay. The faun lifted his eyelids, fighting the poison that filled his body. Now he was looking upon a vision of the Maiden of Ascolot.

"You came back," he murmured.

"You saved my life," she said.

"I never forgot . . ."

Joan let out a wail. "He's dying."

"We have no time for grieving," said Betty. "Look around you."

Chapter 24

The dragon awakes

"Stay still," ordered Betty. "No one must get between the amulet's light beams and the dragon's face."

The children froze, scarcely daring to breathe, and noticing how the strange blue light seemed to mesmerise the dragon.

"Is it alive?" whispered Diane.

"Not yet. If I keep this amulet focused on its face it will slow down the awakening process. But I don't know how long it will last." Betty's voice sounded strained.

Timothy recovered from his ordeal with the catoblepas, breathing deeply to calm himself down, like a long distance swimmer after a traumatic race. But he was angry; so angry with himself. He blamed himself for the last attack upon Eorldormann, in which the faun had been fatally injured. If only he had not been so keen to relax! If only he had checked the chamber for more of those horrid beasts before putting down the sword! He also realised there wasn't time for him to worry about that now, because he needed to concentrate on new problems, such as how to deal with the dragon, and, if they managed to cut the thread, would it bind the dragon? But this time there would be no abath to help, and no faun to summon the beast. Timothy noticed how lines of strain were etching into Betty's face, and he wondered if she would survive the effort of getting to the castle, or would he have to help her as well?

Just then he looked down and noticed his hands were splattered with oozing black blood. It seemed to be everywhere, in his hair, on his face, and fat globules dripping from his coat. Calmly he took out his handkerchief and wiped the messy fluid away, but lifting his head saw his sisters' rising panic. Mark too looked white in the face and in danger of panicking. Timothy had to snap everyone out of it or else he was sure they would all die. He needed to get everyone talking to bring back some sense of normality.

"Hey, Diane? Can you help Mark?" he asked.

"Okay." She broke off. "Oh my! He's going to faint." Grabbing her first aid bag said, "I've got some lemon eucalyptus oil in here; it smells ever so strong. That'll bring him round," and thrust the open bottle under Mark's nose.

"Ugh! That's horrid." Mark jerked back in disgust, pushing the bottle away, but he looked a better colour and less likely to fall down in a faint.

"Thanks, Diane," said Timothy, wanting everyone fit and moving. "Can you help Betty now? She needs to see the rest of the paintings in case she notices something which we've missed."

Betty shook her head at him. "I can't move from this spot, Timothy. I have to keep the amulet's rays trained on the dragon's face to delay its freedom. I'm afraid no one else can do this, only me, since the amulet is mine."

Oh bother! Timothy groaned. If he couldn't take Betty to the paintings he would have to bring the paintings to Betty, and there was only one way of doing that, though it would take much longer, and they didn't have much time left.

"Can Diane describe the paintings to you?"

Diane coloured, feeling important. "Oh, yes, I can do that. That's a terrific idea."

"Thanks. And Mark, are you up to doing a bit of walking too?" Mark nodded, but he had gone a green colour and looked very sick.

"Could you do a final count on those ugly beasties from the wall? See if any are left, and warn us if they are coming to life, and especially if you think they might suddenly leap out." He shuddered. This was like the worst nightmare he had ever experienced. Turning to his youngest sister he winked. "I won't say it, *here*," he said meaningfully. "But if you could do it, behind the wall over there, Joanie." He left the words hanging, hopeful and despairing, watching as Joan nodded, her heart thumping nervously, anxious to do her part and prove her worth. She crept away until she was out of sight of the dragon, clutching her bag with its special contents.

Betty watched intrigued, but could do nothing, she had to keep her whole mind fixed on the dragon and endeavour to ignore the tiredness washing over her.

Mark made his way around the walls, counting the round piles of rubble where the catoblepas had burst out of the chamber wall. *One. Two. Three.* He felt his nervousness mounting, looking for twelve piles of rubble. He remembered counting them on their last visit. *Eleven. Twelve.* Twelve piles of rubble! Now his heart began jumping furiously, knowing they had all escaped. Which meant there were twelve beasts on the loose, or killed. But where were they? He knew there was only one way to check that; he had to count the bodies.

Ugh! His mind froze. He began counting the bodies of the catoblepas, wondering if each time he stepped near it would wake up and grab him. When he counted the last one he jabbed a happy thumbs up sign to Timothy.

"Great. Thanks!"

But Betty suddenly called out, her voice sharp and excited cutting the air of fear and gloom that pervaded the chamber. "Timothy! Quickly! Bring me the sword. I've got an idea."

Timothy felt his chest constricting in horror. The sword had been thrown down beside the body of Eorldormann. To lift it up he would have to step over the faun.

"Quickly," commanded Betty.

Timothy snatched up the sword, averting his eyes and took it to Betty. She immediately burst out laughing.

"That's it! That's the reason it wouldn't cut the thread! I should have thought of it sooner."

"Why?" said Timothy mesmerised by Betty's chuckles.

"Yes, why?" asked Diane.

"This sword is Clarent. Not Excalibur!"

Suddenly everyone realized they had found the wrong sword. There were two swords, but they had brought back the wrong one.

In her excitement Betty's hand slipped and the rays slid off the dragon's face. Instantly it began groaning.

"Whoa!" Betty called, and jolted the amulet back, once more training its powerful blue rays into the dragon's eyes. The creature fell quiet. But in that instant of freedom the beast understood everything. *Clarent*! The children had found Arthur's sword. But, what did it mean? Why were they upset that they hadn't found Excalibur? And what hadn't worked?

A wily look came over the dragon's face as it tried to understand how it might still break free. So, the children needed to find Arthur's military sword, and they still had to look for Excalibur. *Good*. And the dragon began to plot.

"Shh!" Timothy put his finger over his lips and hushed everyone to silence. He could sense the dragon's interest. "Not another word. Nothing! From now on everything must be in writing," and he flicked open his notebook, found a stub of pencil and scribbled a note, which he passed to Betty. *'I think the dragon can hear us. We mustn't talk out loud. Where is Excalibur?'*

Reading it Betty shook her head, *I don't know"* but quickly scribbled a message that she passed to Diane. *'What scenes are painted on the back walls?'*

Diane scribbled her reply and the notebook went back. *'Fighting'*, *'knights dying'*, *'Mordred and Arthur fighting'*, *'Arthur in boat'*, and *'ladies and Arthur'*.

Betty slid her eyes over the words, broke into a huge grin, and begun scribbling again. *'Draw the picture of Arthur in the boat'*.

"Oh!" Diane hesitated; would she be able to draw well enough? Taking the pencil she made an outline sketch with matchstick figures for the knights. She gave King Arthur a circle above his head to show the crown, then a rough canoe shape to represent the boat he was in, and finally a sketch of his hand holding a sword. As she did this Diane suddenly realised what she was doing. This picture of the sword was the most important because it held the answer they were looking for. She was sure of it. Diane rushed to the wall to stand beneath the painting of Arthur in the boat. There it was. The sword which would play such an important part in this prophecy. Carefully she drew the sword as large as she could, emphasising the shape of its handle, the shaft, and how Arthur was holding it. When it was complete she rushed back to Betty.

"Is this it?" she mouthed, grinning, knowing the answer and thrusting the picture beneath Betty's face.

Yes! Betty's beaming face said it all. The sword Arthur was holding in the painting was Excalibur, and it looked completely different from the one they found beneath the tunnels. Excalibur had been with Arthur in the boat, and the boat had been moored at the edge of the lake before he had been cast adrift. Which all meant that the sword had been cast into the lake just like it said in the Arthurian tales.

The children were so excited it took them a few minutes to realise they were no nearer to finding Excalibur and cutting the magical thread.

"Caradon?" began Diane.

"Shh!" said Timothy, gesturing to the listening dragon. He bit his lip thinking hard; the abath had been reluctant to help before, would it help them now? And it was important they make a new plan to find Excalibur, away from the listening dragon. They had been lucky to find the other sword even with Eorldormann's help, and Caradon's, but would the abath come if they called, rather than his old friend Eorldormann? Where would they begin?

Timothy ripped out three sheets of paper, giving one each to Diane, Mark and Joan. At the top of his notebook he wrote, *'Where was Arthur put into the boat?'* They shook their heads, looking vague. Betty looked at the words, took the pencil and wrote underneath *'Beside the lake of Camelot. Get my ancient map and look for the old rivers.'* Timothy shook his head and wrote. *No time. Plus cannot go home. Wild boar in the forest. We need to plan, away from the dragon. Can we leave you? Will you be all right?'* He frowned, not wanting to leave her in the guardian's chamber alone with the dragon, yet what else could he do? He needed everyone to be able to discuss their options quickly, and they couldn't do that with the dragon listening and having to write everything down.

Betty looked so vulnerable facing the dragon with her magical amulet in one hand and her walking stick in the other, but she shrugged away his concerns; the children had to do this on their own.

Hurrying back to the outer chamber Diane let out a deep sigh. "Good, at last we can talk again."

"The dragon gives me the creeps," piped Joan.

"Me too. And Betty doesn't know how long the power from the amulet will last. We must find Excalibur, and quickly!" Timothy wasted no time. "Has anyone any ideas?"

"We must find Caradon," Timothy muttered.

"Perhaps we could look in the tunnels again, but on our own," suggested Diane.

"Too dangerous," declared Timothy. "For one thing we don't know what is down there. I heard weird noises last time. Anyway, Mark is too tired." And indeed Mark looked too exhausted to go anywhere.

"Why don't we look for the river Arthur sailed on?" said Joan.

"That's the river that flows to Avalon and Glastonbury," added Diane.

"What rivers can we think of?" asked Timothy.

"Oh, I know some! We're looking at rivers in our geography lessons at the moment," said Diane excitedly. "There's the Yeo, named after Yeovil. The Cam, called after Queen Camel and West Camel—or are the towns named after the river?"

"A good start Diane, but we're looking for an ancient river. One that was here in King Arthur's time."

"I think the rivers would have been here long before Arthur," said Joan slowly. "Do you remember, just outside of Castle Cary there is 'Alfred's Bridge'. Surely that is named after King Alfred. And he's pretty ancient." She said it so seriously everyone burst out laughing, even Mark, who was trying not to slip onto the floor in exhaustion.

For a few seconds everyone started to feel brighter and their dreadful predicament was forgotten. But Timothy soon reminded them of it.

"Have you any idea how far it is from Crewkerne to Glastonbury? Even if we find an ancient river, and we have no idea how we are going to do that, how will we get time to walk the whole length of it, *and* search for Excalibur? We've no idea where Arthur's sword was thrown. It might not be as easy to find as Clarent." It was a sobering thought. "And how do we get past the wild boar? Remember, Betty said they are trying to get us, and they will be waiting outside in the forest. If we try to find the sword we have to do it from inside the castle."

"We'll have to go underground again." Mark breathed the words. There was so much horror and repugnance in his voice he nearly swooned.

Timothy's face was pinched and white. Everyone was looking to him for a solution, and he didn't have any ideas at all. They wanted Betty's ancient map but they had no time to get it, and neither could they get past the wild boar. They wanted Caradon to help them, but he had disappeared after they found the first sword and showed no signs of wanting to help them again. They wanted to ask Eorldormann questions, but he was dead. They wanted to be able to bind the dragon, but they still could not do so, without finding Excalibur.

All options seemed closed to him. Then Joan spoke up, pulling something green from her pocket.

"I haven't had a chance to use this thread yet. Do you think it's good enough? It might fool the you-know-what for a while."

"Wow, Sis, that is great. The colour match is perfect." Timothy beamed at her, and she thought that all her hard work had been worth it. "We will keep it in case of emergencies. It might work better than we know."

Her 'thread' looked just like the magical bundle that was in front of the dragon, though of course much smaller. Last night Joan had taken the whole reel of their mother's 'magic' thread and coated it in a mixture of green oil paint, coal dust and cornflour. Then she dried it thoroughly in the rayburn. The result was impressive. Joan had struggled to produce the exact colour of green, and the strange thick consistency that the thread appeared to have. In fact she had taken a variety of green leaves back with her yesterday and forced herself to remember that particular shade of green that was neither one green nor the other, but was in fact a shade darker, a touch lighter, a fraction brighter than those she had. She was pleased with the result and wanted to try it out on the dragon right away. If it worked they could all go home!

Timothy saw her enthusiastic face but knew that even if the dragon was fooled for a short while he would soon realise that it was only nylon and break through it in seconds. It would depend on how Joan tied it in amongst the real magical thread and what they said to the dragon as to how long they could fool the beast. Timothy hoped they would not have to use Joan's thread at all; as he had said to her, it was only to be used in the case of emergencies or if they couldn't find the sword.

But none of them expected what happened next, and everything became a series of emergencies.'

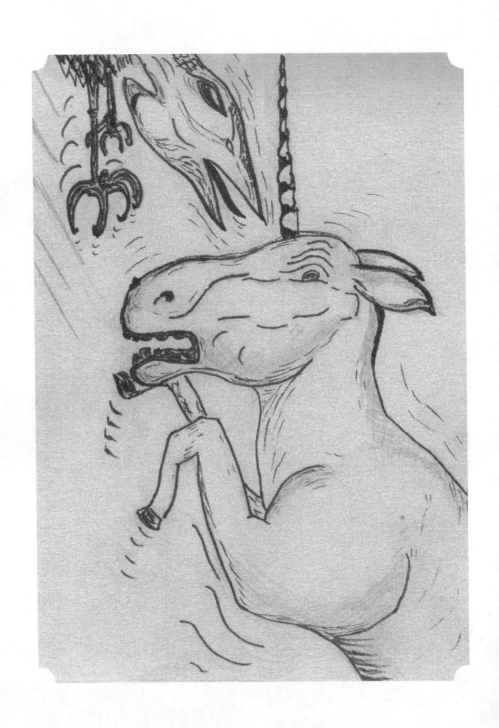

Chapter 25

Caradon returns

Timothy motioned them to sit down, realising he needed to plan his next strategy. But his head felt heavy and he could hardly focus his mind on where to go next. Knowing that their best chance lay in going into the tunnels, and hoping the tunnels went all the way to Glastonbury, what were the chances of them existing centuries ago, when King Arthur sailed away for the last time? Timothy rubbed his forehead; there were so many problems to be overcome. Where could he start? He felt utterly bewildered and deflated. He had celebrated his fifteenth birthday this October, so how could he be expected to deal with dragons, Arthurian castles, and magical thread? His head drooped and then he felt Joan tugging frantically at his sleeve.

"What do you want me to do with my thread?" she asked, popping open her little bag so Timothy could see inside. "Shall I tie it in with the real stuff?" Her chin wobbled as she tried to hide her fear.

"Can you tie it amongst the main pile and leave two ends hanging? Then the dragon will be fooled into thinking it has been cut. We can also make things better by pulling the pile of thread further away, then the dragon won't see Mum's special thread tucked in amongst it."

And that was what they did. Diane and Timothy dragged the pile of magical thread into a shadowed corner whilst Joan wove her painted thread amongst it, to leave the two ends hanging ominously. Then they dragged the thread in sight of the dragon. Betty winked in approval and did her best to pretend all was well with her. But it wasn't. Timothy saw how the least effort to move made Betty drag on her reserves of strength. She was fading in the same way Mark had been fading since he first used the key; the exposure to magical powers ate into their own strengths and left them weak. Betty wouldn't last much longer.

"Where do we look for Excalibur?" Timothy wrote on his notepad and passed to Betty. She shook her head. She didn't know; they would have to find the sword themselves. In the dark recesses of her memory she thought she could see an image, and once upon a time she might have been able to direct the children to the sword, but that was when she had been young and strong. At the present moment she felt old, weak, and vulnerable, and the images of Arthur's last journey had faded from her mind. She could only hold her amulet and direct its rays upon the dragon a while longer.

Timothy took a final piece of paper and wrote. 'We're going to look in the tunnels. Wish us luck."

Betty nodded towards the darkest tunnel at the far end of the chamber. That was the way to go. Timothy gave the thumbs up, signalled to the others, and they were off.

Leaving at a trot, and keeping together for safety they hurried towards the forbidden tunnels, noticing how waves of dank air wafted to meet them and enfolded them like a cold black envelope. But they kept running onwards, desperate to find Excalibur.

After a few minutes Diane passed everyone a pasty remembering mother's words; *you always feel better when you're not worried about food.* If only mother were with them now.

Timothy took the lead, with Diane, Mark, and Joan following in crocodile fashion. There was no time to lose. Everyone could feel a rising sense of panic remembering how frightened they had been when they were in the tunnels with Caradon.

Timothy stopped. He signalled them to silence. Could they hear something? Nothing. A few more seconds passed in silence, but it was an unnatural silence, and reluctantly Timothy led them on again. This time he led them more slowly, peering into the dark and listening for, he didn't know what.

Every time they entered a new tunnel Timothy marked the walls showing which direction they had come from, and which direction they were going. He marked 'B' for returning to Betty, and 'O' for Onward and also took regular compass readings since he remembered that Glastonbury was to the north east of Crewkerne. Therefore he always led them into the north-easterly tunnels, hoping they were heading towards Glastonbury, and Excalibur.

After what seemed like hours they came to a large opening. A bitterly cold wind whistled through as if a storm had been unleashed.

Diane tucked herself deeper into her coat, not liking the feel of the place. She looked up and realised that the place seemed to have no roof, or else it was lost in darkness. "This place feels really creepy," said Diane.

"I agree," replied Timothy, balancing the lance in his right hand and tightening his grip on the sword in the other. Now he felt ready to defend everyone, and turned to find his way into another tunnel.

Before he could move however a high pitched scream ricocheted high over their heads. It was deafening. Jamming their hands over their ears and looking up the children saw the most terrifying bird diving straight towards them.

"Hide!"

Chapter 26

Danger in the tunnels

Miles away from the tunnel where the children hid in fear there existed a deep underground canyon. The lofty place looked like a forest idyll, full of soft tones of burbling water which raced and skipped over ancient rocks and gentle musical echoes tinkled around the large forest glade. The sounds, smell and sights of the forest were like an endless first day of spring. In one part a warm spring bubbled up, with steam rising and filling the grand branches of ancient oak, beech and ash trees. In another part of the canyon swathes of bluebells carpeted the floor, their bright heads and lustrous flowers filling the air with sweet perfume. As clouds of steam rose above the spring, halo-like amongst the topless cavern, vast rainbows arched and flickered through the ponderous trees, like crystalline droplets of colour exploding overhead. Underfoot lush grass and banks of bright gold and soft rose pink flowers gave the forest garden a wondrous exotic feel. Nearby a burbling waterfall splashed on the back of a magnificent one horned creature, as tall as a tower and strong as an oak. This was his domain, his home, and his land.

His silver thickset head was shaped like a magnificent stag and his splendid mane shone with red and golden tints in the sunlight like a fringed sheath of studded gems. Caradon, the last unicorn descendant of legend, raised his head and listened. Ever since he had taken the children to find the sword he had found himself listening to the sounds of the dragon and the giant, as both began to stir. His heart pounded with anger and exhilaration. The time was coming to pass. The children had found the castle and now the dragon was coming to life. He resented the children coming into his world because their coming meant the disturbance of his master the giant. Yet he knew the prophecy had to be fulfilled. If they did not succeed in their quest the end of the world would follow.

Sadness washed over him. He loved his home, this secret glade nestling deep beneath the earth's surface. And though his ancestral unicorns had been killed and it had been a lonely home, yet he cared that it would be lost forever. Oceans of sadness welled through him; everything was coming to an end.

His musings were brought to an abrupt stop by a terrifying screech which sent tremblings rushing over him. It was the sound he never wanted to hear again, and which he had last heard when Arthur sailed the ancient river to his final resting place. The sound of the Cikavac. This birdlike monster belonged to the Eastern dominions and survived from a time when the world had been covered with tropical forests. They had patrolled the skies looking for prey to gorge upon. Nor had they fed upon carrion, they had killed prehistoric creatures as large as the Tyrannosaurus Rex. They were royal birds at a time when birds were prized above rubies, and in return they remained faithful to their master, killing and maiming at his command. Now the last surviving cikavac had been awakened in its nest and was screaming in hatred and fury. Caradon imagined its hideous beak with the fat, swinging sack beneath, twisting and thrashing against the walls of its cavern as it prepared to attack.

But whom or what was it attacking? Like a bolt of thunder the answer came to him. *The children.* They had returned, in spite of Eorldormann's warnings, and were braving the horrors of the dark tunnels. Caradon knew they would be alone, without protection, and that they had carelessly stumbled upon one of the most savage prehistoric creatures still inhabiting the earth. What could have possessed them to enter the tunnels? They would be torn to pieces. He had to help them.

Caradon swished his great mane and whirled into the tunnels, exploding into the darkness like a phantom. Would he reach them in time?

His thick horn flashed, growing in power with every stride, building up for the coming fight. He was searching for one cavern which he had avoided over the centuries; the Cavern of the Cikavac, the home of the creature he feared and loathed the most.

Ploughing into the cavern he immediately saw the children were still alive, though backed into a tiny corner. Then he noticed something amazing, for in front of the rock behind which the three younger children sheltered, Timothy stood, screaming wildly, though fear cracked his voice, gesticulating fiercely at the cikavac. In his hands he swung the medieval lance, jabbing the pointed end towards the cruel talons and fangs of the bird, and on the floor beside him lay the sword Clarent, thrown defiantly at the creature in a rage of hatred.

"You won't take us, you beastly, hateful creature," shouted Timothy, as the creature flew, hovered, bucked and dived at them.

When Caradon first met the children he resented them for their foolish games of make believe and adventure, yet as he watched Timothy yelling at the prehistoric cikavac in a suicidal attempt to protect the younger children, and saw the younger ones screaming like little demons and doing their utmost to keep the cikavac at bay, he felt the first murmurings of admiration for them. How brave they were! How determinedly they fought! He had to save them!

Uttering a vast bellow that filled the cavern Caradon surged forwards, his great body skidding to a halt a short way in front of Timothy, then thrusting his head to the birdlike beast wheeling and screaming overhead, he twisted his horn in anticipation of a desperate battle.

The cikavac broke off, surprised by this new aggressor. Its vast beak and gulping sack flapped hard above the cowering children whilst its wings cracked with the effort to delay its deadly swoop. Recovering from its loss of momentum it prepared to dive again. This time the cikavac ignored Timothy and thrust out its talons to gouge the head of the abath. With an ear-piercing screech it drove its talons down, down, towards Caradon, ready to scrape out unprotected eyes. Caradon twisted violently, his proud horn swinging widely from side to side to swipe away the talons, then with a deft movement swung its stiletto shaped horn into the underbelly of the cikavac. The flying creature screeched in agony as its belly was ripped, then swung to the right, cart wheeling uncontrollably as Caradon's horn sent it mercilessly away. But it righted itself, flapped savagely and prepared to attack again.

Caradon was waiting for it. Raising himself high on its back legs the abath pawed the air like a raging stallion then with a crash dashed its hooves on to the ground, whirling about in a mad frenzy like an unbroken colt. The cikavac was surprised by the swiftness of the abath and with a resounding bellow the thunderous beast sliced its horn across the breast of the wheeling cikavac, laying it open like a sliced melon. The cikavac crashed to the ground beside the terrified children and with a deliberate aim Caradon stamped upon its ghastly head until it ceased to move.

A dreadful hush filled the cave until Timothy staggered over to the abath, his face exhausted but grinning hugely, and he clapped the beast upon its flanks.

"Well done! Thank you. I couldn't have gone on much longer." And he patted the abath's heaving flanks as if he were patting one of his father's favourite cows.

The abath nodded its head in acknowledgement.

Diane crept across, carefully avoiding looking at the bloodied mangled mess nearby, noticing a pool of blood below the abath's shoulder.

"You're hurt!" she cried and leapt into action, seeing an opportunity for first aid, and an opportunity to say thank you to this beast which looked like a unicorn. She whipped out a heavy crepe bandage and started binding the soft material over the bleeding edges of the wound.

Timothy dropped his arms to his sides, his lance banging on the ground, feeling completely exhausted. "Thank you," he said with hardly strength left to speak.

Mark and Joan came creeping out of their shelter behind the rock. They too patted the abath, murmuring words of thanks. Since they were used to being amongst animals they weren't afraid, only thinking that this animal was extremely large, and they remembered how he had helped them to find the first sword.

"Thank you for coming to find us," said Joan. "I think you saved our lives." She let her fingers trail through the abath's wiry coat.

Caradon nudged her, standing quietly whilst Diane bandaged its shoulder. Then rubbed its muzzle into each of the children in turn to thank them.

"Follow me. We need to move quickly," he said.

"We have to find Excalibur," said Timothy. "We found the wrong sword before; it was Clarent, not Excalibur. Do you know where it is?"

Caradon shook his head, thinking hard. "I can't tell you these things; those secrets were not mine to have. However, I know of a dark chamber where you can see more pictures like those you saw above."

"They might help us," exclaimed Diane, snipping off the bandage and pulling the knotted ends with her teeth.

"Will you take us there? Quickly!" asked Timothy.

Caradon nodded. "The fauns inhabited these tunnels many centuries ago and they filled the walls with their beautiful paintings telling everyone of the lives of Arthur and his court. Some of these Eorldormann completed, in the chambers above, but the others were forgotten. I will take you to them now."

"Thank you for helping us; even though you don't like us" said Timothy breaking into a weak and tired smile.

Caradon winked at Diane and Joan and gave a happy shake of his head. "I might be changing my mind," and with that cryptic comment indicated the way out of the cavern, carefully avoiding the dead cikavac.

"Have we got to go far?" Timothy asked.

"Not far. First I need to take you to my home in the glade, it will help you to get refreshed and renew your strength. You will need it later," and the abath swung his head to look at Mark who had slid into an exhausted heap.

Nudging him awake and telling him to swing upon his back, the strange group moved off with Caradon and Mark taking the lead, followed by Timothy who still carried his lance and sword, and then the two girls.

Caradon led them deeper into the tunnels. Down they went, on and on in darkness with only a glimmer of murky light to show them the way. It seemed as if several hours had passed and eventually the children fell silent. Timothy no longer took compass bearings; shamefully aware he had been leading everyone in the wrong direction.

When they thought they could walk no further Caradon led them into his own beautiful glade. The children gaped. Everything looked so peaceful that even the horrors of the wild boar in the forest, and the black catoblepas in the Guardian's Chamber, and the prehistoric cikavac, slid from their memories. This was a place where they could relax.

"I'm hungry," complained Joan rubbing her stomach longingly as she noticed some crisp green apples in the trees overhead. "Can I eat one, please?" she asked, hurrying forward to where Caradon had stopped and Mark was sliding off the beasts' back.

"Of course. Just think of your favourite food when you bite into it," the abath suggested, and reaching up knocked several of the delicious fruit into Joan's outstretched hands.

Timothy took one of the apples and burst out grinning. "Wow! Sis, this is the craziest apple I've ever tasted. It's like my favourite sausages mixed in with Mum's rich, creamy mashed potatoes, with lashings of gravy. Mmm!" And he quickly munched another mouthful, and another, and before long he was reaching for a second apple. Joan sunk her teeth into her apple and it tasted of vanilla ice cream and strawberries. Oh, and how she enjoyed it; it made her feel so much happier and stronger. Diane and Mark did likewise and each of them thought the apple tasted of their favourite food. What a wonderful place they had come to!

When they were all rubbing their stomachs with pleasure they began noticing the thick green trees with ponderous branches, the vibrant plants with lofty spikes of flowers, and nearby a quiet stream scarcely moving in the noon day sun.

"This is super," said Joan flopping down in a patch of dappled sunlight and inhaling the aroma of the trees and flowers. Tilting her head she could hear fresh sparkling water burbling somewhere in the background reminding her of tiny bells. And within moments she was asleep. Timothy soon followed suit, but Diane, after getting out a fresh and heavier duty bandage, waited for Mark to curl up before asking Caradon if she might look at his wound again. It was clear the abath was pleased with her request, and when Diane ripped off the first bloodstained dressing he scarcely moved.

Diane gasped. The wound was much deeper than she had realised and knew they ought to have a vet to stitch it up. *Oh well*, she thought, she would just have to manage by herself. Taking hold of the two sides of the freshly cut flesh she carefully drew them together, covering the ghastly bleeding wound. Then she took a deep breath, knowing she must stitch the wound to keep it closed, and knowing it would hurt the abath. Caradon seemed to know what she was thinking and stamped a hoof loudly, sorely, and said, "Go ahead. I will not move."

Diane was very careful to make sure the knot at the end of the thread was strong, nor did she want it breaking as she pulled the thread through. Taking a firm grip on the needle she shoved it through one of the edges of the wound. She could feel Caradon quivering, but true to his word he kept still. Then she pulled the length of thread through, tugged it carefully until the skin was pulled together and pushed the needle back through again. Another pull made it tight, and she knotted it off. *Phew!* One stitch. The needle went back into the flesh, again and again, until she had a tiny row of stitches, each knot and stitch as neatly made as if she were indeed a vet.

Giving a final snip, making sure she was as careful at the end as she was in the beginning, she finished stitching the wound, tucked the needle into her sewing kit, patted Caradon softly, and within moments she curled up beside her brothers and sister and fell instantly asleep. She thought she heard Caradon breathe the faintest sound, "Thank you, kind girl," before drifting off into a wonderful sleep.

What was it about that sacred glade of Caradon's that made them sleep so soundly, so that when they awoke they were as refreshed as if they had slept for a whole day? Who can tell? The children only knew the sleep gave each of them a sense of healing and renewed strength.

Timothy awoke first, instantly alarmed. How long had they been asleep? *They should be finding Excalibur.* "We have to move now," said Caradon nudging him gently. "Now I shall take you to the wall of pictures. It may help in your search for Excalibur. It's not far from here." The abath nuzzled into Diane's sleeping head; aware of how much pain she had tried to spare him and realised he had always based his dislike of man upon his knowledge of those who had killed his ancestors. He had never met anyone like Diane before; someone who could care for animals. He remembered also how in the cikavac's cavern he had felt a feeling of respect as he watched how bravely the children fought, and now Diane's kindness engendered other feelings within him.

Diane awoke, leaping up, eyes wide, aware she had slept for ages. Gently she touched the wound on Caradon's shoulder and to her surprise found it no longer bleeding. In fact it had nearly healed over and a scar was beginning to form. She felt confused and elated. What a wonderful place this was. Picking up her bag she gave one last glance as she followed everyone out of the beautiful soft glade, would she ever see it again, she wondered. Would Caradon survive if they didn't find Excalibur and couldn't cut the magical thread? She shook her head, trying to get rid of the sense of desolation; it was too awful to contemplate.

They began to walk quickly. Even Mark could walk now he had had a rest, and he tried to keep up with everyone else. Joan tucked herself close to Timothy, feeling some sense of reassurance from his bulk beside her. Again Caradon led them into unusual tunnels, turning so many different ways that Timothy was sure they were backtracking themselves. Then he realised they were moving downwards and the tunnels became a series of spirals and slopes. The grumbling sounds of the dragon and the giant faded away and eventually Caradon brought them to a large well-lit chamber. He stopped, and nodded towards a wall where a painted map with shapes, arrows and objects shone out through the darkness. The children were open mouthed.

The map was carefully drawn with the narrow and wide flowing strokes of a master calligrapher, it showed a large river, whilst along either side were drawn the drooping trees.

"Weeping willows," explained Timothy. Then pointing said, "Look! Look at this! A small hut on the riverbank. I wish we knew where it was."

"It's wooden, so it won't be there any longer," said Diane practically.

"It's got a cross on top of the roof. Isn't that a chapel? And if it is, don't you think it might have been replaced? Perhaps by a stone chapel? And if so, might not that stone chapel, or its ruins, still survive?" Timothy spoke eagerly, looking at every mark upon the wall, hoping each was a clue they could use. "Do we know of a chapel by a river?"

"Many monasteries were built beside rivers hundreds of years ago; so they had a good water supply," said Joan, who had read about such things at school.

Diane pointed. "King Arthur! There! And beside him there is a tiny boat, in the river. And above I can just see a sword! Could that be Excalibur?"

Suddenly all the children were pushing to get closer to the picture, each one eager to see the legendary Excalibur.

"You're right," shouted Timothy, feeling as if he would burst with excitement.

"I can see it too!" said Joan.

"This is important," said Timothy. "We now know Sir Bedivere didn't throw Excalibur into the lake at the beginning of Arthur's journey because Arthur had the sword with him in the boat. Perhaps Sir Bedivere went into the boat with Arthur whilst he was alive and threw the sword into the lake afterwards, when Arthur had died. Then finally sent Arthur off in the boat alone," said Timothy.

"Two boat journeys," stated Mark who seemed to be acknowledging something he already knew.

"But we still don't know when Bedivere threw Excalibur into the river. Or where."

"Look at this," said Diane excitedly, pulling Timothy further along the wall to a different part of the picture. "If you follow the river this way, it leads you to . . . . why, Glastonbury is there! See, the large cross, and there is Arthur's boat again! He did make a second journey!" Mark's face twitched but he said nothing.

"This time he hasn't got the sword!" Timothy broke in, getting louder with excitement. Then Mark pointed at something none of the others had noticed.

"A lake. Look, a lake. The river has flowed until it becomes a lake."

Could that be Avalon?

"And it's here that Arthur throws the sword."

"Sir Bedivere threw it," said Joan softly. "Arthur had to order him three times to do it. When he finally throws it in the water a Maiden of the Lake catches it, raises it above the water, and disappears."

"If only we could find it. It must be at the bottom of the lake, just like the first sword we found," said Timothy. "But which lake? We've searched beneath our pond. How do we find this lake? It must be a special lake."

Caradon began pawing the ground. "Come with me, I know of a special lake. It is an ancient and sacred place, where no one can go. I know of Maidens who guard a lake, but to go near it means death. There is also a monster that guards the lake. He is known as Afanc. Centuries ago he was supposed to have been killed by Arthur when he found Excalibur, but the creature recovered and keeps watch over the lake and the maidens like an evil guardian. Perhaps Excalibur is at the bottom of that lake, though I can't be certain. I do know however that you must be careful if you decide to go to the lake, because the afanc kills everyone who approaches. I will take you as far as I can though I am not allowed to go to the lake. Nor can anyone unbidden walk past the point where I will leave you. The legend says only one being is allowed to the lake, which must be the Chosen One. Or else they die."

"The Chosen One!" said the children, feeling tremors running up their backs.

"Will this afanc attack anyone who goes there?" asked Timothy.

"Yes, anyone. However, there is a short period each day when he is rendered helpless by the heat of the noon day sun. Legend tells us that noontime is very magical because at that exact moment young Arthur found Excalibur and became king to the Britons. Since then the afanc is punished every noon by the maidens of the lake, as his punishment for losing the sword. His strength diminishes until he seeks out the cooler waters below the lake. It is at that precise moment when the sun is at its fiercest and the afanc dives to the bottom of the lake that the Chosen One may creep past and steal the sword Excalibur."

"We still don't know who the chosen one is!" Timothy said crossly. "Betty thought it might be one of us. But which one?"

"You must discover that for yourselves, I can only help by taking you into the final tunnel. After that it is sacred territory, past which even I dare not go. The chosen one must go the lake alone." Caradon whirled away, forcing the children to follow, fretting with their own thoughts. The Chosen One. Was it one of them? And if the wrong person went to the lake they would die? Many other problems swirled around their minds such as 'sacred territory', Maidens of the lake, a lake monster called an afanc and magical noon day suns. What hope did they have to do anything, let alone find Excalibur?

Caradon walked ahead whilst the children followed, talking furiously, their voices a cacophony of uncertainty and fear.

"According to Caradon we have to choose one of us to go ahead and find Excalibur. Has anyone any ideas how we can decide who should go?" asked Timothy. He paused. Secretly he felt that being the oldest and the strongest the task ought to fall to him. After all, he reasoned, Mark had looked ill for a few days, and Diane and Joan were girls and not as old or as strong as him. In fact he was going to suggest they might be more useful caring for Mark whilst he, Timothy, went to the sacred lake. He gulped nervously suddenly feeling sick, and wondering what ordeals lay ahead.

Diane stamped her foot crossly. She had other ideas. "I think you should stay behind Timothy, so you can look after the others, in case of attack." Then she delivered her *coup de grace*. "After all, you are the only one who can wield Clarent, and without you defending us we wouldn't have survived that horrid cikavac thing. You have to protect the ones who are left behind."

"Uhh." stumbled Timothy, gulping at Diane, suddenly bereft of words. He had not expected that line of attack, assuming he would be the one chosen to go, and thereby elected as the chosen one.

"Perhaps I ought to go," offered Joan shakily, feeling herself breaking into a sweat with terror. She felt terrified of leaving the others, but realised she knew more about Arthurian legends than the others and might notice something the others didn't understand.

"No," declared Timothy firmly. "Not you." She was far too small to carry Excalibur back, even if she found it.

Caradon stopped, his nose quivering and his ears swivelling like antennae. "Listen!" A great buzzing sound came racing towards them like the angry hum of a thousand of bees. Moments later the humming sound was amongst them and diving at them from all sides of the tunnel. "Cover yourselves," barked Caradon. He raised his front legs and began sawing the air around the children like a demented windmill. But whatever it was attacking them the children couldn't see anything. They could only hear the awful hum. Now Caradon began a terrifying dance, seemingly thrashing his head from side to side whilst the children looked on in confusion. Finally they could see a vast swarm of hornets streaming through the tunnel, racing towards them like a dive bomber. Then the swarm began breaking up into arrow shaped formations, and like that they dived at the children with their gigantic stingers fixed forwards like stiletto points.

Joan began screaming and threw her coat over her head hiding from that terrifying sight. Diane raced for cover, crazily swatting the insects with her bag, then leaping down beside Joan. Timothy held Clarent in front of him, the tip touching the bottom of his chin like a warning shield, but the hornets kept coming in to attack. Only Mark remained still. He turned to face the deadly formations as if he would speak to them. Everyone could see the hornets were diving directly at him and yelled at him to take cover, but Mark appeared oblivious of their warnings.

Caradon spotted Mark and realised he was in grave danger. The abath began a terrifying dance working his way over to Mark to try and protect him. He started twisting his head from side to side so that his gigantic horn sliced through the air with a hundred different movements and at each twist of his head knocked hundreds of the hornets senseless. Nevertheless many were still getting through and time after time they attacked the group of children, their vicious stings probing through jackets and clothing. The children were losing the fight.

Then Diane remembered she had a can of pain killer in her first aid bag for insect bites and quickly pulled this out. As she did so she depressed the button, firing the powerful spray directly into the heart of the swarm. At first they didn't take any notice, but after a few moments shrivelled up in mid flight and began falling on the floor like hard pellets of black and yellow rain.

Diane kept spraying the can until the can was empty. Only then did she take her finger off the nozzle and shuddered as she looked at the thousands of insects beneath her feet. "I hate wasps," she exclaimed as the horror of the last moments washed over her, and instantly began stamping on the black mass in front of her to make sure none were left alive.

"Well done, Diane," said Timothy clapping her heartily on the back. I'll never laugh at you again when you want to bring your first aid kit. In fact I'll offer to carry it myself."

Joan smiled, that would be a sight worth seeing she thought.

Timothy saw Caradon look steadily at Mark and his face fell. "Have you been stung?" he asked.

"Are the stings poisonous?" Mark's voice was calm, casual, as if the answer was of no interest to him.

"They can be; if the stings are left in. Has anyone else been stung?" No one else had so Diane made Mark lift off his jacket and show her the stings. There were six, and at each location Diane carefully sought out the actual stinger, though these were far larger than she had ever seen before. When she drew each sting with her tweezers she put some antiseptic cream on the wound which would also help to mask the pain. After she finished Mark was left with twelve tiny pinpricks of blood, which oozed slightly as if he had pricked his finger on a needle. Diane wiped this away. Mark smiled his thanks, but it was clear the stings had taken more of his failing strength and now he felt so weak he could hardly feel the pain of the stings above a general feeling of unwellness. He couldn't understand why he felt so lethargic and drained, almost as if he were going down with a bad bout of influenza. He wished he was at home, by the fireside, with a hot steaming cup of hot chocolate made with thick creamy milk from the farm. Would he ever see the farm again, he wondered?

Chapter 27

The maidens of the lake

As soon as Mark's stings had been treated Caradon hurried the group on until they came to a large dark cavern with only one other exit. It was here Caradon stopped. "We have arrived," he said. "I can take you no further. Now is the time for you to decide who will be going to the Lake and attempt to bring back Excalibur. The others I will take back to the Guardian's Chamber."

"I'm going on," said Timothy.

"I am as well," said Diane defiantly, though her nervous voice gave her away.

Mark set off across the cavern.

"Not you," said Timothy rushing across. "You're not strong enough," and he tried pushing Mark back. But Mark shrugged his older brother off, broke free, all the time grumbling and stomping bad temperedly towards the far exit.

"We both know who is the chosen one. It's me. I am the one who must find Excalibur. I was given the special key into the castle. My hand fitted the silver knight's which opened up the inner door into the Guardian's Chamber, and I was the one the hornets stung. I am the Chosen One."

Everyone stared. He was right. Timothy had realised it earlier though wanted to ignore it. His younger brother looked so weak and small; so frail.

Caradon clattered across to Mark. "I can give you some helpful advice," the abath said. "The lake you seek is not far away and this tunnel will take you directly to it. But it is a very sacred place, and only the

Chosen One can enter it. When you see the sword Excalibur be careful to remain hidden. That is most important if you want to see your family again. Remember the afanc will be watching over the lake until noon and when he disappears you will have a short time to get the sword."

Mark nodded, his eyes wide with fear.

"One other thing you must remember," said Caradon. "Listen to any words of advice you may be given, and make sure you do as you are asked. I will be waiting here for your return and will take you back to the Guardian's Chamber."

"What if I can't find the sword? What if I fail?"

"If you are truly the chosen one you will find it. And one more thing to remember," the abath's voice dipped, "When you really need your strength it will be there."

"When you really . . . . ? Mark checked a sudden need to cry. "Thank you for saying that; Mum always tell me the same thing. I'll try to remember it! Goodbye." He whirled into the dark tunnel and never looked back.

Once inside Mark could feel wet moss squidging like sponge underfoot and he wondered if a river sometimes ran where he was now walking, and if so was this the river King Arthur sailed on as he left the land of the living. Overhead Mark could sense ghostly branches as if the tunnel had suddenly opened into a huge cavern, but when he looked up but he could see nothing. Only thin rivulets of water could be heard trickling in the distance and he felt as if he were enclosed in a fathomless space, trapped beneath a vast ocean.

His shoulders throbbed where the hornets had stung him, and his whole body ached as if he still carried the key. Yet that was ridiculous; he had left the key on the floor beside Betty. He could feel time passing and knew he should be hurrying, but could scarcely lift his feet. He knew he was getting slower and slower but felt lost in a strange world where all he could think of was the pain in his shoulders, and an overwhelming desire to curl up and fall asleep. He had to keep on moving. Step after step, one in front of the other. His mind began to close down. Soon he would stop and never move again. He didn't mind; the thought of doing nothing ever again began to sound rather inviting.

His footsteps faltered. It was all too much trouble to think of doing anything. He would sit down, just for a moment, then he would get up, he assured himself, and walk on. But he realised he didn't know why he was walking in the tunnel in the first place. What was he doing there? Everything seemed hazy. All strength fled from his limbs and he began sliding to the ground. As he did so a tiny pinprick of light entered his mind. It was nothing. It was so small he wondered if it were there at all. But in his numbed state he felt intrigued. The light was beautiful. He wanted to see it again. Where had he seen that light before? Then it changed colour. Now it was bright gold and twinkling like a fiery star in the night sky. What was it? Before he could blink the golden colour moved into a tall shape and a graceful arc of a twin handled sword forced its way into his thoughts. This was Arthur's sword, Clarent, raised like a burning crucifix, and branding itself onto his mind. In that moment the whole purpose of his mission flooded back and with it a new found strength.

Mark struggled to his feet. He was still tired but he remembered a trick they used to play on the farm when they had to walk to the farthest field to get the cows in, and it was a bitterly cold day with the rain driving into their face, and the distance had seemed too far to walk. The trick was to count each step until they got to one hundred. Then having reached one hundred to begin counting again. And then again. Mark started it now. One, two, three, four, five, six, seven . . . eight . . . nine . . . He would count to one hundred, then stop, for a brief rest. But on the one-hundredth step he missed his footing and nearly slipped on the mossy ground.

The jolt brought him into wakefulness again. So, he would walk another hundred paces. One, two, three, four, five . . . .

Suddenly he was there. Ahead of him he saw a large clearing, similar to Caradon's sanctuary, but larger, softer, and filled with a thin green sunlight. Sunbeams dappled over a large lake, whilst ancient weeping willows drooped their feathery branches over the edge of the lake making the whole scene a growing, living, green and blue canvas. It was so peaceful; the soft shadows spread over the lake like thick cream. Even the willows scarcely moved but hung gracefully as if communing with the fathomless water beneath. This is Arthur's lake, Mark thought. This was where Arthur's sword was thrown on his return to Camelot and right in front of him, seemingly on cue, in the middle of the lake a silver arm rose out of the water and held aloft a gleaming sword, whilst all around the clearing became suffused with silver rays and soft music as if played upon an angel's harp.

Mark ran forward, forgetting the abath's warning, and dropped down on the edge of the water. Excalibur! The sigh escaped Mark's lips before he realised he shouldn't have spoken. He clamped his hand over his mouth but it was too late, the sigh began to fill the magical world with a myriad of echoes.

Then Mark heard a splash. It came from across the lake and within moments a large shape loomed beneath the water. The ghastly creature raised its head out of the water, its horrid eyes swivelling like an optical radar, searching out the farthest parts of the lake. Then it bellowed loudly and the sound was like nothing Mark had seen or heard before. This was the afanc. Mark froze, too scared to move or to dive down amongst the plants beside the water and hide.

At the centre of the lake the large reptile, with an alligator's head, and larger than a horse began to swim around the lake. The afanc kept its head above water, its football eyes unblinking as it listened for the intruder.

Mark remained motionless, holding his breath, wishing himself miles away. He could hear his heart thumping loudly in his chest and was sure the ugly afanc must be able to hear it also.

The creature circled the lake several times, its tail swishing angrily, sending plumes of water shooting up. Its flat nose rose above the water line, twitching from side to side. When it grew near to Mark it stopped; smelling something; then with a sharp strong beat of its tail it began to swim to where Mark lay.

Mark felt his heart shrivel up in his chest realising there was nowhere to run and nothing he could do; the creature was coming directly towards him.

Mesmerised into watching as the afanc got closer Mark noticed an apparition building up into a large cloud of colour, as if it were a screen of light, on the other side of the lake. Slowly it began gliding over the water towards him. He closed his eyes, afraid of what he was seeing; then opened them again. Still the apparition kept coming closer until it swept onwards and over the afanc. Then it stopped. Mark felt his mouth frame an Oh with wonder and fear as the colourful apparition revolved above the lake, swirling on top the afanc like a splendid tornado, then slowing down until the vortex of colour became three beautiful maidens.

Each one appeared to be dressed in a flowing gown, and all of them with long hair streaming behind them, thick, heavy and rope like. One maiden was the colour of a turquoise bird's egg, the other as bright as a shining silver cup, whilst the third was as magnificent as spun gold. They were the most beautiful beings Mark had seen.

For long moments the three maidens hovered above the afanc, their flowing gowns teasingly touching the monster's head, whilst the aggravated beast snapped angrily at them.

Laughing the maidens whirled away. By now the afanc forgot the noise it had heard earlier and it twisted and snapped at the trailing gowns again that were as irritating as flies. The maidens laughed and spun again. Again the afanc followed them, snapping crossly. This happened several more times and each time it followed them the maidens led it further from where Mark lay. In doing so they had saved his life.

A short while later a shaft of blood red orange pierced the silvered sunlight, and instantly the arm and sword disappeared beneath the lake. Sunset! The sword had gone. Mark had missed his chance. He wanted to shout out "Hey! I'm here. The Chosen One. I've come for the sword. Please may I have it? Please!" But deep in the depths the afanc was stirring the water of the lake and Mark hesitated, wondering how he would get the sword.

Burrowing into the fern and large leaved plants around the side of the lake Mark let the angry tears of frustration and failure spring into his eyes. He had failed, just like he knew he would. He had let everyone down, and for a moment he believed he wasn't the chosen one after all.

That was until an image of Caradon slid into his mind. The beast seemed to be there, beside him, and looking at him with the wise way he had of twisting his head to one side, and Mark suddenly remembered him saying that the afanc disappeared every day at noon, and that he could get the sword then. So, he wasn't beaten! Okay, he hadn't been successful today, but there was always tomorrow. Having made that decision Mark curled into a tired ball and promptly fell asleep.

As he slept the ghostly image of three gossamer maidens came floating towards him to stand and watch over the sleeping boy.

"He is fair," remarked one.

"Young," remarked another.

"Brave," commented the last.

A fitting tribute to Sir Galahad they implied and one worthy to carry the sword. But on one thing the maidens agreed; the sword once given to him, must be returned by him.

They spread fine cloaks of silk upon the boy and disappeared as gracefully as they had come, leaving a warm sigh to flow through the branches of the trees. At last the ancient prophecy was looming closer.

Chapter 28

Outwitting the afanc

Mark knew he had overslept beside the lake of King Arthur. He could feel the hot sun burning his eyelids before he opened them. At once memories of the afanc came streaming back and with it the terror of being chased. Mark had only been saved by the quick actions of the three maidens and realising it he said a silent thank you. He would have to be more careful if he were to succeed in getting the sword today. Breathing out slowly, and preparing to begin his quest, he began looking round his temporary secluded world. He seemed to be in a small green hideout of interwoven reeds. *I'm safe*, he thought, and then grimacing began to get up, feeling as if every part of him was bruised and tired from the events of yesterday.

Keeping his head below the level of the reed tops, and desperate to remain hidden, he checked his watch. Ten minutes to noon. Soon the afanc would disappear for a short while and that would be his opportunity to get the sword, if it was there. But at the moment Mark had no clear idea how to do it or how to bring it back safely. Hopefully something would turn up.

Peering through the reeds Mark noticed swathes of willow trees sending arcs of golden sunlight flitting like swallows above the lake, and the whole scene seemed peaceful and, empty. Then he noticed something amazing and nearly burst out laughing with relief, for right in the middle of the water the silvered arm was holding Excalibur. But there was something else which made him smile. Something he hadn't expected.

And so unexpected and out of place he wasn't sure whether to laugh or feel terrified, because within a few metres from his hideaway a small rowing boat had been lashed against a rickety piece of planking, and beside it appeared to be a landing stage where other such boats might have been tied many years ago.

It must have been the small boat that he had heard a few moments earlier, bouncing and slurping softly against the landing stage.

Mark sucked in his breath, the beginnings of hope flooding his mind. He could use the boat to get to the sword. But one thing worried him, where had it from? And more importantly, who had put it there? But in this world of magic, strange lakes and stranger beasts, Mark thought that if it wasn't a *who*, then *what* had put it there, and where were they now?

Desperately frightened he dropped to the floor, shoving his hand in his mouth to stop crying out in fear. There might be something waiting for him outside his green den. And he had to go out and face it.

Counting slowly to a hundred he listened, alert, heart hammering, waiting for the slightest sound. Silence. He began another hundred, but feeling impatient, and thinking he was safe, he began wriggling through the reeds to get a closer look.

Suddenly an angry splash echoed across the lake. Mark dropped like a stone. At the far end of the lake a column of water rose like a mountainous fountain and crashed back upon the still water. It was the afanc. The creature had just dived to the bottom of the lake. Now! This was it, the opportunity Mark needed to get the sword.

Leaping up and pushing through the reeds as if he were in the hundred metres sports competition Mark headed for the boat. He didn't know much about rowing, or even how much time he had before the creature returned, but he felt exhilarated; at last he felt he was getting somewhere and he began to hope he might really be able to get the sword. His first thought though was to get in and row as fast as he could. Slipping the wooden oars into the row-locks, he pushed off firmly, dipping the oars rapidly, heading across the lake.

After a few jerky movements he found that sometimes the oars skimmed erratically over the water, and then the boat bucked wildly from side to side taking him off course. He bit his lip, knowing time was running out and trying not to panic. He took several deep breaths, then, once again dipped the oars into the water, left, then right. Left, then right. This time the boat began to move to the centre of the lake and within two minutes he reached the silver arm. He was there. *Grab the sword and not drop it!*

Balancing one of the oars on the edge of the boat Mark swung out. He could just about touch it. He curled his fingers around it, gripping it fiercely, preparing to pull with all his strength, but the sword slipped into his hands and Mark nearly fell backwards in shock. At once swirling palpitations flowed through his body; sensations which made him feel powerful, invincible, and like a king! Mark's muscles seemed to throb and grow beyond anything he could have imagined. Was this how King Arthur felt when he had Excalibur? A bit like Superman and every comic hero rolled into one. This time he held the true sword Excalibur. He knew it, and he felt so excited he wanted to race straight off and show the others!

But reality cut in; he had to row back, and then find his way through the tunnels.

Sobering suddenly Mark placed the sword in the bottom of the boat. There wasn't time to relax; the afanc would be coming up. He had to get back as quickly as possible. He struck the oars into the water but it was already too late. He could see the lake starting to swirl around him as the afanc began to come up from the depths. It began like a vortex, surrounding the boat, moving faster and faster, tossing the little craft from side to side.

Mark clung to the oars, his fingers biting around the smooth wood until his knuckles went white. Beads of sweat slid in sticky lines down his face as he dipped the oars into the water, pushing faster, and harder.

Very slowly the boat began to move towards the edge of the lake, but not quick enough. All around the water was being sucked into a tidal vortex and Mark knew he would be tossed out.

Almost crying now with fear and desperation he dipped the oars, again and again. *Only a little farther.* He was almost there.

Far away in the castle beneath Henley Forest the dragon felt the surging power of magical forces being released into the world, and quaked in dread and hope.

High above this dreadful dragon another ancient being began to move. This was the giant of the forest, the one who had slept for a thousand years waiting for this moment when the prophecy seemed doomed to happen. The wide eyes flickered once, then sprung open. The giant growled bad temperedly like a great bear, and shook himself crossly until it seemed as if a mighty hurricane ripped through the forest, tossing the trees like confetti. The same trees that had formed the giant shape now threw themselves into a massive line of moving parts as the giant gathered himself together and took the shape and nature of a true giant. The prophecy which told of a fight between good against evil inched nearer.

A mile southwards of the forest in the town of Crewkerne the people were sleeping late on this grey December day, and oblivious to the drama unfolding. But on the small farm mother paced about, looking anxiously out of windows, and calling shrilly for her children. Her desperate voice carried up through the apple orchard, over the fields, towards Henley Forest.

When father had returned from the forest the previous day he had been badly shaken, but confident Betty Vanstone was looking after the children. He was not sure why he was confident of that, but something reassured him and so he had returned and soothed mother's worries.

Father admitted there was an element of confusion in his mind about what had actually happened up *there*, and already the remembrances of the broken tree, the rock fall, and the strange noises of pigs rampaging through the forest were fading and somehow unreal. He also had the distinct impression the old Fergy tractor had been left up in the forest, but after feeding the calves and milking the cows before supper he saw the Fergy parked in the barn. How did it get there? His head ached just thinking of it all. Mother sent him to bed with a hot water bottle and a cup of chocolate. But she sat up, paced and called, and worried all night. Finally, at four in the morning she could bear it no longer, and tried to telephone Betty Vanstone. The telephone rang and rang, but no one answered. Then she felt the earth tremor and her heart thumped harshly; she knew it had something to do with her children and she paced the kitchen, feeling helpless and lost. Once again she tried to telephone Betty, and once again there was no reply. If the children weren't back by lunchtime she would call the police.

Timothy and the girls had returned to the Guardian's Chamber with Caradon. They wanted to wait for Mark in the tunnels but Caradon told them they should help Betty, and Timothy realised the wisdom of this. He remembered the worn look on Betty's face when they left her many hours before and felt a pang of guilt. She was in great danger and without her controlling the dragon through her amulet the beast would soon be free.

"Hurry up," Timothy urged, and Diane, Joan and himself raced behind Caradon, all feeling afraid, and wondering what they would find when they returned. Joan, remembering her dream, blurted out her fears to the others. They ran faster. When they finally burst into the Guardian's Chamber Betty lay slumped against a boulder and the light from the amulet wavered on and off the dragon's face. Now it was focussed on; now it slipped off. Betty struggled to keep the rays still, but after a few seconds her arm tired and the amulet and the light slipped down. Each time it did the dragon became more alert.

Upon seeing the children Betty gave a groan and slipped into unconsciousness. The effort of controlling the dragon had exhausted her. As she fell the amulet dropped to the floor beside her and the blue light disappeared. Timothy stopped, mid stride, aghast at the strained face of Betty, and completely horrified. He should have come back sooner. Rushing over he scooped his powerful arms under Betty's shoulders, raising her back into position. Betty slipped sideways like a rag doll. Timothy had to try something else. Thinking quickly he snatched the amulet and thrust it towards the dragon. Nothing happened. The blue light didn't work. Timothy cursed. What else could he do? Then he realised that he wasn't a magical person whilst Betty obviously was. Perhaps the amulet was powerless in his hands, but it would still work in Betty's. Providing he could get Betty to hold it. Taking up the amulet he pushed it into one of Betty's hands, then with his hand underneath hers he held it up, towards the dragon. Immediately the amulet began to glow and within moments a hard shaft of blue light pierced the gloom of the chamber, seeking out the dragon again. The tiny movements of the beast slowed once more, then finally ceased.

So, thought Timothy, I will have to stay here with Betty and keep her hand held up until she has recovered. But it was difficult to do on his own and already his arm was aching with the odd position he had to hold it.

"Diane, help me. Quickly." he called. "I can't hold Betty on my own."

Diane rushed over and caught one of Betty's arms.

"That's right, Diane, now take her weight on that side and help me move her so she is sitting with her back against the wall."

It was easier said than done, but with a little more effort Diane managed to partly lift Betty up. Timothy smiled weakly. "Good, you're doing fine, now, after three lift. Two three. Lift!" It worked. Betty lay half propped up against the wall and Timothy could angle the amulet to shed its rays upon the dragon.

"Joan! Try tucking some coats behind Betty to make her more comfortable; it will also help to keep the light shining." Joan raced around collecting coats as they wriggled out of them and tossed them to her.

For a few moments there was chaos and suddenly they heard Caradon's hooves clattering from the dark tunnels.

The abath skidded to a halt, his eyes flaring to see such devastation in the chamber. The last time he had been here was with Eorldormann. The beast looked around sharply. Where was his friend? Then he noticed the crumpled form of Betty, and there finally, he saw Eorldormann. But this was not the friend he knew, this was a lifeless form, prostrate and bleeding. Caradon gave a bellow of such distress it filled the chamber as the abath mourned the last friend he had in this ancient and desolate world.

Caradon hung his head as if the weight of the whole prophecy pressed upon him. He felt so tired and empty he wanted to run back into the tunnels and never come back out. But he couldn't do that yet. He had to keep focussed until the quest was solved, and help the children. If not for his sake then for Eorldormann's.

At that moment a huge tremor shuddered through the chamber. The children shrieked, grabbing one another for safety and fearing the whole chamber might collapse upon them at any moment. But Caradon felt something different. He understood the mighty tremor and reared up in joy; Excalibur had been found!

The beast turned. "I must help the child. I will return. Soon. Hopefully!"

The children exchanged glances. *Mark*! They wanted to speak yet dared not with the dragon glaring at them from the far end of the chamber. They could feel it twitching and knew it was breaking free. Nothing could stop it now, not even Betty's blue light.

Although their eyes were round with fear there glimmered a spark of hope which they passed one to the other by nods and grins, wondering, hoping, though not really sure, whether the sword had been found. Did this mean Mark would be coming back? And if he came back, with Excalibur, would it cut the thread, and would it stop the dragon escaping? Or, and here their thoughts and hopes failed them, would the sword fail again?

The dragon tensed. It had to break free; now or never. Breathing deeply so that a thin ripple like a million tiny castanets echoed in the chamber, the dragon forced itself to stare into the brilliant blue shaft of light and by doing so began to leech away at its strength, and leech into the strength of the woman who held it.

It could almost taste freedom. It flexed its muscles in expectation, and more of its imprisoning wall fell away as far above them the medieval castle began to crumble.

Chapter 29

Betty disappears

Joan began getting restless. The chamber had gone quiet and the dragon seemed to have gone back to sleep. She wanted something to do. She could see Timothy helping Betty with the amulet, Diane fishing for flapjacks from her bag and handing them around, and somewhere in the awful dark tunnels Mark was finding Excalibur, yet she had nothing to do to help. Or so it seemed. Suddenly, remembering the thread she had painted and woven amongst the magical thread, she wondered if the mound of thread would be more threatening to the dragon if it was moved closer. Surely if it was nearer the beast would be able to see it, and feel its power. But, and here her heart thumped painfully, if she took it closer to the dragon, the beast might suddenly leap out, or blast her with molten fire. It was a terrifying thought. All the children had been lucky so far in escaping serious injury, would her luck run out now if she took the thread closer to the dragon? She thought it would, and felt a pang of fear, regret even, thinking how if she died taking the thread to the dragon she would never see her brothers or sister again. And she could never tell them how much she loved them and enjoyed playing these adventures with them.

Her sad thoughts only lasted a moment; being seven she soon focussed on the next task and fixed her mind on what she proposed to do to help everyone. She began walking towards the thread, and as soon as she was close enough she tried pulling it towards the beast. But the mound of thread wouldn't budge. Its weight took her by surprise. She tugged hard, grimacing with the effort.

Timothy stared at her and frowned. What was she trying to do? Didn't she realise it was dangerous to go too close to the dragon? He tried to attract Joan's attention, wagging his head at her and shaking in an angry way, but she refused to look at him.

Grabbing a large handful of thread she finally managed to start her fearful journey towards the dragon, and the mound of magical green thread came inching and sliding very slowly behind her like a giant deflated balloon. She realised with a sick sense of dread how quickly the beast was coming to life. The scales down its front were beginning to bristle and take on a more life-like shape, even the great feet and legs of the dragon were beginning to look like living flesh. Within a few moments the power from Betty's amulet would be exhausted and when that happened she realised the beast would be free to move. It was up to her to do something. Now.

Gritting her teeth, and hauling arm over arm like she had seen the fishermen do on the television, she dragged the bundle of green thread to a spot directly below the dragon. *There*! She dropped it with a thump, exhausted by the effort. But she hadn't finished yet. There was still one more thing she could do to try to delay the dragon's escape. Rummaging carefully through the magical green bundle she found the two cut ends of mother's special thread, and she quickly pulled them up to stand like sharp points. Now they looked as if they were the cut ends of the thread, which was just what she wanted. She slapped her hands, cocked a cheeky grin at the dragon, and raced back to the others as if chased by demons.

The dragon could see the thread ready to be used; miles and miles of it, tangled together in a swirling mass of green and he felt sickened. It promised eternal imprisonment. He had no wish to endure eternity wrapped like a moth in a cocoon. If only he could break free, he thought desperately. He wanted to escape and terrorise the people on earth as he used to do. He ground his teeth in anger; only one lady and four children lay between him and eternal freedom; surely there was something he could do to escape. But he had to act cautiously; any movement before he was completely free might destroy his chances forever.

He lowered his eyelids, plotting wickedly; let them think he was sleeping. Though one thought kept nagging at his mind; where was the fourth child? And what was he doing?

Deep below ground Mark rocked and rowed the boat back to the shore, his heart pounding, exultant and fearful, expecting the afanc to appear at any moment. The boat scraped against the edge and rocked up against the rickety planking. He dropped the oars in the bottom of the boat, picked up Excalibur, and prepared to leap from the boat, when suddenly the three Arthurian maidens appeared beside him at the water's edge. He nearly slipped in fright, shifting so sharply the boat bucked wildly so he nearly fell into the lake.

"Who are you?" he gasped, steadying himself and leaping for the shore. Two things sprang to mind as he landed amongst the reeds and whirled to face these strange visions. Would they harm him? And, should he run? But the apparitions smiled kindly and Mark remembered their help the day before. He gulped. "Thank you for saving me yesterday. I'd like to stop and chat for a while; but I've got to run. Back to Caradon," he blurted foolishly. "Please let me go past. The afanc thing is coming up again."

"You are too late, stay where you are!" the turquoise maiden commanded, blocking his path and flinging her arms over him. Mark ducked, hugging the sword against his chest to keep it safe.

"Please! I've got to hide!"

"There's no time," said the silver maiden, and she too flung up her arms. Lastly the golden maiden reached over Mark until all maidens touched hands. At once a diaphanous mantle spun about Mark as if he were in a tent, and he became invisible.

The afanc exploded through the surface of the lake, its dreadful head snorting angrily. Mark hardly dared to breathe, realising he had been saved, again. Then turning to the lake he almost burst out laughing for there in the middle, where once he had seen Excalibur, he could see the silver arm now holding a stumpy piece of silver birch.

The maidens sighed and pulled faces, their images appearing to quiver as if they understood the joke and laughed with him. "The afanc, like its descendants the alligators, is short sighted," explained the gold maiden, and a short tinkling sound echoed around them.

"Then it doesn't know I've taken it," said Mark grinning, watching the monster disappear onto the far bank, and wanting to shout in delirious joy. "That's great!" And instantly he began thinking he might be able to keep the sword for himself.

The maidens said nothing but their smiles grew still, as though frozen in time. Mark could feel their thoughts seeping into his mind, exposing his own thoughts and weaknesses.

"Welcome, Chosen One. We have been expecting you for a long time. We are the Ladies of the Lake, guardians of Excalibur since the death of King Arthur. We know of your great challenge and are willing to entrust Excalibur into your care, for a short time. However, we hold you to one condition, which you must not fail; you must return to us the sword of magic and truth before forty-eight hours have passed, or else our world will end. It is written that no human can keep the sword of legend; it must remain here. We will prevent the afanc from discovering the truth but can only do so for two days, before then you must return it to us. Will you so swear?" Their gentle eyes grew insistent as if they would burrow into Mark's mind and read his thoughts. Mark gulped, feeling ridiculous and naïve. Had he really thought he could keep the sword for himself? He threw them a beaming smile, and found himself nodding to each of the ladies in turn. They gave him one long look before joining into a perfect rainbow and then simply melted away. Mark found himself suddenly impatient and eager to be on his way.

Hurrying from the lake he entered the tunnels, whistling and feeling great to be much stronger. He kept a firm grip on Excalibur, marvelling how easy it was to carry the legendary sword, and how powerful it made him feel. But as the last glimmer of light faded he began feeling drained, just as he did on his journey towards the lake. He took another step, and another, and as he moved further from the magical lake his strength flowed out of him. Suddenly he understood what was happening, the source of his strength came from the lake, and the further he moved from it the weaker he became. The weight of the sword dragged at his arm like an iron chain. He tried shifting it from one hand to the other, but it didn't help, soon he would only be able to drag it. His breathing came in short painful gasps as he dragged the sword behind him, for minute after minute. He could feel his head becoming dizzy with the effort. How much longer could he continue?

Finally he reached the slimy walls of the deepest tunnels and the dank smell of rotting moss made him cringe; he was near where he had left Caradon. If only he could reach him before his strength drained away. And what about Timothy and his sisters? Were they all right? What had happened to the dragon? To Betty? The fears grew deep within him and he tried to hurry; he had forgotten how important it was for him to get the sword back to the dragon. Had he been away too long?

Just as Mark felt he would slip to the ground with exhaustion Caradon stood in front of him. The ancient abath gave a bark of gladness when he saw Mark and noticed the gleaming sword. "You have found it! Good. Come. Get up," he said to the exhausted boy. "I will take you back."

Grabbing a handful of the abath's shaggy mane Mark pulled himself up, and suddenly they were off, twisting this way and that in the tunnels, and very soon it seemed to Mark they were entering the Guardian's Chamber.

Seeing Mark and Caradon the children shouted in delight, waving furiously. Behind their happy faces the dragon glowered, then the beast noticed something that made his mind boil with fury; Excalibur! Instantly the dragon realised the two ends of thread in front of him were false. The thread hadn't been cut at all. It was still one continual piece of useless thread. The cut ends had been a hoax and the children had tricked him until they found Excalibur, and like the prophecy had said, the finding of the sword would bind him forever. With every ounce of his strength the dragon braced himself, gathering his strength into all of his muscles, screamed with frustration, and proceeded to burst out of the remaining tons of rock still imprisoning him.

Joan saw the moment and her heart leapt into her mouth. She could feel the hatred, and the venom flashing into the dragon's face and realised that at that moment he was breaking free. She opened her mouth to scream; she had to do something, Mark had to cut the magical thread. There was no time to lose.

Betty saw the sword in Mark's hands, felt the last of her strength ebb away, dropped the turquoise amulet and collapsed. Timothy was taken by surprise and slumped forward also and the amulet bounced out of her hand and out of sight. The shaft of blue light was extinguished; the dragon was free.

Caradon heard the explosive sound of breaking rock as if a thousand bombs were going off at once and saw the dragon lunging forward. Without breaking his gallop Caradon carried Mark straight over to the green thread, which thankfully Joan had carried right into the path of the now free and escaping dragon and Mark dropped from his back. In one movement Mark thrust Excalibur into the centre of the thread and then stood back and watched in amazement as the magic and power of

Eorldormann's thread took over. It began rising up, higher and higher, entwining itself like some mythical vine around the dragon. Faster and faster it grew, impaling the dragon in the midst of its first step of freedom, entwining the legs, tail and head until the dragon was covered in the strange green fibre. Finally the last green dragon stood before them, completely covered. They had done it! A shout of elation went up as each child saw the dragon captured for eternity within a web of thread. Eorldormann had done it after all. Betty had done it!

Then they stopped, aghast, Betty was lying motionless.

"Is she dead?" whispered Joan, voicing everyone's fears.

Caradon nuzzled his head into hers. "I think I may be able to save her. I shall have to take her away from here, quickly." His voice thickened with misery, seeing another of his old companions dying.

"You can't go back!" Joan burst out. "It's too late! I can hear the castle falling in upon itself! We haven't saved it after all! You'll die if you stay," cried Joan.

"Your brother made a promise," said Caradon, looking directly at Mark. "Which he has to keep."

A promise? Mark stared.

"Did you? What was that?" asked Timothy who was trying to revive the unconscious Betty.

Mark looked suddenly confused. His elation at having cut the thread with Excalibur and watching the dragon being trapped by the thread had left him with a strange feeling of not understanding what was going on. "Did I?" Then it hit him. "The sword. I have to take it back. Within forty eight hours."

"You can't," cried Diane snatching at his arm. "The tunnels are collapsing. You will be killed."

"Perhaps we can return it for you," said Caradon, nuzzling Betty whose eyes remained closed. "The Maidens will understand. They will know what has happened."

"But you're not allowed in their world. You said so yourself," said Mark, who was now feeling anxious he did not endanger the abath, who after all had risked his own life on many occasions to help them, and who was going to an almost certain death by returning inside the collapsing tunnels.

"I think if you can find the turquoise amulet and we take it with us, we will be allowed inside the sacred place. After all, this lady here is a lady of the lake," Caradon replied enigmatically.

"I belong to the lake." Betty's eyes fluttered open. Her face looked ethereal, radiant, as if she were already contemplating the sight of that perfect glade. "And we shall take Eorldormann. Something may yet be done for him." Caradon walked to the body of his unusual friend and waited patiently while Timothy placed him and Betty on his back.

"I must leave you now," said Caradon. "Goodbye." He took one last glance at Diane who immediately felt tears welling in her eyes. She had come to love this strange magnificent creature.

"Take care," she said, and patted the abath before quickly turning away.

Then beside them a huge part of the roof broke off and smashed upon the floor, dust splattered everyone.

"Quick! Run!" called Timothy, pushing Joan towards the exit with Diane following. Mark touched Excalibur one final time, before passing it to Betty, then brushed Caradon's forehead. "Thank you," he mumbled, his eyes so full of tears he couldn't see, and he raced out of the Guardian's Chamber after the others.

Chapter 30

Christmas comes to Crewkerne

The heavy thunder that had rolled back and forth over the hills and brought with it thick dark clouds moved away without bringing a drop of rain. Everyone in Crewkerne agreed the weather was unusual for this time of year and they would prefer a crisp frosty morning, and perhaps a little snow before Christmas for the children to play in.

Timothy, Diane, Mark and Joan were never able to explain the sounds of thunder and rumblings to their parents since if they mentioned sleeping giants and dragons walled up in castles they would have been accused of being fanciful. As it was both parents were very glad this particular adventure had run its course.

When the children had walked back home from Henley Forest on that rather unusual morning their mother had wept with relief, and even had to wipe her eyes in her apron. She had been so worried, she explained to her children, who said in trying to soothe her that they had had such fun, and they were sorry, but they had fallen asleep in the old rifle range and didn't wake up until the dewy grass eked through their coats and woke them. And that was all they could remember. Or so it seemed.

Diane was rather upset since she had lost her first aid kit somewhere, and confessed to her mother later that she had also lost the 'special' thread and Mum's 'bestest' scissors. But as it was nearly Christmas she was forgiven and promised a new first aid kit for her Christmas present.

What did the children remember of their Arthurian adventure? It was strange they never talked of it. One morning a few days after they had returned from the castle Diane pointed up across the hills to Henley Forest. "Look, you can see the sleeping giant." Timothy heard her and told her not to be so silly, there was no giant, it was only a bunch of trees looking like a sleeping giant, and anyway one day some men were sure to come along and cut the trees down.

On the afternoon before Christmas their father had said he was going to market and would any of them like to come with him. They all declined; Diane wanted to make mince pies, Joan wanted to make cards for some of her friends at school and the two boys decided to try their hands at making a sledge, in case of snow they said. After their father had left, the children gathered in the warm kitchen munching Mum's lovely fruitcake when one of them said, "Shall we have an adventure? Or shall we play off-ground tig?"

"Oh, off-ground tig is better. The last adventure was much too . . ." Timothy broke off and scratched his head. What was he going to say?

The others looked at him rather strangely. "The last one was . . ." And Diane also came to a halt. What was she about to say? Yes, what was their last adventure? When they tried to think of it it was like chasing an elusive dream, or a bit like catching a rainbow that faded softly away as colours on a sunny day. Now, where had he come across something like that, thought Mark, who had fully recovered from an early bout of influenza in a very short time. He frowned in concentration then his brow cleared. They could always go and try to find the old rifle range again. Yet the thought never appealed to the others and it was invariably left for 'another day'.

"Oh, by the way, before you all go dashing off, I've got something to say to you all," said mother wiping her floury hands in a tea towel. "I've heard around town that Betty has gone away to stay with relatives."

"Betty?" Timothy said in puzzlement.

"Yes, Betty, Miss Vanstone. You remember, your friend you took on your last adventure." Their mother hurried into the sitting room and came out with a parcel that she handed to Joan, so she never saw the confused expressions on her children's faces. "She left this. She said Joan would probably like it best of all of you, and said to thank you for all your help the other day. She also left a tiny gift for each of you, which I wanted to keep for Christmas, but she said as you had already had a real Arthurian Christmas you might like to open your gifts now. Now what did she mean by that?" she asked. But none of them could answer.

When Joan opened her gift it was a bound copy of Morte Arthur. Joan looked inside, eager to read another story similar to those she had been reading at school, but found the language difficult to read. *Middle English* her mother explained to her, though couldn't help her to make any sense of it. Perhaps she might like to keep the book to read when she was older. So Joan popped it into her book cupboard and forgot about it for many years. Diane found a new reel of nylon thread, and some real suture needles in her gift. 'With thanks from Caradon' the note said. "Caradon? Who is that?" Everyone was puzzled, though everyone experienced a shiver of remembrance, but rather than tell the others they each decided to keep quiet. And the moment passed. Timothy opened his gift to find the medieval spear head that he had lost recently, though he didn't know when he had lost it; but somehow Betty had found it, and wasn't it thoughtful of her to send it back? However, Mark's gift was the most remarkable. It was a half sized sword with the inscription 'Rex Arturus'. He loved it, played with it, but as he grew older he outgrew it and put it in a box in the attic.

One day they would go into the attic and see all the wonderful things that were lodged there. But for now, they were all rather confused, and if now and then they had a dream of Arthurian knights, dragons, and ladies of the lake, none of them remembered it sufficiently to share it with the others. And as with all things in childhood, if they are not shared they are soon forgotten.

"Come on, Joan," shouted Diane and Mark as they raced out of the kitchen with a great piece of fruitcake in their hands. "We're playing off ground tig and Timothy is 'on it.'"

Epilogue

Well, the adventure *might* have ended like that if Joan hadn't had another dream a short while later, which jogged her memory about those crazy days of their Christmas adventure.

The dream occurred after she heard the buzz of heavy duty chain saws felling some trees in Henley Forest. She dreamed of a lady being taken through some dark tunnels by a strange beast, while all around the air throbbed to the sound of mighty walls crumbling. The lady and the beast were going to be killed.

Then the dream ended and Joan awoke shivering.

Twisting sideways she saw her new gift, the book Morte Arthur, and seeing it in the first light of day finally realised its significance and remembered Betty Vanstone. Betty was the lady in her dream.

Another thought chased after the first namely that if Betty had died in the tunnels then who had sent her the book?

Uttering a large 'Oh' Joan breathed two words into the cold room, '*she survived*! And from that moment onward knew their adventures in the Arthurian castle were just beginning, for after all the legend in Crewkerne had talked of a sleeping giant. Joan smiled to herself, if the giant had awoken once already . . . . and left the thought unfinished.

The End